Peaceweaver

ALSO BY REBECCA BARNHOUSE

The Book of the Maidservant
The Coming of the Dragon

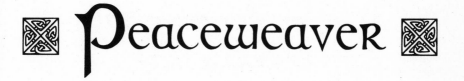 Peaceweaver

REBECCA BARNHOUSE

RANDOM HOUSE NEW YORK

Text copyright © 2012 by Rebecca Barnhouse
Jacket art copyright © 2012 by Mel Grant

Visit us on the Web! www.randomhouse.com/kids

Educators and librarians, for a variety of teaching tools,
visit us at www.randomhouse.com/teachers

Library of Congress Cataloging-in-Publication Data
Barnhouse, Rebecca.
Peaceweaver / by Rebecca Barnhouse. — 1st ed.
p.   cm.
Companion book to: The coming of the dragon.
Summary: Sixteen-year-old Hild hates the perpetual fighting between men of her kingdom and others, but when she is sent to marry a neighboring king, supposedly to ensure peace, she must tap into her own abilities with the sword and choose between loyalty and honor.
ISBN 978-0-375-86766-8 (trade) — ISBN 978-0-375-96766-5 (lib. bdg.) —
ISBN 978-0-375-89848-8 (ebook)
[1. Conduct of life—Fiction. 2. Clairvoyance—Fiction. 3. Sex role—Fiction.
4. Wiglaf (Legendary character)—Fiction. 5. Beowulf (Legendary character)—Fiction.
6. Mythology, Norse—Fiction. 7. Scandinavia—History—To 1397—Fiction.] I. Title.
PZ7.B2668Pe 2012   [Fic]—dc22   2010045284

Printed in the United States of America

10 9 8 7 6 5 4 3 2 1

First Edition

Random House Children's Books supports the
First Amendment and celebrates the right to read.

For my parents

Peaceweaver

ONE

Smoke.

The smell reached Hild's nose, filling her with a sense of unease. Then a door shut—somebody letting a cat out—and she saw it was just smoke from a cooking fire, not the sulfurous fumes that had hung over the lake a few weeks back. Good. She wanted nothing to spoil this day, of all days.

Past the last houses, the lane narrowed as it neared the Lake Gate. Hild crunched over the gravel, increasing her speed as her excitement grew. At the gate, she raised her hand in greeting and watched in surprise when one of the guards waved back, his dagger flashing in a shaft of early-morning sun. It was Brynjolf, her friend Beyla's brother. He gave her a broken-toothed smile and called her name. Hild shook her head. How many times would Brynjolf forget that he was no longer a boy but a member of the king's army, required to stand silently at full attention? A more experienced warrior, menacing behind his masked helmet, stepped out of the guard tower to admonish him. Hild winced. At fifteen, a year younger than Hild, Brynjolf had been promoted to the men's troop only a week before, but knowing him, it might be years before he remembered to take all the rules seriously. If he remembered them at all.

Past the gate, Brynjolf's troubles behind her, Hild could see blue lake water glittering as the sun caught tiny wavelets in its net. A breeze carrying the faint smell of fish riffled over her eyelashes and lifted strands of her dark hair into flight. Was that a smudge over the water? No, just her eyes playing tricks on her, and the memory of the wind-driven cloud that had settled over the lake. Dragon smoke, Ari Frothi had insisted, but the old skald's words had been ignored. Not in living memory had a dragon flown over the land of the Shylfings, and Bragi, the new skald, had announced with smooth certainty that no dragon would dare attack the kingdom. The cloud was soon gone, leaving only an acrid odor and flakes of ash drifting down like dark snow. Most people had forgotten it—but Hild couldn't. Strange tendrils of smoke wove their way through her dreams, embroidered by words she could almost catch in a voice she didn't know, a woman's voice, harsh and commanding. They left her with a longing for something she couldn't identify, something just beyond her grasp.

She blinked the cloud away, reminding herself why she was out so early. She could barely wait to tell her eldest sister the news. Her exuberance returned, mirrored by the diamonds dancing on the lake, and making her want to rush forward like the waves. Surely, if anything would get Sigyn back into the hall, it would be the sight of Hild standing on the dais beside their uncle, the king.

When the path branched, she turned toward the group of dwellings clustered together on the shore, allowing her feet to skip a few steps. Small boats lined the beach, some of them right-side up, some of them upside down, a few with people gathered around them unloading their early-morning catch as the water shushed onto shore. Far out on the lake, boats bobbed, their bows winking in and out of view, and Hild stopped for a moment to watch them, shielding her eyes with her hand. Beyond the boats, on the lake's far shore, red and gold birches swayed, too distant to be more than a tossing blur of bright color.

Closer by, on the near shore, a boat sat waiting, eager to be out on the water. Hild gazed at it, memorizing its contours and the way the prow tapered upward, graceful as a drinking horn. It was just the image she needed for the banner she was weaving—the one that would someday hang in a place of prominence in Gyldenseld, her uncle's splendid mead hall.

A slave woman hurried by, lugging a basket filled with silvery fish so newly caught that some still slapped their fellows with their tails. Hild peered into the basket as the slave passed her, bound for the king's kitchens, where the fish would become part of the feast at tomorrow's harvest festival. When Hild reached the cluster of cottages where the fisherfolk lived, she stepped around a pair of little girls chanting a clapping game and nodded to the women and white-haired men who hunched in their doorways, mending piles of nets. A weather-beaten woman squinted up at Hild's approach. "Good harvest to you, my lady. Come to see your sister, have you?"

At her words, others raised their heads; some greeted Hild, and some turned immediately back to their nets. A little boy peered around an open doorway with sleepy eyes, but when he saw her, he pulled inside again. There was nothing grand about these people her sister had chosen to live among, and they would feel out of place in the hall. They kept to themselves, to their boats and their nets, providing fish for the kingdom and receiving in return protection from enemy tribes. Yet despite their isolation from those who lived inside the wooden gates that surrounded the fortress, one couple had been different. Hild heard in her head Ari Frothi's lay about how the fisherman and his wife had seen their young son's talent for war craft and sent him away from boats and nets to be trained instead with sword and spear. And then, through his exploits, Wonred had risen high enough to become one of the king's hearth companions. So honored had he been that he was given the king's sister-daughter—Hild's sister Sigyn—in marriage. The lay ended with Wonred's death, but it didn't mention that he'd been killed in a senseless skirmish with a tribe the Shylfings weren't even at war with. Nor did Ari Frothi sing about the way Sigyn had barricaded herself in her mother-in-law's cottage, the two widows alone together with a third companion: grief. Two winters had passed since the old skald first sang that lay at Wonred's funeral, and the memory of his body's being consigned to the flames still brought Hild pain. For Sigyn, the pain was far, far worse.

Yet today, Hild was sure, her sister would throw off her mourning and rejoin the women who gathered in the hall. And Thryth, Sigyn's mother-in-law, would accompany her.

A shorebird shrieked and beat the air with its wings. Hild watched as it hovered, then dove into the waves. When it rose from the water with a minnow glittering in its beak, Hild turned and approached the dark cottage. It was larger than the others, and better built—Wonred had seen to that. Yet unlike the others, with their doors open to catch the morning light, it was silent and shuttered. She knocked on the door, two short raps followed by another, the signal that would let her sister know who it was.

But Thryth, not Sigyn, opened the door, just enough to let herself out. She put a fleshy arm around Hild and drew her close, peering up at her with dim eyes from under a wool cap. "It's a bad day," she whispered, shutting the door behind her and leading Hild away from the cottage and the people who might be listening. "She's still abed; won't see a soul."

"She'll see *me*," Hild said, turning. "When she hears my news, she'll get out of bed."

Thryth shook her head and gently pulled her back. "Come, dear one. Tell me instead." She led Hild toward the lake path, sharp-edged grasses sawing at their skirts.

Hild's shoulders slumped, and the bright promise of her news lost its luster in the shadow of Sigyn's grief. Her sister's bad days had grown worse, not better, as the seasons since her husband's death had faded into the past. Sometimes Hild wondered if the two women fed off each other's grief, growing more ravenous with the passage of time, yet she knew that wasn't fair. After all, here was Thryth, walking alongside her.

Hild looked down at the older woman, at the white curls peeking from under her cap, at her broad nose and the cloudy eyes sunk deep in wrinkled skin, and felt a rush of warmth for her. "Well, if Sigyn won't come to the hall today, perhaps you will," she said.

"So your mother thinks you're ready to serve the mead, does she?"

"How did you know?" Hild asked in surprise.

"How?" Thryth shook her head in amusement. "My dear, you've talked of nothing else since your mother started training you."

"That's not true." Hild stopped and took a step back.

"I've talked about my weaving, and about my friend Beyla, and all sorts of things, I'm sure."

Thryth smiled and reached up to touch Hild's cheek with her rough fingers. "Of course you have, dear one." She started walking again and Hild, embarrassed by her childish outburst, fell into step beside her. Across the lake, hills rose in the distance, and beyond them, mountains swathed in mist. Giants walked there. Somewhere beyond the mountains lay the kingdom of the Heathobards, the warriors at whose hands Wonred had died. If Wonred had been from a noble family, the king would have demanded vengeance and the Shylfings would have gained yet another enemy. But Wonred's humble beginnings, and the fact that Sigyn hadn't petitioned the king for redress for her husband's death, had kept the lakeshore a place where Hild could walk without fear of enemy longboats plying the waters.

"Can you remember the days of the queen?" Thryth asked.

Hild turned her attention back from the mountains. She started to speak, then saw that no response was needed. The old woman's eyes were almost closed, as if she were watching a scene from days gone by, not the path in front of her.

"Back then, before she fell ill, she'd serve the mead horn to the men." Thryth's voice took on a singsong quality, as if she were chanting a lay. "I don't think half the warriors in the hall noticed how much she guided them, but the women did, you mark me."

"Did they?" Hild asked, even though she knew the answer. She never tired of Thryth's stories about how things used to be.

"We'd watch from behind the beams while the queen said, 'I know you want to end that feud,' or some such—she had a way with words, she did. And then she'd hold out the mead to a warrior"—Thryth held out her own hands, pantomiming the passing of the horn—"and he'd hardly know that when he accepted it, he was pledging to carry out the queen's words. But we women knew."

Hild nodded. She could remember the queen moving about the hall, speaking to the king and his hearth companions, even if she'd been too young to pay attention to the words that passed among them.

"It wasn't just the warriors she counseled. The king listened to her, too. Of course, she had Ari Frothi to help her. He'd pull out his harp and sing something that went right along with what she'd said, some lay about a feud that had ended, or whatever it was the queen was talking about." Thryth shook her head, making a *tsk*ing noise with her tongue. "But now it's that younger skald, Bragi, who counsels the king. With him it's always power and fighting and war. His words make all of us unsafe."

The sound of honking made them both look up to see skeins of wild geese stitching seams across the sky. They watched until the birds' melancholy calls faded into the distance. Hild had always liked Thryth, not just because she was so comfortable and comforting, but also because there were many things they agreed about. Hild's mother, who had taken over the queen's duties, was far less willing to try to influence the men than the queen had been. "It's not my place; I'm not the queen," she protested to Hild whenever they talked about it. But as bearer of the mead, it *was* her place, Hild argued. Someone needed to counter Bragi's influence. Ever since the queen had fallen ill, the atmosphere in the hall had changed. Feuds were prolonged; raiding parties went looking for fights, not just gold and slaves; boys became warriors too young, before they were ready; and far more times than they should, funeral pyres sent their greasy smoke spiraling into the sky. The last funeral hadn't even been a full season past—the grain whose harvest would be celebrated at tomorrow's festival had already been tinged with gold when Harr's pyre had been lit. Hild hadn't known him, but she'd recognized the grief on his widow's face all too well.

It had to stop. And it would, Hild vowed to herself. Starting today, she, not her mother, would be serving the mead in the hall, and as she did, she would find ways to break Bragi's hold over the king. She'd show both the king and the skald—and all the warriors, too—how the women of the kingdom saw things. She would make things like they'd been before, when the queen still served the mead.

They came to the bleached skeleton of a boat, long since abandoned, one side buried in sand. A bird sheltering behind it took flight at their approach. They stood looking out over the lake for a moment. When a fish leapt, slapping the water, they turned back toward the cottage, walking silently, each sunk in her own thoughts. "Will you tell her?" Hild asked when they neared the door.

Thryth nodded. "Of course I will, dear one." She stopped at the herb bed, reaching down to pick a sprig of mint, its late-season leaves curled and brown. As she handed it to Hild, she squinted up at her. "But don't look for Sigyn in the hall. Not today, anyway."

Hild rolled the leaves between her fingers and brought them to her nose, wondering how such a withered plant could hold so firmly to its fresh scent. She gave Thryth a quick hug, then headed back to her uncle's fortress, her head down, weighted by Thryth's words.

At the Lake Gate, she looked up and smiled. Brynjolf stood stiffly at attention, square-jawed and resolute. Hild knew she shouldn't speak to him, or even look at him—it would be far too easy to get him into trouble a second time. But at the last minute, she couldn't help herself. Glancing quickly to make sure the other guard wasn't watching, she made a pig face. When Brynjolf's lips quirked, she did it again, this time sticking out her tongue, too. Before the other guard turned, Hild had wiped all expression from her face and passed through the gate with a queenly bearing. Behind her, Brynjolf snorted with laughter, and she hurried onward, trying not to snort herself. It was just like Beyla always said, grinning, every time she led her brother astray: "Someday Brynjolf will make a fine warrior. But today is not that day."

Inside the fortress, Hild stepped off the path to avoid an oxcart rumbling toward her, and greeted her cousin Skamkel, who rushed past her importantly, his helmet hiding his face. Her route led her past the Old Place, the little wooden shrine to the gods that had been left to crumble when newer temples, one each for Odin and Freyja, had been built back when Hild's mother was a child. Weeds poked from between boards. Under an eave, a bird had long ago built a nest, now as dilapidated as the temple itself. Still, no one would dare tear the shrine down; it was up to the gods to do so when they chose, using their tools of weather and time. Hild laid the mint sprig on the shrine, bowing her head briefly.

Beyond the Old Place, a group of women called to her, and Hild waved, wondering whether they'd heard her news, and whether they would come to watch her. As she rounded the corner near the Thordsby Gate, a commotion made her stop. The guards had pulled the fortress gates wide open to let five horsemen—a newly returned raiding party—ride through. The sun glinted off their helmets, and the horses' hooves sprayed dust and gravel over a group of children who stood near the gate, cheering. Hild narrowed her eyes to make sure she could trust what she was seeing, then widened them with delight. She could hardly believe her good fortune. On her first day to serve in the hall, not only would she get to celebrate the homecoming of a raiding party, but one of the warriors standing in front of her would be Garwulf. Had her uncle suspected that Garwulf's troop would be returning when he'd decreed that she would bear the mead to the men today?

The wooden gates shut, pushing in front of them a band of bedraggled people roped together—new slaves for the kingdom. Mord, the leader of the horsemen, wheeled his horse around and rode directly at the slaves. They startled back, their eyes wide. Their ropes made them pull at each other and cry out in confusion as they tried to get away from the horse's hooves. Mord's laughter rang out over the din. Just like him to make sport of helpless slaves, Hild thought, and all to earn the praise of an audience of children. He seemed to have forgotten what everyone knew: the gods might decide who would be slaves and who would be free, but they expected free people to care well for their property.

Another horseman turned, and she breathed out heavily in anger, unwilling to witness a second warrior acting so dishonorably. But it was Garwulf, and instead of repeating what Mord had done, he dismounted as he neared the slaves. Hild watched, gratified, as he put a hand on a male slave's shoulder, speaking words that she couldn't hear but that obviously calmed the man, who in turn spoke to the others.

As Garwulf mounted his horse again, he looked in her direction.

Her breath caught in her throat. Had he seen her?

He had! He bowed, then raised his head, his eyes meeting hers, before he rode for the stables.

A thrill ran through her and she looked down at herself, wondering how she had appeared to him. She still had on her everyday gown. She had to go home now if she was to get to the hall in time. If she was to welcome Garwulf with the mead horn.

She picked up her skirts and ran.

TWO

At home, they were ready for her. There was a joke in the kingdom that if an invisible dwarf spoke to you wordlessly in a lightless cave, three people would already know what he'd said before he finished his message. That was how hard it was to be the first person in the kingdom to hear something. Hild thought of the joke now as her mother stood at the door watching for her, urging her to hurry, somehow already aware of the raiding party's return.

Inside, Unwen, the slave who had served the family for years, was brushing out Hild's good red gown. A clean linen shift lay over the bed.

As Hild struggled to unfasten the brooches that held up her everyday gown, the door opened and her sister Siri rushed into the room, a stream of sunlight illuminating her from behind. "Did you see them ride in? Aren't you excited?"

"We don't have time for chatter," their mother said, then pushed Siri toward the stool. "You sit and rest so your baby will be healthy."

"I don't need to rest. I didn't with my first three, and look how healthy they are," Siri said as she reached for the shift. "Here, Hild, raise your arms."

Hild smiled at her, the two of them amused by their mother's solicitude. It was an old story, the way she tried to keep Siri from working during every pregnancy, and the way Siri always did exactly what she wanted to do.

"I know you girls are laughing at me," their mother said. "But we don't have time to joke. This is too important."

The shift went over Hild's head and she inhaled deeply. The linen garment had been washed with lavender, and the scent quieted her agitation.

"You were at the lake early," her mother said, holding out the red gown. Again, Hild thought of the invisible dwarf. She hadn't told anybody where she was going when she'd left that morning.

"Did you see Sigyn?" Siri asked, her voice quiet.

Hild shook her head. Neither her mother nor her sister needed any explanation to know what that meant. Hild was hardly the only one Sigyn had turned away without seeing. It was hardest on Siri—it wasn't her fault that she had three children and another on the way, while Sigyn had miscarried twice, once just after Wonred's death. Besides feeling rejected by her sister, Siri suffered in other ways. When she'd heard the raiding party ride in, she had no doubt run to see if it was her husband returning. Hild knew that her sister's cheerful face hid her disappointment that it hadn't been him—and her fear that he might follow Wonred and Harr and too many other warriors to an early funeral pyre.

As Hild's mother and sister worked at the brooches that held up her gown, Unwen, standing behind her, tried to comb her hair.

"Turn this way," her mother said, pulling Hild toward her so she could get a better grip on the brooch. When she did, Unwen sighed noisily. Hild and Siri exchanged another smile at the familiar sound. Unwen had been their slave since Hild was a little girl. She could barely remember the newly arrived Unwen, who'd wept silently and fumbled through her tasks, not at all like the Unwen of today, with her brisk authority among the other slaves, and her way of showing her opinions through her wordless sighs and grunts of disapproval. When Hild had gotten older, she had come to understand that Unwen hadn't always been a slave, that she'd been among a group of people—Hild wasn't sure from what tribe—who had been captured by a raiding party headed by Hild's father. Unwen ought to consider herself lucky, Hild thought; not only did her captors speak the same language she did, she served a noble family. The gods didn't always see fit to give captives such a fate.

She felt the comb on her scalp again. Now that her mother and Siri were through with the brooches, Unwen worked with swift, sure strokes to tame Hild's hair and tie it into the complicated knot at the nape of the neck favored by the women of the kingdom, letting the remainder fall loose and silky down her back like a horse's tail.

While Unwen put the last touches on Hild's hair, her mother looked her over and pronounced her fit for the hall. She led her to the door, Unwen running after her with the comb while Siri picked loose threads off Hild's sleeve. She would make it just in time.

The way to the hall was crowded, but when people saw the king's sister—Hild's mother—approaching, they stepped off the path. Hild craned her neck as they neared Beyla's house, but she couldn't find her friend. She must already be in the hall, trying to get a good place in front of a beam. Hild's fingertips tingled with anticipation.

"This way," her mother said, leading them the back way into the hall, through the kitchens. It might be the quickest route to the dais, but they had to be careful not to run into someone heaving a bucket of water or pulling a steaming pot from the fire. Kitchen workers rushed past them, barely acknowledging Hild and her mother and sister in their haste, but none of them so much as touched their skirts.

At the door to the hall, Hild paused while her mother checked her over once again and patted a stray hair into place. Then she smiled at Hild, kissed her on both cheeks, and pushed her in the direction of the dais.

Hild fought the impulse to look back at Siri. Instead,

blinking as her eyes accustomed themselves to the firelight, she moved toward the group of men who clustered near the front of the hall. Bragi, his harp tucked under his arm, looked her up and down from the corners of his eyes, but he didn't otherwise acknowledge her. She held her head higher and kept going, pushing past Hrethel, a high-ranking earl, who smiled at her and inclined his head graciously. Hild smiled back. She moved past two thanes, who were so deep in a whispered conversation that they didn't notice her, then winced as Olaf the Peacock trod on her toes. "So sorry, my dear, so very sorry," he said, but he was brushing off his embroidered tunic, not looking at her, as he spoke.

She was almost to the dais now. Where was her uncle? She wondered if she should wait for him, but when a man held out his hand to her and bowed regally, she let him guide her up the steps. It was one of the queen's kinsmen, a visiting Bronding whose name she couldn't remember. Her eyes still scanning the crowd for her uncle, she thanked him.

Then she was on top of the wooden platform, alone. She breathed in, then out again to quell her nerves. A slave handed her the long, curved drinking horn and she took it, careful not to spill the mead. She stood uncertainly at the back for a moment, then moved forward, taking her place at the front of the dais, hoping she was doing the right thing.

How different the hall looked from here. She had never seen things from the king's perspective before. At the far end, daylight streamed through the massive oak doors, shining on the guards' spear tips, while a group of grannies sat making thread in the hall's north corner and three little boys chased each other around one of the brightly painted beams that held up the roof. Her eyes traveled up the beams to the banners hanging from the rafters. Even they looked different from this perspective, torchlight illuminating the woven images of Odin, of Freyja, of the lesser gods. She pictured the tapestry just taking shape on her loom at home and realized she should be considering the role fire and shadow would play on the design. That was where it would hang when she finished it, she decided, choosing a prominent position easily visible from where she stood. The story the banner told would remind the king of the women and children left behind when he sent his warriors into battle.

She looked down again, at the men who stood beside the long wooden mead benches on either side of the blazing fires, the slaves hovering in the background waiting to serve. Women, among them her aunts and cousins, crowded the walls. Her mother and Siri leaned against a beam, their heads bent toward each other. They were too busy whispering for her to catch their attention. But there was Beyla, her hair in her eyes, standing with a group of girls and ignoring their chatter as she waited for Hild to notice her. They gave each other a solemn look before Beyla grinned. She pantomimed taking a slurp from the horn and wiping her mouth with the back of her hand. Hild hoped her friend had heard how she had made Brynjolf laugh earlier.

When a tall warrior moved, blocking Hild's view of Beyla, she turned her focus back to the heavy drinking horn in her hands. It was full to the brim. Tiny bubbles on the edges of the golden mead winked at her, and firelight danced on the polished silver fittings. Her arms were starting to ache from its weight. She hadn't anticipated quite how heavy it was, and she prayed to the goddess that she wouldn't spill it—or worse, drop it.

A hush fell over the crowd. She heard footsteps coming up the stairs. The boards shuddered beneath her feet as her uncle moved across the dais to stand beside her. Just behind him came Bragi. Hild watched her uncle shift his eyes to the skald. Bragi inclined his head, as if he were giving the king permission to begin.

Then her uncle looked out at the hall, and as he did, Hild followed his gaze, finally allowing her eyes to settle on the five travel-stained warriors, who stood closest to the dais, their mail shirts clinking lightly as they swayed around the men's legs. She tried to make herself look at the others, but her gaze kept straying to Garwulf. Firelight reflected off the metal band that encircled his arm, a gift from the king for his prowess.

Then their leader stepped forward. Mord, one of the king's trusted thanes, but hardly one of his shoulder companions, wore two rings to Garwulf's one. *Not for long,* Hild thought, remembering the way he'd treated the slaves that morning, and the way he was always ready to start a fight, or to prolong one.

"Hail, Ragnar, King," Mord said, lowering himself to one knee and holding both hands before him. Gold glittered in his fingers. The raiding party had done well. They had brought not just slaves but also treasure to the kingdom.

Beside her, Hild's uncle raised a hand. "My hearth companions," he said, and when Hild stole a glance at him, she could see that he was letting his eyes rest on each of the five men in turn. "You have performed a great service to our kingdom. You are most welcome."

All five of the warriors bowed, and Mord rose to his feet.

The king turned, his hand going to Hild's shoulder.

It was time. She tightened her belly.

"Hild, our sister-daughter, gives you our greeting."

Hild turned to her uncle, sinking into a careful curtsy. She rose and held out the great curved horn. Her uncle took it, sipped, and handed it back to her. As he did, their eyes met and she could see the humor in his. *Easy for him to laugh,* she thought. He didn't have to descend the dais, mead threatening to spill, skirts threatening to trip his feet.

Nor did he know what she was planning. Beyla knew, of course, and Hild suspected that Thryth did, too. She'd looked for the old woman in the hall but hadn't seen her. It didn't matter. Hild had made her decision, and despite the eyes of the kingdom on her, she would hold to it.

She placed her foot on the first step, realizing belatedly that she would have no free hand to hold up her skirts. At least she had to present the horn only to the raiding party, not all her uncle's earls and highest-ranking thanes. If she had had to serve them all, or the visiting Bronding noblemen, or worst of all, Bragi, she didn't think her courage would have held. She could feel their presence behind her, and smell the oil the skald used on his harp strings, as she made her way down the steps.

At the bottom, she moved quickly, before she could change her mind. A little too quickly—a trickle of mead spilled over the horn's edge and ran down its sides and onto her fingers. She ignored it and moved toward the men. As she neared Mord, he reached out to accept the horn. Gathering her resolve and keeping her gaze directly ahead, Hild passed him, leaving his hands to clutch at empty air.

She thought she might have heard murmuring in the crowd, but she closed her ears and kept walking. She passed one warrior, then another, until finally, she stopped in front of Garwulf.

Keeping her eyes on the torchlight reflected on the horn's silver fittings, hoping no one could detect the trembling in her voice, she spoke loudly enough that the women who stood along the walls would be able to hear her. "Receive this mead, Garwulf, along with our thanks for your service to the kingdom, and for your *honor*." She emphasized the last word. Then she held out the horn.

For the briefest instant, his clear brown eyes met hers and she saw the confusion in them before he looked down. A flush crept up his neck.

She had put him in an impossible situation and she knew it. He had to insult either her, by refusing to drink, or Mord, who not only had led the raiding party, but, with his two arm rings, held a higher rank among the king's thanes. Hild was sure she knew what Garwulf would do, but being sure didn't keep her heart from pounding. She watched him, careful to keep her eyes away from his, trying not to notice the way his dark hair curled around his neck where it had escaped from the leather cord that held it back. She caught a whiff of saddle leather and sweat and autumn leaves. In the now-silent hall, she could feel everyone looking at her, and she hoped her own face wasn't coloring.

Hurry, she urged him silently. With her arms outstretched, the horn was getting heavier, but she didn't want to pull it back or people might think she was changing her mind. She shifted her weight to steady herself.

The movement broke the moment. Garwulf dipped his head. "My lady," he said, and reached for the horn.

When he gave it back to her, she lowered herself into a curtsy. She wanted to look at his face, to see what he was thinking, but now her courage failed her.

Instead, she returned to Mord, who was rubbing his thumb over the white scar on his upper lip, just below his mustache. As she approached him, he gave someone behind her—Hild couldn't see who—a look of withering contempt and took the horn before she even began her greeting. He drank, then thrust it back at her so roughly that mead sloshed over the sides. "My lady," he said, the tone of his voice making his opinion of her perfectly clear to anyone with ears.

Anger made her resolution return. She met his eyes and held them. "We thank you, Mord, for your service to the kingdom." She kept her voice icy calm.

She approached the three other warriors according to their rank, first Lyting, then Halga, and finally Gizzur the Loud, a small wiry man whose "my lady" was so quiet that if she hadn't seen his lips move, she wouldn't have known he'd spoken.

Then she turned to climb the steps, steeling herself to meet the king's wrath. She was prepared for it; she knew exactly what she would say.

But he didn't give her the chance. Instead, he was smiling at her.

Smiling?

As she came to the top of the stairs, he turned her to the crowd, his hand again on her shoulder in a protective gesture. "A first try is often difficult," he said, warmth in his voice. "This was Hild's first time passing the mead to my warriors. I'm sure Mord will forgive her."

Mord bowed briefly, but Hild didn't look down at him because now her own cheeks were flaming.

The king wasn't through. "May the next time be without flaw." Then, raising his voice and pushing her forward, he called out, "I give you Hild, my sister-daughter."

The crowd roared its approval, but Hild stared stonily ahead, humiliated. It hadn't been an error. She'd meant to serve the man with the most honor first, as a message to her uncle. But he hadn't even noticed. And now everyone saw her as a child who didn't even know the order of rank among the men.

From the corner of her eye, she saw her cousin Skadi standing with the other women, laughing. Hild ground her teeth and stared at the open doors at the far end of the hall, willing herself to be through them.

She couldn't wait to be dismissed.

THREE

"HILD, WAIT!"

She heard Siri calling her, but she kept going. After the dim hall, the sunlight made her blink and the crisp air cooled her flushed cheeks. She pushed through a flock of geese that crowded the lane. Both they and the slave boy driving them toward the kitchens were too surprised to react, but she heard them honking and clattering by the time Siri got to them.

"Ow! Stop it!" her sister cried out, and Hild turned to see her batting ineffectively at a hissing gander. Hild sighed irritably. There wasn't much that bothered Siri, outside her worry about her husband, but she had a long history with geese. Hild couldn't simply leave her sister to deal with them on her own, and the slave seemed too young to be much help. She rushed back, shooed the birds away, and pulled Siri down the lane. They passed a girl carrying a huge basket and a man leading two nanny goats, everyone busy preparing for the harvest festival, before Siri stopped and brushed at her gown. "I hate that goose."

"You hate all geese."

"But especially that one. He needs his neck wrung."

"He's not the only one," their mother said, hurrying toward them, her eyes on Hild. She stopped to catch her breath. "How could you do that?"

Hild's chest swelled with indignation. "He's more honorable, Mother. Any woman would agree, especially if they'd seen them when they rode in this morning with the slaves."

"It's not about honor, it's about rank, and you know that." Her mother's brows knitted in anger. "You embarrassed me and our whole family—and that includes the king."

Hild shifted uncomfortably and looked back at the geese. The gander was hissing at his harem, his strong neck snaking around to keep them in line. It gave Hild great satisfaction to know he would soon be somebody's dinner.

Her mother started down the path again, her shoes drumming against the packed dirt. "I told the king that you were ready for this, that you knew the rules of precedence." She looked back at Hild. "I told him I would train you."

Hild lowered her eyes. She hadn't thought about how her actions would reflect on her mother.

"If she'd been able to," her mother said, "the queen would have done her duty. She would have served Mord first, because he's higher in rank—no matter what she thought about his honor."

Anger flared again, as it always did when Hild and her mother had this argument. "If she'd seen what he did to those slaves, she wouldn't have served Mord first. Besides, he picks fights over nothing—he thinks it's fun to start a feud. The queen would never let him get away with that." Why had her mother never been able to see the obvious? When the queen had taken to her bed several years earlier, she had abdicated her power and her right to influence the king with subtle persuasion. In doing so, she'd taken away the ability of any of the kingdom's women to sway the king's opinions. Instead, the king was guided by Bragi, his chief skald, whose love of war was no secret. Before the queen fell ill, there had been feuds with the Geats and the Helmings—not open war, but lightning raids across borders on both sides. Now that Bragi had the king's ear, however, Hild had lost track of how many tribes the Shylfings were hostile with.

"The queen would have talked to the king later, in private, if she was worried about Mord," her mother said.

"No, she wouldn't. She would have done exactly the same thing I did." Hild knew she shouldn't speak to her mother this way, but in her anger, she couldn't stop herself.

Siri pushed between them, laughing and grabbing their hands. "That's not what this is about."

"What?" Hild whirled, her chin raised.

"Mother, don't you see? This doesn't have anything to do with rank or honor or duty." Siri looked from their mother to Hild. "This is about Garwulf."

Her mother's features softened, but Hild wasn't ready to give up the fight. Besides, what Siri was saying wasn't true, not in the way she meant it.

"He's a good man," her mother said.

"An honorable one," Siri added, giving Hild a wink.

Hild bristled. "He *is* honorable. That's why I served him first."

"Don't tease your sister, Siri," their mother said. "He's from a powerful family. Your uncle approves of him; young as Garwulf is, the king already values him. And he's handsome, too." She put her arm around Hild's shoulder, but Hild shrugged it off.

She'd never made any secret of it—she did have her eye on Garwulf, and she was happy that her mother and uncle believed a match between them was a good idea. But it wasn't why she'd served him before Mord. It was because if the king was going to elevate some thanes above others, and listen to their counsel, he should put Garwulf far above Mord. How many times had she seen Garwulf breaking up a fight between two ale-headed warriors, joking with them until the heat of anger was gone? And the way he had treated the slaves that morning showed exactly how much better he was than Mord. If her mother wasn't willing to take a stand, Hild was.

They got to Siri's house with the argument still hanging in the air. Before Hild could say anything else, though, the door opened, and her two nephews dashed out. Behind them, she could hear the baby wailing.

"Careful of my herbs!" Siri said, but the little boys ignored her, trampling the late sage in their haste to get to Hild.

"Aunt Hild! Look what we found!"

Hild brushed aside her anger and knelt to admire the rock that Faxi thrust at her. It glinted in the sunlight.

"Ooh, it's beautiful," she said. "Do you think dwarves made it?"

Faxi nodded, his blue eyes wide, before he took it back.

"Come, younglings, and watch where you step," Siri said, and a slave ran forward to usher the boys back inside.

As Hild rose, she heard her aunt Var's deep voice greeting them from down the path. "I thought I'd find you here."

She suppressed a groan. *Goddess help me.* She had to get away before a new round of faultfinding began.

Careful not to let her eyes meet her aunt's, she called a bright "Greetings, Auntie!" and gave a little wave before she turned and hurried back down the path toward the geese. She could hear her aunt calling her name, but she waved again and kept going, her lips turned up in what she hoped was a convincing smile. Just beyond the geese, the lane branched. With a last glance behind her, she turned.

Although her loom beckoned and her fingers itched to

get back to the pattern she was weaving, it wasn't worth hearing more about how foolish she'd been. And who knew how many other women—neighbors, aunts, cousins—would show up to offer their opinions. She couldn't go home yet. She needed to talk to Beyla, and she knew just where her friend would be.

At the stables, she paused in the doorway, inhaling the pleasant scent of horse and hay. A boy hurried over, bowed, and stood waiting for her instructions, but she waved him away and headed for Fleetfoot's stall. As she approached, she could see her horse baring his long teeth in a ridiculous face of bliss. Beyla, who had no horse of her own, was currying him.

"You're spoiling my horse."

"Of course I am." Beyla didn't look up from her work. "Let your auntie Beyla spoil you," she crooned at Fleetfoot, who slobbered his approval.

Hild laughed and touched her forehead to her horse's nose, letting his warmth steady her after the tension in the hall.

"I saw your mother running after you. What did she say?" Beyla asked.

"What you'd expect."

Beyla shook her head and reached for the horse's front foot, pushing the battered silver arm ring she wore as a bracelet over her elbow when it threatened to fall off her wrist. "Someday she's got to see that you're right."

"But today . . . ," Hild began, and when Beyla grinned up at her, they finished the line in unison: ". . . is not that day."

They laughed and Beyla straightened, brushing horse-hair from her skirt and blowing her own hair, which had come loose from its knot, out of her face. "You didn't know Garwulf would be there, did you?"

"Not till this morning when I saw him ride in. Turn around." Hild took Beyla's unruly brown hair in her hands, retying the knot. Her work wouldn't last long. Beyla spent a good part of her life being told to stand still while somebody knotted her hair again or repinned one of her brooches or straightened her gown.

"I wish I could have seen his face when you gave him the horn," she said. "From where I was standing, I could barely see the back of his head."

"He blushed," Hild said, smiling.

Beyla turned, her grin revealing the gap between her front teeth. "I'll bet he did."

"You should have seen what happened at the gate this morning, what Mord did."

A woman's voice from the stable doorway interrupted her. "Beyla? Are you in here?"

"Goat's breath," Beyla whispered. "It's my turn with Granny." She called out, "Coming, Mother," before lowering her voice again and speaking apologetically. "I want to hear what happened, but not now."

"I know," Hild said. She wouldn't see Beyla for the rest

of the day—not when she had to care for her grandmother. It was hard to believe Beyla's granny had ever been young or happy, so difficult and unpleasant was she now, demanding the undivided attention of the person caring for her. From experience, they knew it was easier for Beyla when Hild didn't try to help. "I'll tell you tomorrow at the festival."

Beyla nodded and gave Fleetfoot's mane one last tug before she ran from the stable.

Hild watched her go, trying not to mind. She needed Beyla to help her sort out the events in the hall, and to tell her how people had reacted.

Fleetfoot nickered softly and nudged her head, turning it toward the stable doors. Light spilled through them, illuminating dust motes and reminding Hild that their days of galloping freely were numbered; winter would soon be upon them. She turned back to her horse. "You want a ride, don't you?" When she pulled the bridle from the hook, Fleetfoot pricked up his ears and danced in his stall, making Hild laugh. She called the boy over to help her with the saddle and then rode out of the stable, taking the path to the Thordsby Gate, where the guards dipped their spears in acknowledgment. Because she was the king's sister-daughter, it was Hild's right to come and go as she pleased, as long as she kept to the patrolled lanes.

As Fleetfoot cantered past, a slave girl, her blond hair in braids, jumped out of the way, spilling the contents of the bucket she was carrying. She said something that Hild didn't catch. Whatever it was, it didn't sound nice. Hild should have reprimanded the girl for her insolence, but she didn't care enough to go back. Now that she was away from the weight of her family's disapproval, the bright autumn day reached out to her with open arms and the road ahead beckoned.

In a rocky field beside her, the boys' troop was practicing archery. She found her cousin Arinbjörn in the midst of the group and frowned when he raised his bow. Wasn't it too high? She hoped none of the other boys were snickering at him. He might be the atheling, the king's heir, but they wouldn't hesitate to show their scorn. It was bad enough that his father had made him start training when he was younger than the other boys, but the fact that he wasn't very good at it made it worse.

She shook her head and looked down the road. Fleet-foot shook his head, too. He wanted a good gallop, the same as she did, but too many people and carts lined the way, and the field beside the path was too rocky. Far ahead, Hild could just make out the thatched roofs of Thordsby, the farm the townspeople would visit for the harvest festival, to celebrate the bringing in of the last grain. "Let's wait till we're at the farm," she told her horse. "Then you can ride as fast as Sleipnir."

He tossed his mane in agreement.

It turned out they didn't have to wait that long. They were still halfway between town and farm when the road before them cleared. "Now!" she said to Fleetfoot, who didn't need to hear more. Hild bent low, feeling the wind pick up her hair and send it streaming behind her like Freyja's winged cape. Down the road and through the farm's gates they went without pausing, then thundered across a field, cold air filling Hild's ears and stinging her face.

At the edge of the field, the ground was strewn with rocks and Hild slowed Fleetfoot's pace. Reluctantly, they turned, Hild's breath still coming fast, her ears aching from the wind that had filled them, her heart pounding from exertion, her exultation barely dimmed. Fleetfoot picked his sedate path back toward the farm buildings. In the distance, men were harvesting the golden grain, and beyond the buildings, she could see workers erecting logs for the huge bonfire that would honor the gods during the festival.

At the gate, a rider sat watching them, but from this distance Hild couldn't see who it was. As she neared him, the horseman started toward them. Garwulf.

She watched him approach. Why was he here? He still hadn't changed from his travel-stained clothing.

As he got close enough that she could see his face, her spirits fell. The straight line of his mouth spelled disapproval. Was he going to admonish her, too?

She looked away, her focus on the rows of stubble the harvesters had left behind in the dirt. Garwulf had every right to be angry at her for the position she'd put him in. She wished she'd thought more carefully about that earlier, back when serving him before Mord had seemed like a good idea.

When they were so near to each other that she could no longer avoid it, she looked up again. "Garwulf," she said, and swallowed.

"My lady." He dipped his head in acknowledgment, then met her eye. "You ride well, my lady. But if there had been a rock or a fallen limb, you could have been thrown."

"Fleetfoot and I ride here often," she told him as he turned his horse to ride alongside her. "They keep the way clear for us."

"Oh," he said. "I didn't know. That's good, then." He reached out to stroke his own horse's neck.

She watched him surreptitiously, unsure of his mood. His mail shirt jingled softly as he rode, but he said nothing. Then he turned to her.

"What happened in the hall today—" He stopped.

She looked down, preparing for his words. If it hadn't been humiliating enough to have her uncle misunderstand her and her mother upbraid her, now she was about to be chastised by the man she planned to marry.

"Hild," he said. His voice was so low it rumbled in her chest.

She forced herself to look at him.

"I thank you for what you did, my lady."

She stared at him in surprise. When she realized her

mouth was open, she snapped it shut. He had ridden all the way out here to thank her?

"May I accompany you back to the stable?"

She smiled. "Of course you may." She couldn't wait to tell Beyla.

FOUR

ONCE GARWULF LEFT THE STABLE, HILD STAYED WITH her horse. He might have already been thoroughly brushed, but she needed to think, and currying Fleetfoot was a good way to do so—even if it did get dirt on her best gown. She hoped she could get the gown into Unwen's hands for cleaning before her mother or one of her aunts saw the mess she was making of it.

She was glad she was wearing it, though. She and Garwulf must have looked impressive riding back from the farm together, he in his warrior's garb, she in the red gown that drew attention to her dark hair. She had seen people watching, and she'd kept her back straight, her pace measured, as she'd asked Garwulf question after question about his raiding party, keeping the conversation going all the way through the gates and back to the stable, despite his willingness to ride in silence.

At the stable, he had called a boy over to help her unsaddle Fleetfoot, then given her a low bow before hurrying off. As soon as he was gone, she sent the boy away, pulled out the comb, and considered her next move. When it was time to serve the mead again, she would follow precedent precisely. She'd forgotten that her uncle still considered her a child. Once she'd proven that she knew the rules, she could start to break them. If she was going to influence his opinion, she would need to go about it with greater subtlety than she'd shown that morning.

Her thoughts flickered back to Garwulf and she smiled. *He* approved of what she had done.

As for her uncle, she had time, and plenty of it, on her side. Unless the queen left her bed, Hild would be the only one to pass the horn in the mead hall. Not until her cousin Arinbjörn married would another woman take her place, and that wouldn't be for years.

All his life, her uncle had been guided by others. His mother, the old queen, had advised him from the time he was crowned as a very young man. When he married, his mother stepped aside, making way for his wife, as was expected. "A queen must serve the mead to her lord first, and be ready with advice for him," the saying went. But when the queen had become ill and people were distracted by their worry about her, Bragi had slipped into the king's confidence, taking the place that should be held by a woman. He'd elbowed out Ari Frothi, too, whose age brought him wisdom. It wasn't right. And more than that, Hild told herself, it wasn't good for the kingdom.

She laid her cheek against Fleetfoot's neck, breathed in his horsey scent, and stroked his nose one last time before she left the stable, heading for home—and her loom. She hadn't gotten there yet when she heard women's voices. Her cousin Skadi's unmistakable giggle pierced the air just as the group turned the corner and saw her. There was no escape.

"Hild, come and help us," her mother said, giving her dirty gown a quick look of appraisal. Instead of remarking on it, however, she smiled, the lines around her eyes crinkling. "We're going to the goddess's house."

Hild joined them, happy to be forgiven. Aunt Var's expression was sour, but with Aunt Var, that was customary. Skadi's smirk, however, was clearly meant for Hild, her dirty skirt, and her behavior in the hall. Skadi herself looked as beautiful as she always did, her chestnut curls and wide blue eyes making her the image of the elf-bright maiden in the old stories. She was insufferable.

Beyla's little sister tagged along behind them, singing some private tune to herself. "Inga, come walk with me," Hild said, holding out her hand. The little girl ran to catch up, slipping her fingers into Hild's, and they swung their arms back and forth together, laughing, until they reached the wooden temple dedicated to Freyja. On the other side of the lane, outside the larger temple to Odin, a puppy pawed the ground, inviting them to play, its tail a blur of wagging. When Inga dropped her hand and ran to greet it, Hild recognized it as Brynjolf's dog.

"That hound had better stay away from me," Aunt Var said, clutching at her skirt.

Hild caught her mother's eye and smiled. Aunt Var, her father's older sister, was as prickly as her chin and elbows were sharp, and her eyes were the same color as her iron-gray hair. Only her voice belied her features; it was low, warm, and melodious.

"I'm sure the puppy won't come near you, Aunt Var," Hild said. "And look, there's Brynjolf. He'll keep it under control."

As the young warrior stepped out of Odin's house, Hild lowered her chin and pouted in apology for getting him into trouble earlier. When he saw her, he laughed, then bowed to them all before kneeling in the dust to play with Inga and the puppy.

Aunt Var glared at both boy and dog before she entered the temple.

Hild followed her, ducking under the lintel, and paused, blinking, while her eyes adjusted.

"Watch out," Skadi said, bumping into her as she came through the door, and Hild took a step forward. There was scarcely enough room for all four of them in the temple, especially when the slave girl who accompanied them came in to hand them their tools. Hild grabbed the sheepskin before Skadi could get to it, leaving her cousin the whisk, while her mother and Aunt Var began to take down the summer tapestry that hung on the wall.

While Skadi stooped to sweep dust from the corners, Hild polished the small altar, starting on the edges and working her way toward the center, where a metal bowl sat in front of the stone statue of Freyja. As they worked, Aunt Var began to hum. She kept a vast hoard of lays in her head. *Women's songs,* Bragi scoffed when he heard them. When he chanted in the hall before the king's hearth companions, he chose the histories of the tribes and lays of feuds and wars and heroes. Aunt Var's songs told the other side of things, the side that said there were no feuds or wars or heroes without women sorrowing in the background.

"Sing about the baby in the boat," Hild said. "Please, Aunt Var?"

Her aunt made a coughing sound that was the closest she ever came to laughing. "I've sung that one so often for you the goddess herself is tired of it."

"Don't anger the goddess," Skadi said, looking around in mock terror.

Aunt Var hummed again, but instead of Hild's favorite lay, she began one about a woman waiting without hope for her lover to return from war.

Hild picked up the metal bowl from the altar and rubbed it until she could see the light from the open door reflected in it. She was glad Siri wasn't here—ever since Wonred had been killed and Sigyn had sunk into her grief, Siri had taken to creeping away whenever Aunt Var sang this song. Especially when her husband wasn't home. It wasn't the sort of thing Aunt Var noticed, but Hild did.

Her aunt shifted into a song about a woman who had been married to the enemy in order to bring peace between two feuding tribes. Hild shut her ears to it; she'd never liked this lay, with its emphasis on just how many kinsmen the lady had lost when the peace she'd been sent to weave couldn't withstand the men's hunger for vengeance. Her husband, her son, and her brother had all perished in the bitter swordplay. Hild wondered if there were any lays about successful peaceweavers. She'd have to ask her aunt to sing one of those next time.

For now, though, she was relieved when Aunt Var cut the song short and started a harvest chant. Hild's mother joined in as the two women lifted the tapestry, with its images of Freyja blessing the sheaves—a tapestry Hild's great-grandmother had woven—onto its hooks on the wall. Seeing its craftsmanship made Hild hunger for her own loom. Half listening to the chanting, half picturing the tapestry she was working on, Hild turned from the bowl to the stone figurine. She ran the sheepskin over its surface, brushing away dust from the carved features. As her palm covered the top of the goddess's head, sudden dizziness made her sway. Holding on to the edge of the altar to steady herself, she waited for the sensation to pass, but it didn't. Instead, the light-headedness became an impression of warmth and power—tinged with something else. Then it was gone.

Hild stood unmoving. What had happened? It seemed familiar, like a memory that hovered just beyond her reach. She had felt comfort, perhaps, and strength—the kind of strength she'd experienced earlier when she and Fleetfoot had galloped across the field so fast her eyes had watered from the wind. Warmth, too; she'd felt warmth like a stone heated in the ashes and tucked under the blankets on a winter's night. And light. Light like a stream of golden mead poured from the drinking horn, pierced by the glow of the hall fires. But snaking behind it all were the tendrils of smoke that invaded her dreams.

For an instant, the sensation returned.

"Are you finished?"

The words brought her back to the world. Hild looked up to see her mother handing the rolled-up summer tapestry to the slave. They were all watching her: her mother, Aunt Var, Skadi.

She looked back down at the statue and swallowed. "I'm ready."

The others went out, but her mother lingered for a moment, giving Hild a searching look. Hild met her eyes, but she didn't speak. Finally, her mother turned and Hild followed her out of the temple, emerging from the shadowy interior into the afternoon sun. Momentarily blinded, she stepped directly into the path of a man walking down the lane.

"Watch where you're— Oh! Forgive me, my lady," the man said, and she looked up to see one of the Bronding noblemen, the one who had offered her his hand in the hall.

She curtsied to him and his companions and felt the other women dropping into curtsies, as well. The Brondings responded with curt bows before they resumed their conversation and walked on. Although the Shylfings were at peace with the Brondings, the queen's illness had made their alliance fragile. Hild's mother had told her the Brondings wanted their interests expressed in the hall, which was why they'd sent the queen's kinsmen to Gyldenseld. Few Shylfings agreed that the Brondings should have any say in the kingdom's affairs. And although the queen was well liked, her kinsmen, with their ostentatiously fur-edged cloaks, were not.

"Ugh, no mustaches," Skadi said.

"Hush, they'll hear you," Hild's mother said, but Hild heard the amusement in her voice.

Skadi ignored her. "It makes their lips look like slugs. Can you imagine kissing that?"

Her cousin irritated her beyond all bearing, but Hild had to admit that she could be funny. She and her mother laughed, and even Aunt Var looked like she was suppressing a smile as the little party broke up, Skadi and Aunt Var heading in one direction, Hild and her mother in the opposite.

Now that the two of them were alone, Hild steeled herself for what her mother had withheld in the presence of the others. If she didn't scold her for the dirt on her gown, she would at least ask her questions about what had happened in the temple. But Hild was wrong.

"I must attend the queen," her mother said, touching Hild's arm lightly before she turned down the path that led to the royal quarters.

Relieved, Hild headed for home. It was past time for the midday meal and she was hungry. Now that the flurry of attention to her behavior in the hall had died down, she could eat and weave in peace.

But peace, it turned out, had to wait until Unwen had made known her opinion about the condition of Hild's gown. Although she didn't say a word, her expression made up for Hild's mother's silence on the matter.

"It will come clean," Hild said as Unwen fastened the brooches on her everyday gown.

Unwen grunted her disapproval so low that if Hild hadn't grown up hearing it, she might not have recognized the sound.

Finally, having eaten the bread and salty cheese Unwen prepared for her, Hild sank onto the stool in front of her loom. Images from the lay she had tried to get Aunt Var to sing, the story of the baby in the boat, were beginning to emerge in the threads. In the weave, the top of the mother's head was just coming into view: she was running from danger, her infant in her arms. On the left side, enemy warriors with spears were already beginning to threaten her, and in the foreground, the boat rocked on the waves. Hild recalled the boat she had seen earlier, out at the lake. Yes, she decided, running her fingers over the fabric; she could make those same graceful curves appear on her boat's prow.

It was still too early to tell, but Hild thought this might be the best tapestry she'd ever made. And that was saying something.

She bent to her work, a ray of sun turning the cloth to gold under her fingertips.

FIVE

A SHADOW FELL OVER THE LOOM. HILD FROWNED BUT SHE didn't stop working. Freyja was with her, guiding her hands, taking the threads places she wasn't aware she wanted them to go until she got there. She didn't want to lose her concentration.

The shadow moved, this time blocking even more of her light. She looked up in irritation—which turned to laughter.

Her cousin Arinbjörn leaned against the doorpost, smiling.

"What are you doing here? Why aren't you at training?" Hild asked.

"My father granted us a holiday for the rest of the day." His father, the king.

"Well, not a holiday. We're supposed to be helping get

a bonfire ready for the festival, but there were too many of us." He sank to the floor beside her loom, wrapping his arms around his long legs. For an instant, Hild was transported to an earlier time, before her cousin had begun training with the boys, when the two of them had been inseparable. After his mother had fallen ill, Arinbjörn had spent most of his time with Hild. She might be three winters older, but he was good company. He could listen quietly while Aunt Var wove stories and Hild wove threads, but he was always ready for fun, too, joining in their adventures when Hild and Beyla allowed him to.

"Come help me," he said.

She looked at her loom, but her concentration was gone and she knew it wouldn't return while her cousin was here. Spending time with him was a rare treat now that he was part of the boys' troop. Still, she had to make a show of resistance. "I can't, I'm busy."

"Please?" He gazed at her beseechingly with his wide gray eyes, the lashes thick as a girl's.

Finally, judging that she'd made him wait long enough, she turned to him and smiled.

"Hurry," he said, standing and pulling her up with him. Laughing, they emerged into the light.

"Look how tall you are!" Hild said, making Arinbjörn stop so she could measure herself against him. "You must have grown overnight—you're almost as tall as me."

"But not as tall as Garwulf," he said, giving her a sly

look, and she knew he must have seen them riding together earlier.

If he meant to embarrass her, it didn't work. "Not nearly as tall as him. You're no Garwulf, youngling," she said, and tried to tousle his hair, but he ducked out of the way. "Where are we going?"

Without answering, he led her toward the path that wound behind the hall. They passed the smithy and the cheerful ringing of hammer on anvil as the blacksmiths shaped weapons of war. Just beyond the smithy's well, Arinbjörn ducked off the path and headed down a weedy trail where rows of smelly sheepskins were stretched out to dry. Hild hurried to keep up with him as he picked his way around a trash heap. Her cousin could get anywhere he wanted to without using the stronghold's main pathways; he had shown Hild and Beyla so many shortcuts over the years that they were almost as good at it as he was.

When they came to a wooden wall, Arinbjörn put his finger to his lips, looked both ways, leaned down to pick up something that had been hidden behind a rock, and then beckoned Hild forward. She stifled her laughter as he moved a loose board aside, stepped through the wall, and ended up on the dusty lane that led out the East Gate, the one hardly anybody used except farmers bringing their grain to the stronghold.

They could have gotten here directly in half the time, but Hild had to admit that her cousin's way was more fun.

Once they were on the lane, she looked to see what he had picked up. A sheathed sword. "You've already got a sword," she said, gesturing to the weapon that hung from his belt.

"But you don't." He looked back at her and laughed. "Hurry up!" His voice squeaked on the word *up*.

Although she was sorely tempted to say something, Hild pretended not to hear it. Instead, she ran to keep up. "Girls don't fight, cousin." She passed him and, walking backward, held out a length of her skirt. "See this?"

"It never stopped you before."

"But that was when—" She stopped herself from completing her thought: *when you still needed my help.*

"When what?" he asked as she fell into step beside him.

"When I was young enough that it didn't matter."

"You mean, when you weren't afraid Garwulf might see you."

"Maybe," she said, and this time, despite herself, she blushed.

"All right, you don't have to. Come watch me instead."

At the gate, the guard stepped out, his spear raised to challenge them. He stopped short, then backed up and bowed as he recognized Arinbjörn, who passed him without so much as a nod of recognition. For all that he was just a boy, Arinbjörn occasionally showed flashes of the ruler he would become, of the privilege and power and expectation of obedience from others. Hild knew it was hard for him to train with the other boys, almost all of whom were older than he was and better with their weapons. She wondered if they resented him and used his weakness with the sword against him.

Not far from the stronghold's wooden walls, a pile of boulders left over from some long-ago party of trolls sheltered a grassy spot where she had taken Arinbjörn on sunny days when he was a little boy. There they'd been away from the noise and dust and smell of town, but close enough that they could call for the guard if danger threatened. So often had they gone there that others recognized it as their private place, and Hild had seen farmers with their oxcarts taking the long way round it in deference to the atheling, the king's son.

Flat farmlands stretched before them, and in the distance, a dark line marked the Wolfholt, the frightening forest that bordered the kingdom on the east. Closer by, on the far side of the grassy area, a stand of birches danced in the breeze, their leaves flickering red to gold to red. The same breeze tugged at Hild's hair and she pushed it out of her eyes. A harsh *caw* announced a raven that landed on a high branch, flapping its wings to steady itself. Another flew in just behind it and settled lower on the tree. "Look." She pointed. "Odin's watching us."

"Which one do you think is Thought and which one is Memory?" Arinbjörn asked, and Hild watched them for a moment, trying to decide. The birds' black feathers shone in the red leaves against a piercingly blue sky. The scent of hay from afar mingled with the odor of cow manure and the sharp smell of goat. Even if she'd had to leave her loom, she was glad she had come.

When she turned, Arinbjörn had dropped into a fighting stance. She sank into the grass and leaned against a lichen-covered rock. The cold of its surface crept through her gown. She shivered.

In front of her, Arinbjörn stretched out his sword. His footwork was fine, Hild thought as she brought a critical eye to his movements. But the way he held his sword . . . If *she* could see how bad he was, what must the other boys think?

"Try raising the point," she called, and he looked over at her.

"Like this?"

She caught herself just before she started to frown. Her features blank, she said, "Elbow closer to your body—don't expose your flank."

He jammed his elbow into his side.

It was all she could do to keep from sighing out loud. Arinbjörn was far from stupid. Why was it so hard for him to learn the basics of defense? *Because he's growing so fast,* she told herself. He was like a foal becoming a horse, awkward and ungainly. The moment his muscles learned a move, his bones grew again, pushing him off-kilter. *As soon as his body catches up with the rest of him,* she thought, *he'll be fine.* She'd seen it with her cousin Skamkel. But still, it was hard to believe Arinbjörn had forgotten everything she had practiced with him, the things her father had taught her. And had he learned nothing from his daily drills with the other boys?

He stretched out his blade again, and once again, his position left him open to attack. Unable to restrain herself any longer, Hild rose and stood behind him, holding her arm parallel to his, making him mirror her moves. "That's it, good," she said.

"It's easy when you're standing there, but when I have to spar with someone—"

"Don't move." She walked to the boulders, where he'd set the other sword, and unsheathed it. "Point up," she said, looking back at him. "Don't let it waver." She took her place in front of him, knees bent, her own blade just touching his. "Ready? Go."

He hesitated, so she attacked, hoping his arm would remember the defensive position. Instead, his blade came under hers, and before she knew what had happened, her own sword was spinning out of her grasp. She watched in astonishment as it landed in the grass a spear's length away.

She looked back at Arinbjörn, who caught her eye, then pounded his thigh with his shield hand as he staggered with laughter.

Comprehension dawned. "You—you planned this, didn't you?"

He gulped for air and wiped at his streaming eyes, but he was laughing too hard to answer.

Her hand went to her mouth; no need to let him see that she was laughing, too. She picked up her sword and strode back to him. "Get in position."

"Girls don't fight," he managed to say as another fit of giggling overtook him.

"In position. Now." She raised her sword.

Trembling with amusement, he raised his own sword. The point was barely in the air before she attacked. It took him two exchanges this time to send her blade flying. Even the ravens in the birch tree cawed with mirth as she picked it up, and she couldn't help laughing along with them.

"So you've learned one trick," she said. Grinning at him, she took her position again. "Let's see if you know any more."

His smile was still broad, but she could tell he was concentrating, watching her as carefully as she was watching him. He was coming *under* her blade and she couldn't let him do that again. "Ready? Go." As fast as she could, she slipped her point underneath his and advanced. He backed up, eluding her easily. She kept her eyes trained on the point of his sword, feeling the way he was leaning forward, letting everything her father had taught her, and all her experience from years of practicing with her cousin, guide her hand. He'd always been hesitant for fear of hurting her, and she would capitalize on that. Again, she advanced, keeping her weapon below his, but instead of retreating, he stepped forward, his blade moving so quickly she couldn't follow it.

And there she was, again, walking across the grass, laughing, to retrieve her sword. He'd learned to fight. She didn't know when or how, but he had, and she was glad of it.

She leaned over to pick up the sword, shaking her head in amusement at the way he'd fooled her, wondering how she would get him back for it. And how had he done that with his blade? Was it something they taught all the boys, or was it a special move of his own? Whatever it was, she'd make him teach her.

She stood, pulling a long piece of grass from her sword hilt, and looked back toward Arinbjörn—just as three men stepped out from behind the boulders. The Brondings.

Arinbjörn was watching her, laughing; he hadn't seen them yet. They moved toward him, smiles on their faces.

Then he heard them and looked at them, his lips slightly parted, in surprise or speech, she wasn't sure. A wave of dizziness made her catch her footing. As she steadied herself, the sky seemed to brighten, and she blinked. The odor of smoke, acrid and burning, bit at her throat, and in that moment, she knew without knowing the why of it that the Brondings' smiles were fox grins, far from friendly. The man closest to him raised his hand toward Arinbjörn.

Within Hild, something snapped. White-hot fury filled her, and without realizing what she was doing, she grabbed her skirt in one hand, her sword in the other, and ran blindly toward her cousin. In less time than it takes a hawk to plummet from the sky after its prey, she was across the practice area, shouldering Arinbjörn aside and pushing with her sword. Her arm jolted as the weapon met resistance, but she shoved back against something she couldn't see, then shoved again, pushing her blade in front of her as it buried itself in something solid.

Everything stopped. Insects in the grass quit their chirring mid-note, the breeze in the birches held its breath, the bright autumn sky blanked into white—

—and then a weight was on her sword as the man standing in front of Arinbjörn staggered.

Now her own lips were parted and she stepped back, taking her blood-spattered hand from the sword, which was still embedded in the man's guts, and looked over his shoulder at Arinbjörn. A tuft of her cousin's hair was sticking up on one side, she noted incongruously. It gave him a comical appearance.

A raven cawed, unlocking the stillness, shocking the world back to life.

"Hild, what have you done?" Arinbjörn said, and his voice sounded different than she'd ever heard it before. Then his face caught up with his voice, and he gave her a look of such horror snaked round with contempt that she didn't think she could bear it.

He was going to kill you, she meant to say, but no words came out before the man crumpled to the ground, almost taking her with him.

He was dead.

SIX

Hɪʟᴅ ᴄᴏᴜʟᴅ sᴄᴀʀᴄᴇʟʏ ᴄᴏᴍᴘʀᴇʜᴇɴᴅ ᴛʜᴇ ғʟᴜʀʀʏ ᴏғ action around her. Shapes and colors rushed together. Her knees gave way and she found herself sinking to the ground, but someone grabbed her elbow and hauled her up. Men came running—guards, she thought, but she couldn't seem to focus—and a hand took her other elbow, squeezing it so tightly she would have slapped it away if the world had still been real. But it wasn't, and the pain in her arm was just another sensation she couldn't interpret, any more than she could comprehend why her body wouldn't stop shaking.

She knew enough to recognize the gate when they marched her through it. When she next opened her eyes, she was in the hall, surrounded by images that resolved themselves into people, a whole group of them. She felt as if she were a small child trapped in a press of grown-ups, their wool garments cutting out light and sound, or as if she were lost in a forest so thick that fir branches pressed into her body. Only fir branches wouldn't reek of blood, would they?

There were voices, voices so loud they hurt her head, and then a finger pointed at her, jabbing toward her face. She sank to the floor again, and again she was yanked upward. Why was she here? She couldn't remember.

Then the pain in her elbow stopped and a gentle arm slipped around her and a scent she knew and loved filled her nostrils. Her head fell to her mother's shoulder, and even though she didn't hear the words her mother was saying, relief washed around her as if she were waking from a nightmare. She slipped into darkness.

When she opened her eyes, she was in her own cabinet bed, carved cats chasing mice in an endless procession around the wooden trim. The bed's doors hung open and firelight cast shadows on its ceiling. Hild lay silent, listening, wondering. Something had happened, but she couldn't remember what, or why she was in bed when the fire was still dancing on the hearth. Her head pounded. Had she been ill?

A movement made her turn. It was her mother, crossing the room to look down at her, her face grave, one finger on her lips, warning her to silence. Why?

Hild gazed across the floorboards to the loom beside the door. Her loom—she had been working at it when Arinbjörn had come looking for her.

Remembrance came flooding back, and she looked at her mother. Without thinking, she opened her mouth to speak.

Her mother's hand came down quickly, gently, cool fingers covering her lips, quieting her. She held Hild's eye until Hild nodded that she understood she was to remain silent. Then her mother walked toward the closed door and stood listening. Seeming satisfied, she moved back to Hild, silently pulled the stool to the bedside, and sat, looking into the bed frame as if it were a window into Hild's world. "Tell me," she breathed, her finger to her lips again.

"Arinbjörn," Hild whispered. "Is he all right?"

Her mother nodded.

Hild stared into her mother's dark eyes, at the golden flecks of firelight illuminated in them, at the creases in the skin around them. "They were going to kill him."

Her mother said nothing.

"I—I knew they were, I don't know how."

Did her mother believe her? Hild couldn't tell.

"The red-haired man. His dagger—the blade was poisoned." Hild blinked in surprise. How had she known that? She didn't remember knowing it before, but now it was a certainty. The fire snapped and she looked up at the bed's ceiling, at the twisting pattern, lines interlaced like a slave girl's braid, carved into the wood. Where they met the trim, the lines turned into cats' tails.

Her mother exhaled; it was the loudest sound she'd

made since Hild had woken. "Your grandmother was a far-minded woman."

Hild looked at her. Of course her grandmother had been far-minded; everyone knew the stories about her. But what did her grandmother, dead long before Hild was born, have to do with her?

"Her grandmother was, too. So they say." Her mother touched the fine wool blanket, smoothing its ridges and valleys into a flat plain. "I've wondered if you might be."

"Me?" Her voice squeaked and she followed her mother's gaze to the door. Nothing happened. Her voice lower than a whisper, she spoke again. "Me? Far-minded?"

Her mother nodded. "Even when you were a little thing, you showed signs of it. Do you remember how you used to stroke your aunt Frea's stomach? Before even she knew she was with child?"

Hild shook her head. She could barely remember her mother's youngest sister, who had died when a fever had swept through the kingdom.

"No, you were too young. But when your father was killed . . ."

Hild closed her eyes. That, she did remember. She'd been nine winters old when her father had ridden out on a border patrol. He was to be gone for weeks, but the third day after he'd left, Hild had thrown herself onto her parents' bed, crying inconsolably. She hadn't known why, but she still remembered the terror and emptiness that had overtaken her. Her mother, her sisters, Aunt Var—all had tried without success to comfort her. Two days later, his men had brought her father's body home.

But why shouldn't the gods have told her about her father? As a late baby whose siblings were almost grown when she was born, Hild had been his favorite, his constant companion, his gift from Freyja to care for him in his old age. Young fathers had no time for their children, but Hild's father, old enough to be her grandfather, hadn't needed to prove himself anymore. He'd had time to make her laugh, to teach her to wield a sword, to show her squirrel and field mouse tracks in the snow. She hardly needed to be far-minded to know that he had died.

But how else could she explain what had happened today? She looked at her mother.

"It can be a blessing and a burden," her mother said. "Your grandmother didn't always understand the gods' messages. She said that sometimes they were clear as a winter day." She ran her fingers lightly over Hild's forehead, pushing a few stray hairs into place. "But sometimes, she said, it was like staring into muddy water."

"Today," Hild whispered, "it was clear. I knew the moment I saw them."

Her mother nodded. "Your uncle will understand. After all, it was Mother's far-mindedness that told us he would be king."

Hild knew the story—the skalds sang it often enough. The youngest of four brothers, Ragnar could hardly have expected to become king. But his mother—Hild's grandmother—had known from the moment he was born, and she'd raised him to expect it, too. Hild had always thought of it as a good story, but she'd seen it from her uncle's point of view. Now, with a flash of realization, she saw what it had meant for her grandmother: if she'd known her youngest son would be king, she'd also known her three older sons would die before him. She raised her eyes and her mother met her gaze with a look of sympathy, as if she knew where Hild's thoughts tended.

"It can bring you great honor," she whispered. "But it can be a heavy load." She reached for Hild's hand and took it between her own. A log shifted on the fire and popped, sending up a little shower of sparks. "We'd best tell your uncle."

After Hild had emerged from the cabinet bed and smoothed her skirts, her mother worked the comb through her tangled hair, the touch of her fingers calming Hild. Her mother retied the knot at the nape of her neck and smoothed the hair that fell down her back. Then, giving Hild a reassuring nod, she led her to the door.

Two fully armed warriors were standing outside, masked helmets hiding the top halves of their faces, spears in their hands. As Hild's mother opened the door, the spears came down to form a barrier. Hild's lips almost quirked into a smile at the way she and her mother both squared their shoulders at the same time—but her smile fled as soon as she saw the grim set of the warriors' mouths and remembered why she was here.

"My daughter will see the king." Hild's mother's voice held quiet authority. "You will take us to him now."

Both men straightened and bowed. Holding her breath, Hild followed her mother, stepping between the two soldiers, who fell into place just to the edges of her line of sight.

It was the Between Time, the day more dark than light, when birds would be settling into their nests, and mothers putting sleepy children to bed. Yet in the dusk ahead of her, a group of children and slaves crowded beside the lane to the hall. She looked at them curiously, wondering what they were doing out at this time of day, before realizing they were watching her and whispering to each other. Of course. They must have heard that she'd killed the Bronding, but they didn't know why. They didn't know how close the kingdom had come to losing the heir to the throne.

Did Beyla know? She was still with her granny, but surely someone had told her.

At Freyja's temple, a group of women stood in the doorway, watching silently. The two nearest her—Groa, her cousin's wife, and Jord, who had taught Hild a complicated knot to use in her weaving—looked away when Hild glanced at them. It wasn't their fault, she told herself;

they didn't know what had happened. She focused straight ahead, wishing she didn't feel so rattled.

Outside the hall, another crowd awaited them, men, women, and children trying their best to see inside the wide hall doors, their faces dark shapes in the twilight. The sight of a little boy jumping up and down repeatedly in a vain attempt to see over the broad backs of the three men blocking his view made a bubble of laughter form in her chest—until she remembered. She had killed a man.

At the broad doors of Gyldenseld, hall guards pushed people out of the way with their spear butts. Garwulf was one of them—he must have had only a few hours of rest before returning to duty. Hild looked at him, hoping for a hint of acknowledgment. He wouldn't think it proper to recognize her while he was standing guard, she knew, but it wouldn't hurt just this once, would it? Angrily, she turned her gaze away.

Her mother, a half step behind her, gave Hild's fingers a squeeze.

Then they entered the hall.

Flickering torches lined the walls, and in the long pit that stretched up the center of the structure, all the fires had been lit. Smoke rose to the holes in the thatch high above. Past the banners and beams and mead benches lining the long tables on either side of the fire pit, men crowded around the dais. Someone must have signaled to them, because as Hild tried to calm herself, they turned to look at her, their faces half red, half shadow in the light of the flames. Silence fell.

Suddenly, a sense of unfamiliarity gripped her, as if the hall where she'd spent her entire life, where she'd played as a child and grown into a young woman, where everyone knew and respected her, were a foreign place. As if she no longer belonged here. Cold air collected around her, fingering at her neck. Somewhere outside a dog barked. Another answered it.

Hild took a deep breath and started forward. As her feet touched the wooden hall floor, the sensation left her and she began to feel at home again, despite the unusual hush. Her shoes barely made a sound on the floorboards—her skirts whispered more loudly. She stared ahead at the group of men and held her spine straight, her head high, willing herself not to look at people's faces. Not to look for Arinbjörn.

Where was he? She didn't remember seeing him after . . . She closed her eyes to erase the memory of the expression on his face, the look he'd given her.

She wished he would step out from the crowd to walk beside her, but neither he nor anyone else did. No matter: soon he would know the truth and everything would be as it was before.

She reached back for her mother's hand, but her fingers met air. She stiffened. There was no one behind her. She was on her own.

Ahead of her, her uncle stepped out of a circle of men to stand directly in front of his throne. Bragi positioned himself just to the side and a little behind the king. As she neared them, she steeled herself, narrowing her focus. None of the men who lined the way to the dais—not even Arinbjörn, wherever he was, and certainly not Bragi—mattered in this moment. She had eyes only for her uncle, the king.

She sidestepped the fire pit and wove around a long bench, careful not to waver in her gaze. She didn't need to look down to find her way, so familiar was the hall to her feet. She remembered to avoid the board that always creaked, and approached the long tables where the king's hearth companions ate their meals. Once she was clear of them and in the wide expanse before the dais, she could hear someone's wheezing breath. Somebody coughed. Men stood on either side of her, watching her, but she blanked them all from her mind and kept her focus on the steps to the dais.

Reaching it, she stopped and sank into a curtsy, not all the way to the floor with lowered head, as would befit a supplicant, but halfway down and then up again, her eyes never moving from her uncle's face.

She swallowed, trying to wet her dry tongue. Then, hoping her voice wouldn't crack, she spoke without waiting for permission. "Ragnar, King. Your mother, my grandmother, was a far-minded woman. She foretold that you would rule."

No one spoke. The king regarded her impassively. Never had he been so good at wiping all emotion, all judgment from his expression. She wished he would give her the barest hint of what he was thinking.

Then she realized he had—by not stopping her from speaking.

She took a shaky breath. "Her grandmother, it is said, was also far-minded."

Again, no one reacted.

"My lord." The muscles in her neck stretched impossibly taut. "Ragnar, King, I, too, am far-minded."

From the rustle of clothing and the creaking of floorboards, she knew that the men who weren't still staring at her were turning to see the king's reaction.

There was nothing to see. He held her eyes, again shielding all his thoughts from her. *Say something!* she wanted to shout into the silence.

Footsteps sounded behind her, the light patter of a woman in slippers walking quickly. Hild flinched as her mother's hand touched her shoulder.

"It's true, my lord. My daughter is far-minded."

The king took a step forward. Almost imperceptibly, the men standing nearest him moved back. "Far-minded Hild may be. Nevertheless, a visitor to my kingdom, a Bronding nobleman, is dead." His gaze seemed to bore into Hild, but she kept herself from looking down or even blinking. "What do you have to say to that?"

"My lord," she said, her voice low but steady. "The Bronding nobleman was planning to kill your son."

"That's a lie!" a man said, pushing his way forward. His words served to unloose the tongues of all the other people in the hall, and in the noise, Hild watched him, recognizing him as one of the companions of the Bronding who had tried to murder Arinbjörn.

The king raised his hand. Immediately, the voices quieted.

Hild watched her uncle's face. Did he believe her?

"Whether or not it is true is not my question," he said to the Bronding, who scowled. Then the king turned to Hild. "If, by some power of far-mindedness, you knew the man's intentions, why did you not call for the guards?"

"There wasn't time, my lord."

"They were within shouting distance."

She stared at him. Hadn't he understood? She had saved his son's life. The life of the atheling, the heir to the throne.

"As you say," her uncle continued, "my mother was a far-minded woman. Yet she gave her knowledge to the king. He decided what to do with it. She didn't kill men she suspected of murderous intent."

"I didn't *suspect* him, I *knew*," Hild said, then added almost under her breath, "my lord." She hated what her uncle was saying, mostly because it was making her doubt herself. Why had she run at the man with her sword instead of calling for the guards? Then she remembered. "He had a poisoned dagger. He was going to stab Arinbjörn."

Her uncle flicked an eye toward a guard, who detached himself from the group and jogged from the hall, his head bent low. To find the Bronding's dagger, Hild understood, to check it for poison.

"And because he had a poisoned dagger, you decided it was up to you to kill him?"

"I didn't decide."

Her uncle narrowed his eyes and cocked his head, as if he was puzzled. "What do you mean, Hild?"

"I—" She fumbled for words, trying to explain. "I knew more about those men than I did about myself. As soon as I knew they were going to murder Arinbjörn, it was like it wasn't even me anymore."

"Go on."

"I was so angry I couldn't see. I didn't know what I was doing—I don't remember doing anything. And then he was dead."

Behind her she heard her mother's sharp intake of breath.

The men around the king began to murmur, their voices growing louder, although Hild couldn't distinguish their words. Bragi leaned forward to whisper into the king's ear, but his eyes were on Hild.

"Mother?" Hild asked.

Her uncle's voice cut through the noise. "Has it

happened before? Or is this the first time you have been possessed?"

Possessed?

Guards stepped to her sides. She could feel that one of them was Garwulf. But she could feel nothing else.

SEVEN

THE KING'S EXPRESSION WAS TERRIFYING. IN HER UNCLE'S face, Hild saw a stranger, someone who felt no tenderness for her.

Her knees locked so tight that if the guard standing beside her had given her the slightest push, she would have toppled.

Bragi stepped forward. His eyes were on the king but his voice was pitched for everyone in the hall to hear. "The choosers of the slain," he said, and Hild heard murmuring from someone near her. "The spirit women who decide men's fates . . ." He paused.

Hild stood rigid, listening.

"They make their choices during battle, not on the practice field. The choosers of the slain are spirits, not living women." Bragi looked from the king to Hild and she stared back at him, unable to move. "They do not inhabit the bodies of living women. Only a malign force could possess a person with anger this way, taking control of her body, making her do its will."

At the word *malign,* the king moved his fingers, and more guards stepped close to Hild, metal rasping as they drew their weapons, until she was caged by a bristling fence of spear points, daggers, and swords. When cold iron touched the back of her neck, she flinched.

There was a movement in the crowd around the king, and for a moment, Hild saw Arinbjörn's face. Then people shifted again, and Ari Frothi, who had been supplanted by Bragi even before his voice had lost its strength, waved his arm for attention, making her lose sight of her cousin. She watched as the king motioned the old skald forward, and Ari Frothi, leaning on his little grandson's shoulder as if it were a cane, shuffled out of the crowd. Age had dimmed his eyes, and Hild wasn't sure whether he could see her, or whether he was deliberately avoiding looking at her. When she was young, Ari Frothi had always had time for her and Beyla and Arinbjörn, to tell them stories of heroes and heroines or test their wits with riddles. She didn't think she could bear to hear the awful things he would say about her, and she tried to look away but found herself stiff, as if she were carved from wood.

Ari Frothi's mouth moved, but no sound came out. He cleared his throat, then cleared it again. People leaned forward to hear him. "Evil spirits may possess a person, as Bragi has told us," he said, his voice hoarse. "But the gods may do so, too."

Men standing near the dais turned to each other and Hild heard snatches of their whispers. Someone said something about Odin; someone answered with the name of the goddess. When Hild's eyes strayed back to the dais, she saw Ari Frothi watching her. The gentleness in his face warmed her.

Bragi stepped closer to the king and gave a backhanded wave that dismissed the older skald. His voice rising over the crowd, quieting it again, he said, "That's not a chance we can take. What if it were to happen again, here in the hall? Which of us might be attacked with no warning?"

The spark of hope Ari Frothi had kindled in her, a spark so tiny that she'd barely recognized it, sputtered out.

"She can't stay here, my lord," Bragi said. "She must be sent into exile."

Exile. The word hung in the air, sapping what little remained of Hild's strength. She felt as insubstantial as candle flame, as if a summer breeze could blow her out of existence.

Then the Bronding nobleman pushed his way past Bragi. "Exile her? No!" His voice echoed through the hall. "We demand vengeance for our kinsman." Other Brondings stepped forward to join him, their fur-trimmed cloaks thrown back to reveal their hands on their sword hilts.

The Shylfing warriors standing near the king threw back their own cloaks and began to draw their weapons.

The king raised one hand, stilling the crowd.

"The wergild will be paid," the king said. "You will be compensated for your kinsman's life."

"You would offer gold for the life of Thorfinn of the Uplands?" the Bronding said. "Gold could never suffice. We demand the life of the one who took his."

Nobody spoke. Gradually, Hild grew aware of her own breathing, the air forcing a ragged path through her throat.

Her uncle looked at the Bronding, his gaze unyielding. "We will pay the price in gold."

The Bronding muttered something and looked at her through narrowed eyes. The air constricted in her throat and she felt caught like a rabbit, unable to look away from him.

"Skamkel, Hadding," the king said. "Escort Hild to her quarters."

The planks beneath her feet vibrated as the two guards stepped forward.

Hild's knees collapsed, unable to support her. Her cousin Skamkel, Skadi's brother, took her by one arm, lifting her, while Hadding Oxfoot, a warrior she barely knew, gripped her other arm painfully, his fingers like shackles. Another guard moved out of their way. Garwulf. Below his helmet, his expression was so twisted with distress that she barely recognized him. Why didn't he defend her, or at least make Hadding loosen his grip on her arm? Why didn't he do something, *anything*? When he saw her looking at him, he averted his eyes.

Garwulf! Hild cried silently as he moved out of her sight.

Then her guards turned her around and the crowd parted. Hild saw faces—faces she knew—but she could recognize none of them. They blurred together like dark leaves—leaves with eyes, watching her, judging her—as Skamkel and Hadding took her on the long march through the hall, Hadding's rolling gait from his clubfoot pulling her down and then forcing her up again with each step.

They passed the fire pit and the tables lined with benches; they trod the board that always creaked. Banners floated above them; beams carved and painted with stories of the gods lined their path, but always the door seemed so far away, hidden in the shadows of the hall. Hild didn't think they'd ever reach it. If it weren't for the pain where Hadding held her arm, tugging it whenever his foot forced them downward, she would have thought she was lost in a nightmare.

Finally, they made it to the door. She stumbled on the threshold, stubbing her toes on the doorstep. Dark had settled around the hall while she'd been inside, but a crowd still lingered near the steps. Another guard fell in alongside them, holding a torch high. It lit first one watcher's face, then another's, the wind-tossed flames distorting their features. They looked like the dead waiting in Hel's underground kingdom.

Hadding tightened his hold above Hild's elbow and it was all she could do to keep from crying out.

"My arm," she said, hating the whimper in her voice.

He didn't loosen his grip.

"Hadding, please," she said again. "It hurts."

If he heard her, he didn't show it. He stared straight ahead, his fingers like talons.

She closed her eyes, then opened them again, a sob forming in her throat. She swallowed it back, but she couldn't stop the shaking in her jaw, her shoulders, her chest.

The people lining the path murmured when Hild drew near. She heard the hissing of the word *possessed* as the news slithered from one mouth to the next.

The torch flared, turning the face of a slave woman scarlet as she spat into her hand and glared at Hild, looking her in the eye in a way no slave should do. The guards must not have seen the slave's action—surely a capital offense against the king's sister-daughter—because they didn't react. Emboldened, the slave woman made a sign with her spat-upon hand, some heathen gesture only her gods would recognize.

Hild stumbled. Neither guard—not even Skamkel, with whom she'd played when they were children—showed her any kindness as they pulled her to her feet again. The guard with the torch brandished his spear at the crowd, and they backed away to let the group pass, then closed round again menacingly.

Just when she thought she could bear it no longer, they reached her house. Hadding yanked the door open and shoved her inside. As Skamkel let go of her other arm, she lost her balance and fell to the floor. She tried to brace her fall with her hands, but they collapsed under her, dead from her arms being gripped so tightly. She went all the way down, her forehead hitting the wood, and lay in a crumpled heap.

Behind her, the door slammed shut.

.　.　.

Hild wrapped her arms around herself and stared into the blue flames. She flinched at the feel of a woolen shawl being settled over her shoulders, but she didn't look up at Unwen.

The sound of voices outside—her mother arguing with a guard—didn't make her move, nor did the creak of the door.

Behind her, she could hear her mother and the slave whispering their worry to each other, but she didn't move from where she crouched in front of the fire. If she could have crawled into her sleeping cabinet and pulled the doors shut without having to face them, she would have, but her body had turned to ice and stone.

She stared at the flames that couldn't warm her, trying to block out everything else, every memory of the day's events, especially the looks on people's faces. On Garwulf's face.

Just this morning, she had thought she might live a long and happy life with him. Now she didn't know whether he would ever speak to her again.

A gentle hand touched her back as her mother came to sit on the floor beside her. Hild dropped her face into the comforting shoulder and wept while her mother rocked her back and forth, back and forth, as if she were a child.

When the tears were finally spent, her mother helped her stand, Unwen rushing to her other side, the two of them as gentle as the guards had been rough. Together, they got Hild to her bed, undressed her, and put her under the blankets. The sheets were as icy as her heart, and she knew she would never sleep.

Possession. Exile. The words swirled round in her head, mingling with images of Garwulf's face, of her uncle's, of Arinbjörn's when she'd killed the Bronding. Exiles were sent from the kingdom, left to wander alone as outcasts, hoping to find another king to take them in—if they survived the sleet and hail, the ravenous wolves and bears. Or worse, the giants that roamed the mountains, the trolls and hags and spirits that lurked in the forests. Yet who would take her in when doing so could bring the fury of an entire tribe down upon them? She could almost laugh at the irony of it. She, who had been so eager to bring feuds to an end, might have started a new one between the Shylfings and the Brondings.

She shuddered at the memory of the Bronding's weight falling against her, the smell of his blood.

If only she'd never left her loom, if only she'd never gone with her cousin, none of this would ever have happened. But if she hadn't been with Arinbjörn, she realized, he would have been killed.

Yet she had had little to do with it. Something had taken over her body to kill the Bronding. Maybe Bragi was right. Maybe something evil had possessed her. What if it happened again, but this time to someone she knew and loved?

She rolled over, shivering.

The movement brought her mother to her side. She pulled the blankets up to Hild's chin as if she were a little girl again, laid her palm on her forehead, leaned down to kiss her cheek, then closed the bed doors, shutting Hild into darkness, away from the rest of the kingdom.

EIGHT

She awoke to shouts and laughter. "For Odin!" someone cried outside, welcoming the god to the harvest festival. The gods must be honored for the season's bounty and supplicated for good harvests to come, Hild knew, but it was inconceivable that anyone could be happy when the world had collapsed.

She shut her ears to the noise until an argument just beyond the door caught her attention. A man—a guard, she assumed—said, "No one, not even you."

"On whose authority?" a girl said. It was Beyla—a very angry Beyla. Hild rose to her elbows, listening. Depending on the guard, Beyla might be able to get what she wanted.

"The king's authority." Hild didn't recognize the voice.

"Did the king mention me, specifically? Because I'm practically family."

"No one means no one, and that includes you," a second guard said. "Now get away from here before I have to make you."

"Hild!" Beyla yelled, but whatever she said next was muffled. She must have taken the guard up on his challenge. The noise of their struggle grew fainter as the guard took Beyla away, probably with his hand over her mouth to keep her from shouting again. If that was the case, he might end up with tooth marks on his fingers.

Hild lay back on the pillow, trying to smile at the image of Beyla biting a mail-clad warrior, but she was too weary to feel anything. After a time, she pushed the bed's doors open a crack. A fire flickered on the hearth, and in the shadows, someone moved. Unwen. Hild's mother was leading the prayers at Freyja's temple, which was where Beyla should have been. So should Hild. Just as she had served the hearth companions in the hall, it was her place to pour the mead into the bowl for the goddess. She wondered who would do it in her stead.

On the east wall, hints of morning sun stole through the boards. Why hadn't Unwen opened the door to let in light? Then she remembered: the door was shut to keep her in. She watched the slave, who stooped in front of the fire, stirring the pot that hung from the tripod. As she did, Hild caught a whiff of something cooking. Fish. Unwen was making her special cod and barley stew, Hild's favorite. She opened the bed's doors all the way and swung her feet from under the covers.

Unwen was at her side instantly. "Here, let me help you, my lady."

Hild took her arm, grateful for the slave's strength, and raised herself shakily from the bed. She didn't mean to let Unwen lead her to the chamber pot or put her shoes on for her, but she felt so unsteady she didn't think she could do it by herself.

Unwen settled her on the stool in front of the fire, then ladled stew into a wooden bowl and placed it in Hild's hands.

For a moment, Hild sat in silence, allowing the heat from the bowl to seep into her palms and the pungent steam to curl into her face. Finally, she ate, savoring the texture of the barley grains in her mouth, the taste of the cod and—

She looked up at Unwen, her eyes wide. "Pepper? Did you put pepper in it?"

The slave gave her a sly look.

"Where did you find it?" Pepper was rare, precious, and usually reserved for the king.

"I have my ways," Unwen said, and Hild recalled that her uncle's cooks would be preparing something special for today's festival. Something with a pinch less pepper than planned, no doubt.

"It's good. Thank you, Unwen."

The slave dipped her head in acknowledgment. She watched until Hild had scraped the bowl clean before she said, "More, my lady?"

Hild felt full, but the expectant look on Unwen's face made her hold out her bowl and say, "Just a little."

Unwen's "little" turned out to be a lot more than Hild could eat, and she stirred her spoon through the stew, watching the lumps of cod appear and disappear beneath the barley broth.

Unwen lowered herself to the floor beside her. Hild frowned. No slave should be so familiar with her owner, not even one who had made Hild's favorite stew. She started to say something, but Unwen spoke first.

"Where I'm from . . . ," she said in a low voice, then stopped and picked up the poker to stir the fire.

Hild waited, watching. She had never heard Unwen mention her home or her life before she'd been made a slave.

"Where I'm from," Unwen said again, her voice so quiet Hild had to strain to hear her, "when the gods choose to send their spirit into a person . . ." Again she stopped.

Hild felt herself going rigid. She didn't want to discuss the subject with anybody, least of all a slave.

"The one the gods choose is honored above all others," Unwen said, stumbling over her words to get them out quickly. She stood and moved to Hild's bed, then pulled up the sheets and folded the blankets.

Hild tried to relax her jaw, but Unwen's words had brought the previous day's events back to her with such immediacy that she felt like she'd been slapped. After a few moments, the soft sounds of the fire and the creak of the floorboards under the slave's feet as she went about her work calmed Hild, allowing her to think about what Unwen had said. The gods sent their spirits into a person? That wasn't what Bragi had said when he'd warned about malign forces. The chief skald was no fool. He had the knowledge and the experience to recognize the signs of a possession by something evil.

Then Ari Frothi's lined face rose before Hild. What had he said? That the gods may possess a person.

Hild stared into the fire. "Unwen?" Like the slave, she kept her voice low enough that the guards outside the door wouldn't hear her.

Unwen crossed the room and crouched before her again. This time Hild recognized that the slave's intention wasn't familiarity; it was secrecy. The closer their heads were to each other, the more privately they could talk.

"What is it like when someone is possessed by a god?"

Unwen shook her head, keeping her gaze on the fire. "I only knew one person who was possessed. They say it's different for everybody, that it depends on the god."

"And the person you knew? How did he act? What happened to him?"

"Her," Unwen said. "She— It was like what happened

with you. She did something but she didn't know why. Didn't even know she'd done it till it were done." She swallowed as if her throat were sore, and closed her eyes tightly.

"Unwen?" Hild said gently.

The slave gave her head a little shake, but she kept her eyes screwed shut.

"Who was she, the one you knew?"

Unwen kept her face turned away from Hild's. She swallowed again, and then, as if the words were scraping against her throat, she wrenched them out. "My daughter."

She rose and went back to the bed, refolding the blanket, tucking the sheets more securely under the pillow, picking up the feathers that had made their escape. Hild watched her stop and lean on the mattress for a moment. Then Unwen closed the bed's doors, brushed her apron, and said briskly, "You'll be wanting your loom over by the fire, where you can see it, my lady. I'll move it for you."

"No, Unwen," Hild said, looking at her as if she were seeing her for the first time. "I'll do it."

The sound of footsteps made them both turn toward the door as it opened, sending sun flashing into the room. Hild's mother stepped in and the door closed behind her, taking the light with it.

As Hild got to her feet, her mother took her by her elbows and peered into her face, her brow furrowed with worry.

"I'm all right," Hild said. Before the words were even

out, she realized how pale and worn her mother looked. Had she slept at all last night? Had people treated her poorly on Hild's account? "Who poured the mead for the goddess? Tell me it wasn't Skadi. Was it?" she asked in a feeble attempt to lighten her mother's mood.

The expression on her mother's face told her she'd hit closer to the mark than she had intended. "I know you were counting on it, Hild, and I'm sorry. I talked to your uncle, but Bragi—" She gave her head a little shake of anger.

"It's all right. Here, let me help you." Hild unpinned the brooch that held her mother's cloak together at her shoulder—the blue cloisonné jewel with runes carved in gold running around the edges and spelling out the words *Valgard had me made for Saxa*. Hild's father had given it to her mother when they'd first been pledged to each other, and her mother wore it only on special occasions—like when she led the ceremonies in Freyja's temple. Hild handed the cloak to Unwen, then scooted the stool over and guided her mother down onto it, watching her.

Her mother sighed and turned her face from Hild's. Hild waited, giving her time to smooth out the bad news.

"They found the dagger." She reached for the poker and stirred the glowing embers. Finally, she spoke again, her voice pained. "There was no poison on it."

A noise in the corner of the room made both Hild and her mother look toward Unwen. The slave was shaking her head in disgust.

"Unwen?" Hild said.

"They're not fools, those Brondings. They would have wiped that dagger clean the first chance they had."

The recognition that she was right kept them from commenting on the slave's presumption. Unwen busied herself again, eyes averted, as Hild turned back to her mother.

"Your uncle may have realized that—especially when the Brondings accepted the wergild in payment," her mother said.

"They took the wergild? That's good, isn't it?"

Her mother nodded, but the way she hesitated made Hild realize there was something else. She hoped the fire's warmth would give her mother the strength to tell the whole truth instead of trying to shield her from it.

Her mother set the poker back on the hearth, giving it far more attention than it needed. "They left this morning. The Brondings."

"Before the harvest festival?" Hild said. It was an insult to the king, but not an unforgivable one.

Her mother nodded, her fingers still resting on the poker.

The oddness of her mother's posture told Hild she still wasn't through. Her insides tightened.

Finally, her mother looked her in the eye. "As part of the payment, your uncle gave them Fleetfoot."

Hild felt the breath go out of her. "Fleetfoot?" she whispered. "He gave them my horse?"

"I'm so sorry, youngling," her mother said, and Hild saw in her eyes how helpless she felt.

Hild strode to the door, her hand stopping when it reached the latch, the touch reminding her why it was closed. She stared unseeing at the doorframe, at the cuts in the wood where she and Arinbjörn had measured their height every winter, a rune scratched beside each cut to identify it. She reached out her fingers and ran them over the wood, digging her fingernail into the last mark they'd made for her, in the year the king had given her her horse.

Leaning into the wall, she touched her head to the wood the way she and Fleetfoot always greeted each other, one warm forehead against the other.

Did Beyla know? Was that why she had been trying to talk her way past the guards? She loved the horse almost as much as Hild did. Hild had to talk to her—*now*. But the way was barred. She could go nowhere.

She tightened her grip on the doorframe. When a splinter bit into her palm, she welcomed the pain.

NINE

HILD HEARD THE CLICK OF THE LATCH AS HER MOTHER let herself out of the house. She lay back on her pillow. Somewhere a dog barked, but she couldn't hear voices. It must be very early morning.

Hild knew how frustrated and powerless her mother felt about Fleetfoot. About everything that had happened. All day yesterday, when she wasn't busy with festival duties, she had hovered, trying to do things for Hild, but there was nothing to be done. No matter how many times Hild forgot and walked to the door, she could never go through it, or even open it, unless Bragi and the king changed their minds.

She closed her eyes and pictured her horse, trying to let thoughts of him keep her from remembering what she'd done. It didn't work.

How could she, who had wanted Bragi and her uncle

to stop sending so many men off to war, who had argued against killings and deaths, how could she, of all people, have killed a man? Try as she might to keep it away, the scene in the field replayed itself on her eyelids. In her fingers, she could feel the weight of the Bronding's body pulling on her sword as he fell. She rubbed at her palm, but the sensation haunted her.

Unwen thought there was honor in being possessed, but she was wrong. And even though Hild's grandmother had been far-minded, Hild wanted nothing to do with it. If it ever happened again, she wouldn't give in to it.

Mice rustled in the leaves on the other side of the wall. She rolled over. Today would be as endless as yesterday. Her mother would try to cheer her, but what cheer could there be? She pulled the blanket over her head.

Again the mice scrabbled beside the wall. "Hild," a voice whispered.

"Beyla?" She sat up so fast she hit her head on the bed's ceiling. "Beyla, is that you?"

"Hild," Beyla whispered again.

Hild knocked on the wall, two shorts, one long, the signal she always used for her sister.

Beyla knocked back, repeating the pattern.

Her heart thumping, Hild moved as close to the wall as she could. She had so much to say to her friend, so much to ask her, but now no words came. It was enough to envision Beyla crouching beside the back wall of the house.

"Guards coming!" Beyla said, and Hild heard her scrambling to her feet. Then she was gone.

She lay listening, hoping Beyla would return, but instead of footsteps, she heard raindrops plunking tentatively on the roof before they built to a steady drumming.

When she finally crawled out of bed, Unwen scurried to help her dress. She was eating when her mother returned. "This rain is a good sign," her mother said, shaking water from her cloak. "It shows that the gods still favor the kingdom."

Despite what happened. Despite what I did, Hild added silently.

Her mother crossed to the fireside and placed a cool hand on her cheek. It smelled of the outdoors, of the rain. "You're cold. Unwen." She gestured and the slave brought a shawl to drape over Hild's shoulders.

Hild let them fuss over her; it was easier for everyone if she allowed her mother to expend her nervous energy. When Hild pulled the shawl more tightly around herself, she felt another one being settled over her, but it couldn't take away the chill of the house, or the gloom. Nor could her mother's funny stories about Siri's boys. Hild did her best to smile about Faxi's learning to dance at the harvest festival, but the tale, and the pleading look in her mother's eyes, only reminded her that she hadn't been allowed to witness it herself. Would her uncle ever relent? If only she could be in the hall to judge his mood or talk to him face to face . . .

Behind her, her mother whispered orders to Unwen, even though there was no reason for her to keep her voice down. And what could she tell the slave to do that she wasn't doing already? When she finally left the house, taking her jittery anxiety with her, Hild was relieved.

· · ·

Beyla came again the next morning, knocking on the wall and speaking Hild's name. Hild was ready for her. She'd woken early and waited in the dark, words she wanted to say tumbling through her head. If she had a chance to tell Beyla only one thing, what would it be? She couldn't decide. As it turned out, she didn't need to. Whispering through the wall made real conversations too difficult. "This rain won't stop," Beyla said twice before Hild understood her, wasting words on something she already knew. She imagined her friend holding her cloak over her head, water dripping onto her face and her hair, which was probably falling out of its knot. Then Beyla said, "Guard," and Hild heard her footsteps diminishing before the heavier tread of a warrior's feet splashed through a puddle.

When she got out of bed, her mother helped her to dress, chattering brightly while she straightened Hild's shift and worked at the straps that held up her gown. Then, as if she had just remembered it, she said, "The queen needs me," and gave Hild's shoulder a squeeze before she slipped out of the house and into the rain. Hild knew that her mother was trying to stay cheerful for her sake, and that it wasn't easy for her. Nor was it necessary.

She found she was becoming more and more satisfied to be left alone with her thoughts and Unwen's dark gossip. As the slave endlessly swept the spotless corners of the house, she told Hild what she'd heard people saying: some men feared that Hild would curse them or that she had the power to blunt their weapons and make their arrows go awry by merely looking at them. "Fools," Unwen said, and it comforted Hild to hear the scorn in her voice.

She watched the slave for a moment, trying to work up the courage to ask the question that bothered her the most, the one she had no one else to ask. Finally, she said, "What's the difference between being far-minded, like my grandmother was, and being possessed . . . ?" Her voice faltered before she got to the words *like me.*

Unwen snorted and looked toward the door. She had taken to wearing her cooking knife at her belt, as if she were protecting Hild from the guards who always stood outside the house.

"You want to know the difference?"

Hild nodded.

"If a woman tells a man the gods favor him, everybody says she's far-minded." The broom halted mid-sweep and the slave turned to Hild. "But let a woman do what the gods tell her, without asking a man's permission first? Then she's possessed." Unwen punctuated her words with her broom, jabbing it into a corner.

Hild wished she could believe her. The slave didn't think

any malign forces were at work, and Hild had been grateful when she had said aloud, more than once, that if evil spirits were what had made Hild save the life of the king's son, then she, Unwen, was a three-headed chicken. But Unwen had also told her that in the king's kitchens, some people were saying it was Hild's fault the queen had never had another child and never left her bed.

A finger of fear twisted around her spine. There were plenty of problems in the kingdom she could be blamed for. And if people didn't think of problems on their own, she suspected Bragi would help them.

If only she could talk to Beyla about it, ask her what the women in the hall were saying. She could just hear her friend arguing with anyone who tried to make accusations against Hild.

The next morning, she was awake long before she could expect Beyla to show up. In every small noise, every creak of the house, she heard footsteps. Not until she'd finally dozed off again did real footsteps startle her awake.

"Beyla," she whispered, rising to her elbows.

The footsteps stopped.

"Beyla?" she said again, louder this time.

There was a noise outside the wall, and then the footsteps receded. What had happened? She strained her ears, but silence met them.

Then a goat bleated and another answered. A boy called them by name and led them past the house, probably taking them out the Lake Gate to graze. Beyla must have been avoiding him.

The sound of the goats faded, but nothing took its place. Hild kept listening. Finally, when she'd almost given up, she heard the patter of footsteps, followed by the three-part knock. Hild felt weak with relief. She hadn't realized how much she counted on Beyla's visits.

"Hild," Beyla said.

Hild knocked in response. Now that Beyla was here, the questions she had wanted to ask faded in importance. It seemed enough to simply know that her friend was on the other side of the wall.

"You there!" a man called.

"Goat's breath!" Hild heard Beyla say, and then there was noise Hild couldn't discern, followed by Beyla saying, "Ow! Let me go!"

A second man said, "Stop struggling and you won't get hurt."

Hild covered her eyes with her hand, but it didn't keep her from picturing Beyla scuffling with the guards.

A third voice said, "Bring her along. Bragi's waiting."

"Hild!" Beyla cried, and Hild could hear the noise of her struggling as the guards dragged her away. To Bragi. She listened until the sounds died out, then lay heavily on her mattress, darkness weighing her down.

She didn't have to be told to know that Beyla wouldn't be coming again.

TEN

Hild picked listlessly at a thread in the pattern her fingers were unweaving. She couldn't remember how long it had been since Unwen had hauled the loom over by the fire. She'd meant to do it herself, but that was before torpor had overtaken her limbs.

As the days had gone by and nobody had told her what was to become of her, Hild had lost her appetite for food, for news, for company. All she wanted to know was what would happen to her. Was she to be exiled? Or had her exile already begun? Were the four walls of this dark room her future?

She tugged at another thread on her loom. The head that had been coming into view—the woman putting her baby into the boat—had disappeared, a victim of her nervous hands.

Her eyes lost their focus and the tapestry became a surface for images of her past life, before her imprisonment. She saw sun and bright sky above brown earth; grain standing in tall shocks; the faces of Beyla, her sisters, her nephews, a laughing Arinbjörn.

The face of Garwulf.

Fleetfoot.

Were the Brondings taking good care of him? Surely they recognized his value, his spirit. She hoped they were currying him regularly, because he loved to be curried. She pictured the silly faces he always made when she and Beyla brushed him. She closed her eyes, feeling her horse's nose against her cheek, the warmth of his flank. Then, with a great effort, she blinked away the emptiness that tugged at her heart.

It was dark, as it always was now, the room lit only by the fire on the hearth. Wasn't it time to sleep? Unwen wouldn't let her into the bed if it wasn't evening, but Hild no longer knew whether it was day or night. Laboriously, like an old woman, she rose from the stool and dragged her body to her cabinet bed.

"Not yet, my lady," Unwen said, taking her arm and leading her back to the fire. "You haven't eaten anything today." She lowered Hild to the stool again. "I'll get you something from the king's kitchens. What would you like?"

Hild forced herself to look at the slave, but speaking

took more energy than she could muster, despite the desperation she read in Unwen's eyes.

"I'll be right back. Just you wait and see what I'll bring with me." Without bothering to throw her cloak over her shoulders, Unwen hurried away.

As the door opened, Hild shut her eyes against the stabbing light. It wasn't even bright out, but compared to firelight, daylight seemed harsh and threatening.

Her mother still brought her tales of her nephews, and Unwen still whispered the latest gossip, but Hild had stopped even pretending to pay attention. None of it seemed real anymore. None of it mattered.

Being enclosed was the worst of it, and never seeing the sky. It seemed like it must already be the darkest part of winter, when the clouds encase you and the sky is as white as the snow. She felt as if she had been buried in a cave. And why not, when it seemed as if she were already dead?

The door rattled and opened, letting in light again. Hild held her hand over her eyes and ignored the sound of feet against the wood.

"Look who's come to see you," her mother said.

A visitor? Despite herself, Hild roused herself enough to look up.

Ari Frothi stood by the door, leaning against Hild's mother's arm, a fur-lined cloak over his shoulders, a small harp under his arm. "May I?" he asked.

Manners Hild had forgotten she possessed suddenly

returned, and she rose from the stool so quickly that she staggered from light-headedness. "Please, sit," she said, gesturing.

Her mother smiled at her, not quite meeting her eyes, and led the old skald to the seat beside the fire.

Hild sank onto the floor before the hearth, her legs shaky from the sudden movement. Briefly, she wondered how the skald had gotten her uncle to allow him to come in. Then her torpor returned and she withdrew into herself, watching the old man as if she were seeing him from the bottom of a deep pool.

Ari Frothi reached for her hand and held it in his own, chafing it as he gazed at her.

It was too much work to look at him. Her chin dropped and she closed her eyes.

As she did, he let go her hand and settled his harp into his arms, plucking notes and tuning the strings. He stopped when the door opened.

Hild's lids fluttered, but it was only Unwen.

"Bear meat, my lady," she said triumphantly, crossing the room to hand Hild a wooden bowl filled with thick stew.

Hild held up her palm to refuse it.

"But, my lady, it's *bear* meat!"

Hild shook her head and kept her eyes from Unwen's disappointed ones.

"If she doesn't want it, I'll eat it," Ari Frothi said, and reached for the bowl.

Unwen pulled it back. "You will *not*," she said fiercely. "It's for my lady."

"Let him have it, Unwen," Hild said. She didn't think she had the strength to listen to them argue.

Angrily, Unwen shoved the bowl toward the skald so hard that a dollop of stew lapped onto the floorboards. She wiped it vigorously with her apron, then huffed her way across the room.

Ari Frothi dipped the spoon into the stew and brought it to his mouth. "Mmm," he said, closing his eyes with pleasure. He took another bite and smacked his lips, murmuring, "Bear meat."

The stew's aroma wafted to Hild's nose, and to her surprise, her stomach growled. Maybe she could have eaten it after all—if Ari Frothi hadn't gotten to it first.

"A meal fit for the gods," he said, and set the remainder on the hearth. "If I hadn't just eaten in the hall, I'd clean that bowl for you." He picked up his harp again and plinked one string, then another. "Young was I once, and wandered alone," he chanted, his voice husky and frayed.

And naught of the road did I know.
Rich did I feel when a comrade I found,
for a friend is our heart's delight.

As Hild listened, her eyes strayed to the hearth. The bowl was still half full of thick broth, and she could see lumps of meat in it, too. Before she was aware of what she was doing, she had reached out to pick it up, brought the spoon to her lips, finished the stew, and scraped the bowl clean.

When she set it down, she saw a furtive movement from the corner of her eye as her mother and Unwen turned away, pretending they hadn't been watching her. The meal gave her enough strength to be amused by their studied lack of concern and the twisted lips, a semblance of a smile, that Unwen couldn't hide.

Ari Frothi's voice guttered like a candle flame. Hild looked at him as he swallowed and coughed. "That song's for men younger than me," he said, shaking his head ruefully.

"Sing me another, then," Hild said. "One that's right for wise old skalds."

He looked into the distance, running his fingers over the harp strings. His voice might be weak, but his hands were still supple, and the harp sang for him. Suddenly, its tone changed. "Listen!" he said, the word commanding Hild's attention. The skald beat twice on the harp's wood, then strummed the strings brusquely. "Never have I heard of one so mighty as Ingeld," he chanted, his voice low and stronger now.

It was a lay Bragi often sang, not one Hild would have chosen, but she supposed it was easier on Ari Frothi's voice. Still, hearing about the deeds of the famous Heathobard hero only made her own lack of freedom cut deeper.

The skald struck the strings again and caught her eyes, holding them.

He brought home as his bride Hrothgar's daughter,
That elf-bright lady, blameless and gold-adorned.

Hild blinked. Bragi had never sung these lines—not that she remembered, anyway. They sounded more like one of Aunt Var's songs. Ari Frothi turned back to his harp, dipping his head as he chanted.

To the men on the benches, bright in their mail,
Nobles' sons seated beside ancient spear bearers,
The lady brought mead. She meant to mend old
*   wounds,*
Feuds between kingdoms . . .

The skald's voice dropped so low she had to lean close to hear him. He looked up at her from under his bushy eyebrows and whispered, "Your uncle. He follows Bragi's lead. They have plans but you mustn't trust them."

This wasn't part of the lay. Hild waited for him to explain.

Instead, he coughed and spoke more loudly. "If I had the golden tongue of youth . . ." He turned to the corner of the room. "Do skalds merit no ale in this house?" he asked plaintively.

Unwen hurried over with a cup.

He drained it and handed it back to the slave. "I'll be back when the god of poetry has returned me my voice." As he rose, so did Hild, giving him her arm to steady him. "Take courage, dear heart," the old man whispered, squeezing her arm. Then he opened the door.

It was the closest Hild had been to the outside since she had first been shut in, and she blinked at the sudden slap of cold air against her cheek, the bright sliver of sky visible just above the high roof of the hall. She caught a glimpse of the crescent moon hanging in the blue air, its horns glowing with pale luminescence.

Then the door closed with a solid thud, sealing her in again.

Before, she hadn't felt at all. Now a sense of desperation filled her, making her clutch her arms around herself as if she'd been outside with no cloak.

Her mother must have noticed. "Come get warm," she said, leading Hild back to the fire.

Hild sank onto her stool again, staring at the flames as they danced—now joining together, now separating and dancing alone. The heaviness that had weighed down her limbs left her and a feverish feeling overtook her. She rose and paced across the floor to the west wall, then the east, then back to the fire to gaze into the flames again. She knew her mother was watching her, her brows raised in surprise and concern, but Hild walked past her, straightened a nonexistent wrinkle in the blanket Unwen had left in a tidy square on the chest, and returned to the fire for a third time.

She repeated the old skald's words to herself, trying to tease out their meaning, wondering if the lay was part of his warning. What did Ingeld have to do with her? Or had Ari Frothi simply been working his way around to telling her about her uncle and Bragi? Whatever they had planned for her, she couldn't stay here to find out. Desperate as the exile's path was, she would tread it.

But how would she get away?

She didn't know how closely she was guarded; she'd been sunk so deeply inside herself that she hadn't paid attention.

Night would be best. If she could get past those guards . . .

"Hild."

Her mother's voice made her jump. She followed her mother's gaze to her own hands and saw that she'd been unraveling threads again, this time on the sleeves of her gown.

Willing herself to be calm, clenching her fists to still her fevered fingers, she sat on the stool in front of the fire and tried to quiet the beating of her heart before it gave her away.

She had to break free of here.

She had to escape.

ELEVEN

Until tonight, Hild had craved sleep. She had longed for the moment each day when her mother and Unwen would allow her to crawl into the bed and close its doors. All she had wanted was for her eyes to be shut, for the world to disappear.

Now everything had changed. Although it was deep night, she lay rigid with wakefulness, listening for telltale signs of guards outside the door, trying to determine their habits. She felt as if her thoughts would burst through her skull, yet she couldn't focus them. One idea spawned countless new ones, and from each of those, hundreds more sprang forth. Whom could she trust? Her mother, of course, but Hild wanted to protect her from the anger of both the king and Bragi. She would have to hide her intentions from her mother. Ari Frothi she was sure of, but how could she make any plans with him when he wasn't here? Maybe she could send a message through Unwen—but she didn't know what message to send.

How could she get away? Even if she was able to get through the gates, where could she go? No farmer would hide her and risk the king's wrath. The idea of entering the Wolfholt made her shudder—wolves weren't all that roamed there. Could she take one of the fisherfolk's boats and cross the lake? Doing so would mean hiking over a mountain range, the dwelling place of giants, before she could reach the Heathobards—who would have no incentive to take her in, and plenty of reasons not to.

It was early morning before her frenzied mind finally allowed her to sleep.

She was still drowsing behind the bed's doors when raised voices wove themselves into the pattern of her dreams. What they were saying she couldn't tell, only the tone, and that her mother's voice was one of them.

Heavy footsteps pounded across the floor. Hild startled fully awake.

"Get her up. Now." It was Bragi.

Her heart thumped wildly. Did the chief skald know about Ari Frothi's visit? Did he suspect her plan to escape?

The footsteps retreated and she heard the door open and shut as Bragi left the house. Hild sank heavily back into the mattress, letting out her breath and, with it, all her hopes. Last night had been her chance to get away and she hadn't taken it. It was too late now.

She waited, trying to compose herself. Whatever was to become of her, she was about to find out.

The bed's doors opened. Her mother looked in at her, her face pale, shadows etched under her eyes. Without speaking, Hild rose and allowed her mother to help her dress. She didn't ask why she needed to wear her best gown, the red one she'd worn to serve in the hall. Unwen drifted into and out of her view, trying to assist, but her mother claimed Hild for herself, running the comb through her hair, arranging the knot at her neck, running her fingers through the long black tail that hung down Hild's back. And all with no words.

Asking would do no good; if her mother was going to tell her anything, she would have done so already. But when her mother insisted on helping with Hild's shoes, Hild's apprehension grew close to a breaking point. Desperately, she tried to still her hands and her mind, to accept whatever the gods decreed.

She looked up at Unwen, who stood beside the bed, where Hild sat while her mother knelt at her feet, taking more time than anyone could possibly need to tie a pair of shoes.

Unwen met Hild's eyes with a steady gaze, but her face revealed nothing. Hild wasn't sure how much the slave knew.

Someone pounded on the door, making them all jump.

Her mother rose and took Hild's hands in her own, pulling her gently to her feet.

The pounding came again.

Hild swallowed. With her mother's arm around her, Unwen a step in front of them, they crossed the room.

At the door, Unwen paused and looked at Hild's mother for permission. Then she opened it—directly onto a fist poised to pound again. Bragi's fist. Warriors stood on either side of him, their weapons drawn. Garwulf wasn't among them. For that, at least, Hild was grateful.

The skald looked Hild up and down. Then, without speaking, he stepped onto the path that led to the hall.

Hild and her mother followed a short distance behind him, the guards falling in after them. Hild glanced back to see Unwen standing beside the open door, kneading her right wrist with her left hand as if it was stiff.

She turned her face back to the path, inhaling the first fresh air she'd tasted in days. It was cold. While she'd been shut away, harvest season had ended. The sky was white and hostile. Its brightness stabbed at her eyes, making her lids flutter.

As they walked, a few curious onlookers glanced at them, but the crowd Hild had faced before was absent. She looked for Beyla but couldn't find her. When they got to the hall, its wide doors, flanked by guards whose helmets obscured their faces, loomed before her. She didn't need to see his face to recognize Garwulf standing stiffly at attention.

Sudden tears surprised her and she blinked them back angrily, keeping her gaze before her as she took the steps that led into the hall.

At the threshold, she stopped. She hardly needed time to allow her eyes to adjust to the inside firelight, she'd grown so accustomed to it. But she needed time nonetheless.

Her mother's arm slipped from Hild's shoulders to the small of her back, gently propelling her forward. "I'll be with you," she whispered, so quietly that Hild wasn't sure she'd really heard it.

With her mother behind her, so close Hild could feel her warmth, she followed Bragi through the hall, where people leaned against beams and sat on the benches. They passed the tall fires, which leapt and crackled. People turned to look at Hild, but she didn't return their glances. Instead, she kept her eyes on Bragi's finely furred cloak and the knot of men standing near the dais. Where was the king?

As she approached the men, her mother's hand went again to Hild's back in a comforting gesture, as if to say, *I am here*. Instead of calming her, it made her more nervous.

Then the king broke from the crowd. He raised his head and, seeing Hild, smiled and came toward her, his arms wide and welcoming.

"Ah, here she is," he said, sweeping a hand to her shoulder and turning back to a group of men standing near the dais. "Hild, my sister-daughter." When he pushed her forward, his touch was gentle.

Hild stood dazed at the seeming return of the uncle she recalled from her childhood, the one who always had a kind word for her.

"My dear," he said, looking back at her with a smile. "Greet our visitors from the kingdom of the Geats."

She turned from the king to the three men who stepped forward, and as they bowed, she sank into a stiff curtsy, her head swimming with confusion. Had her mother or Unwen told her about these visitors when she hadn't been paying close attention? Why was her uncle treating people from Geatland—seaweed-eaters—so courteously when the Shylfings were at war with them? Of all the feuds the Shylfings were involved in, the one with the Geats was the longest-standing, stretching back generations. Besides, they weren't just enemies; they were country oafs. It didn't make sense.

"And my sister, Hild's mother," her uncle was saying, and now, beside Hild, her mother was curtsying, too, while the visitors bowed again.

Hild looked at them, three men clad in well-worn clothing neither fashionable nor particularly clean. Two of them were young, no older than Garwulf, while the third, whose thinning hair and crow's-feet marked his age, stood a little in front of the others. As he bowed, one of his arms seemed to dangle beside him, as if he couldn't move it. When he rose, his eyes met Hild's, making her bridle. What right did a mere Geatish messenger have to look her in the eye?

"Our king sends you greeting, my lady," he said. His

voice was soft and husky, and he pronounced the words so oddly, stretching them out unnaturally, that it was hard to understand him. The messenger glanced behind him at one of the other men, who stepped forward, holding out a bag made of rich cloth. As he approached, Hild could see the moth holes scoring the fabric. The older man tugged at the bag's string, then reached in to pull out a handsomely wrought torque. As he held it out, firelight gleamed on the necklace's patterned gold and flashed off its inlaid rubies. It was a kingly gift. She wondered who they'd stolen it from.

The king moved to stand beside Hild and reached for the torque. "As beautiful as the necklace of the Brosings," he said, his voice resounding throughout the hall. He turned it in his hands, holding it up so the men standing nearby could see. Then he gestured to Hild, and she realized by his movements that he meant for her to wear it.

Her mother held her hair aside while the king himself fastened the torque around her neck.

"Let me look at you," he said, smiling as he manipulated Hild so that everyone near the dais could see.

The necklace lay cold and heavy against her skin, and its clasp caught her hair, but she didn't touch it. Instead, she watched her uncle, trying to interpret his intentions. "You mustn't trust them," Ari Frothi had said of the king and Bragi. But except for more smiling than she'd ever seen from him before, the king was acting his courtly self. Exile she had been prepared for, but not a kind and gracious uncle who seemed to have forgotten everything that had happened.

It was as if all were the same as before, except that nothing was the same. She suddenly recognized what was different. It wasn't just her uncle. Since she had entered the hall, everyone, even Bragi, had been polite. And not just to her. The loud laughter and joking, the everyday insults and slurs she usually heard in the hall had been replaced by quiet conversation, smiles, restrained words. There was so much smiling it made her jaw ache. And the hall was far too quiet.

The cold of the necklace crept down her back.

Then her uncle caught her eye, and the look he gave her chilled her even more. He flicked his eyes to a guard, compelling Hild to look as well. The guard's masked helmet obscured his face, but she could tell his gaze was trained on her and on the king as he awaited orders. Hild understood perfectly. She was to comply with whatever her uncle said. She, too, was to smile.

The king held her eyes, warning her. Then he turned to address the crowd and his expression grew serious. His voice carrying to the far corners of the hall, he spoke. "Beowulf, King of the Geats, is dead."

Gyldenseld had already been quiet, but now even the fire stopped crackling. The smiles Hild had seen faded as warriors leaned in to listen.

"A dragon attacked the kingdom, taking the life of its lord."

Hild drew in her breath. The word *dragon* flew through the hall as warriors repeated it, their voices hushed and questioning. Did they remember the cloud over the lake, the one Ari Frothi had said was dragon smoke?

Her uncle held up his hand for silence. "We need not fear the monster," he said. "It, too, lost its life, slain by King Beowulf and the kingdom's new lord."

He turned back to the Geats. "Our peoples, Shylfing and Geat, have long been at war. Your new king argues wisely, saying that the time for a truce has come."

The man with the damaged arm nodded.

The king looked at Bragi, then at the other men standing nearby, his gaze stopping on first one face, then another. Finally, he looked back at the Geats and stepped forward. As he did, he reached for Hild's hand and drew her up beside him.

"To Wiglaf, King of the Geats," he said, holding Hild's hand in a grip so tight it was all she could do to keep from crying out, "I give Hild, my sister-daughter, to serve as a peace pledge between our kingdoms."

Hild stood rigid. Finally, she understood. The lay Ari Frothi had sung her began to make sense. The older Geat said something, but she didn't hear it, because her blood was thrumming so loudly in her ears.

Her uncle's hand crushed hers in its grip as he pulled her down into another curtsy. The Geats were bowing, and now her crushed hand was free again, and her mother was leading her from the hall. They emerged into the harsh air, passing the place where Garwulf stood as straight as his spear. Down the path they went, past the people who turned curiously to see who it was, past Siri's house, and finally, through the phalanx of warriors who stood guard outside Hild's house. Hild scarcely breathed, trying not to think.

This was the form her exile would take. She had thought being confined inside was unbearable, but now, stumbling on the threshold, she knew she would have willingly stayed here forever if she could.

Instead, her uncle was ridding the kingdom of her and her far-minded ways. If the Brondings wanted vengeance for the death of their kinsman, they would no longer find her here. Instead, she would be far from everyone she knew and loved. Her uncle was sentencing her to live out her life in a land full of lumpen, boorish farmhands.

She was being sent to marry the king of the hayseeds.

She crumpled onto the floor beside the fire and sobbed.

TWELVE

MIST PRESSED AGAINST HILD'S SKIRTS. IT WET HER FACE and balled into tiny spheres of moisture on the wool threads of her cloak. She stood stiffly, looking neither right nor left. Fog-shrouded shapes hurried past her, carrying bundles, calling orders in voices she'd known her entire life. Voices she would never hear again. She curled her fingers into her sleeves against the cold.

Siri had been allowed in the previous night, and she'd brought Hild's young nephews and the baby. Hild had held the infant one last time in her arms, cupping her head in her hand, but when she'd felt her heart beginning to break, she'd hurriedly given her back to her sister. Holding this baby was too strong a reminder of the one she would never meet. She wouldn't be there to help Siri in her confinement; she wouldn't watch her funny nephews grow to manhood.

She had spoken to each of the boys briefly, then turned away, unable to comfort them in their confusion, her cheeks throbbing with unshed tears.

Now, standing near the East Gate in the early-morning chill, she stared, unseeing, into the gray air, hoping Siri wouldn't come again, knowing that her mother's presence was both a balm and a trial, threatening Hild's carefully maintained calm. She didn't need anyone to tell her why her mother was keeping so busy supervising the baggage.

The sound of someone running made her turn. Beyla almost knocked her over with a hug. "I didn't think I'd find you," she said, releasing Hild. They stood silently, looking at each other. Beyla sniffed, her eyes filling.

"Don't you dare cry," Hild said.

Beyla looked away, blowing her hair out of her eyes, as she tried to control her emotions. "Brynjolf's going with you," she said.

"He is?"

She nodded. "I always said he'd make a fine warrior. Maybe today is finally that day." She tried to smile, but instead, she teared up again. "I can't help it, Hild," she said, her face crumpling. She covered it with her hands, then lowered them and reached for her left wrist. "Here, this is for you." She pulled off the twisted silver armband she wore as a bracelet and pushed it at Hild.

"Beyla, no! Your father gave it to you."

"He would have wanted you to have it."

"Are you sure?"

Beyla nodded, tears trembling on her lashes and threatening to spill onto her cheeks.

Hild reached to hug her again, but Beyla gave a sob, then turned and rushed away. Watching her disappear into the thick air, Hild rubbed the battered silver piece between her thumb and forefinger, then slipped it over her wrist and pushed it up her arm. It was a warrior's armband that Beyla's father had won in a skirmish before he'd died. Hild was glad she'd asked her mother to give Beyla the small tapestry she'd woven last winter, the one with horses galloping along its edges. Yet silver band and gold-threaded tapestry were no recompense for this parting. She swallowed back her sorrow, lowering her head and closing her eyes.

When she opened them, a horse loomed out of the fog, making her step back and almost trip over a bag on the ground behind her. She steadied herself as a set of long, elegant horse legs stopped directly in front of her. One wide hoof stood for a moment before it rose, then placed itself carefully on the earth again. Hild could feel the animal's warmth, and when she looked up, she saw a rider lowering himself from the saddle.

Arinbjörn.

He held the reins in one hand, his eyes on hers. She couldn't read his expression. Had he grown taller again while she'd been shut up? He passed the reins to her and her hand automatically reached for them.

Her cousin regarded her for a moment longer, then pulled her into an embrace. "He doesn't mean to keep the truce with the Geats," he whispered into her ear.

She fought to pay attention to his words, so grateful was she to see him again.

"You're just a decoy; he'll send an army to destroy them." She could barely hear him, he spoke so quietly. Then he held her at arm's length and said in a voice he meant others to hear, "Fire-eyes can never replace Fleetfoot, but he'll try his best."

Hild opened her mouth, then closed it. "I can't take your horse!"

"No, of course you couldn't *take* him," Arinbjörn said, and laughed, his voice brittle in the cold. "That's why I'm giving him to you."

Hild looked into his eyes and saw no laughter there. Had her cousin forgiven her? For saving his life? She wasn't sure.

He gave her one last look before he walked away, melting into the mist.

She willed herself not to give in to her grief and leaned against the horse's neck. Of course he had forgiven her, she realized. He loved Fire-eyes as much as she had loved Fleetfoot.

The horse whinnied impatiently and Hild knew he wanted to be with his proper master.

Another horse approached, and Hild looked up. Its

rider was Mord. She hadn't seen him since the day she'd served the mead in the hall. He called out to a slave, who scurried over to grab the bag Hild had nearly tripped over. Mord brought his horse closer and looked from Fire-eyes to Hild and back again, not attempting to hide his contempt. "Waste of a good horse," he muttered before pulling on his reins and riding forward again.

Was he going along? Hild hoped not, although it was hard to know whom she would choose if she could. What warrior would trust her now? Which of them would want to accompany her? She wasn't even sure about Brynjolf— what must he have heard about her? The men didn't even have enough confidence in her to let her carry her own table knife. Her mother had told her, in a tone devoid of expression, that her food would be cut for her if need be.

Well, she told herself, she was being sent to be married, not to fight.

Then Arinbjörn's whispered words came back to her. What had he said? That her uncle wouldn't keep the truce? That he would send an army? She was no peace pledge. Her uncle wasn't just getting rid of her. He was using her to trick the Geats.

Two men—one small, one hulking—rode slowly past, and she glanced up to see Gizzur the Loud and Hadding Oxfoot. Both of them had earned arm rings for their skill at tracking game and enemy warriors. They wore bows on their backs and swords at their sides, and she heard the faint jingle of mail under their cloaks. They must be going as scouts. Gizzur, a slight, wiry man, wore a leather cap that fit tightly over his close-cropped hair, and even in the misty light, Hild could see how neat his clothes were, especially compared to Hadding's. Gizzur's helmet, strapped to the back of his horse, gazed at her blankly with its dark eye-holes.

Hadding saw her watching them and leered. Beneath his helmet's mask, the remains of his morning meal were evident in his bushy beard. She recalled the way he had escorted her home from the hall, his clubfooted gait forcing her up and then down again with each step, his fingers bruising her arm. He was obviously more at home on a horse. Without his limp, he seemed to feel powerful, judging by the expression on his face. She thought of his wife, a pale, frightened-looking mouse she'd seen in the hall, and wondered if Hadding treated her cruelly.

"Come, love," her mother said, and Hild turned to see her glaring up at the warrior. Hild looked away from him. Her mother gave her no final words of advice, just warm arms around Hild's body and a cool face against her cheek.

"Let's go!" Mord called.

Hild pressed herself further into her mother, seeking courage, some kind of armor against the uncertain future her uncle had condemned her to.

Hooves sounded behind her, and a hand reached down to pull her away from her mother. Mord's hand.

Hild gave him such a look that he recoiled, dropping her arm. *Good,* she thought, remembering Unwen's words about men thinking she might be able to steal their power. *Let him fear me.*

Her anger buoyed her. She brushed at her elbow where Mord had grabbed it, and squared her shoulders. Then, without looking back at her mother, because doing so would take more strength than she possessed, Hild climbed into Fire-eyes's saddle, found a place for herself amid the bundles the slaves had tied there, and gave the reins a tug.

In front of her rode Mord and the two scouts. A little to the side, Brynjolf sat astride his horse, polishing his already-gleaming dagger, the weapon he'd been awarded when he'd been promoted from the boys' troop to the men's. When she nodded at him, he looked away, pretending not to have seen her. At least Beyla wasn't there to witness it. Hild repositioned the silver band on her arm, making sure it wouldn't fall off.

As they neared the wooden gates, Hild saw the three seaweed-eaters waiting silently, already mounted, just inside. When their leader saw her, he gave her a bow. Startled, Hild returned it, then wondered whether she should have.

Ahead of her, the gate loomed, the door between Hild's past life and the one her uncle and Bragi had decided for her. A harsh sound made her jump. It was just the croak of a raven landing on top of the wooden palisade, a dark shape in the misty air. She tried to calm the fluttery feeling in her chest.

Behind her, another noise made her turn to see the pony she had been meant to ride. Unwen was struggling to mount it.

"Oomph!" she said, sliding to the ground. Finally, a guard stepped forward and helped her up.

The pony trotted forward too quickly as Unwen tried to find her seat. Hild watched them, pulling Fire-eyes out of the pony's path just in time.

"What are you doing?" she asked, more brusquely than she'd intended.

"It's better than us both riding on the same horse, my lady," Unwen said.

Hild stared at her, not comprehending.

"You didn't think we'd let you go alone, not with all these men, did you, my lady?"

Words failed her, but Hild took a shaky breath. Unwen would be with her.

Ahead of her, Mord led the party, followed by the scouts, the three Geats falling in directly behind them. Hild followed the Geats, and behind her came Unwen, her muted gasps making it clear just how unaccustomed she was to riding. Brynjolf brought up the rear.

Then she was at the gate. Despite a wild desire to look back, she kept her face forward as she rode through it, leaving the stronghold, and her old life, behind.

On the other side, fog blanketed the fields and swallowed sound. Except for hooves hitting the path and an occasional "oomph" from Unwen, Hild heard nothing until a hawk shrieked in the trees—a warlike hunting cry. She glanced to her right but saw only ghostly trunks in the distance, beyond the troll rocks. The last time she'd seen those trees, golden leaves had flickered in the sunlight while she and Arinbjörn had practiced swordplay.

She looked away.

Ahead of them, the fog had lifted enough that she could make out the low buildings of a farm in the distance. As they approached, Hild saw a few scattered figures at work. One of them looked up when they neared, a farmer no older than she was. He stood watching her, then bowed low. As he looked up again, her hand, moving as if of its own volition, rose in greeting—and in farewell.

Then he was gone, and they were past the farm and on the rolling, rocky plain that led to the Wolfholt, still a line of dark trees in the distance. Hild laid her palm against her horse's neck, and he gave his head a shake as if he was no more eager to enter the forest than she was.

The mist dissipated into gauzy wisps as the morning wore on, but the sun stayed hidden. No one spoke, and Hild felt the weight of the gray air settle over her. She made her mind a blank to keep away the image of her mother's face, of Beyla's. Arinbjörn's eyes looking mirthlessly into hers. This morning he had seemed much older than the boy she knew. What had changed him? Was it what she had done? Or was it what he knew about the treachery his father was planning?

She shut out the thoughts, refusing to tangle with them. There was nothing she could do. She was a peaceweaver. She knew the stories, and how often they ended in tragedy, even when both sides' intentions were honorable. It took only one old warrior, recognizing a sword that had belonged to his dead friend, and now worn by the man who had killed him, to rekindle the flames of war. He'd point out the sword to the dead man's hotheaded nephew or grandson, who would seek vengeance, and the whole cycle would begin again, leaving grieving widows and lovers and children behind.

But in her case, there were no honorable intentions. The peace she had thought she was being sent to weave would be rent and bloodied before her loom was even in place.

Gizzur and Hadding had broken away from the others and ridden ahead to scout out their path. Hild assumed they were looking for routes an army could take on its way to subdue the Geats. How long after they left her in Geatland would it be before a troop of Shylfing spearmen returned to attack? Would they be fast about it, or would they wait out the winter, until spring hunger weakened the Geats?

But after the fight, they would bring her home! She sat up in her saddle, hope kindling in her heart. Then she slumped again. Bragi had no love for her and he had her uncle's ear. She would not be going home.

A noise made her turn to see Unwen coming up beside her. "Oh, my lady," she groaned. "How do you bear it?"

Hild watched the slave, so unaccustomed to riding, put her hand to the small of her back, then grab for the reins again as she wobbled unsteadily on her perch.

"It gets easier," Hild told her. But she knew it wouldn't get much easier for Unwen. They would be riding every day until they got to the land of the Geats. How long that would take, she wasn't sure, but it must mean many days of riding, and Unwen's body would be stiff and aching until they arrived at their destination.

Ahead of them, saplings marked the edge of the Wolfholt. Gizzur came riding back to confer with Mord. Hild watched as they looked over the rest of the company, making sure everyone was in place before they entered the unfriendly forest. Mord's eyes, glittering from behind his masked helmet, stopped when they got to her face, lingered for an instant, then flicked away. *Does he think my eyes can harm him?* She wondered if Mord feared that she could read his thoughts the way she had read those of the men who tried to kill Arinbjörn. If he did, what would he not want her to know? He was an ambitious man from a powerful family, but not quite powerful enough, not one of the king's closest advisors. Mord always seemed to crave something more. What would he do to get it?

Suddenly, she remembered what had happened the day she had served the mead in the hall. She'd been so intent on honoring Garwulf that she'd hardly thought about Mord at all. But Mord would have seen things differently. To his mind, it must have seemed that she had insulted him in front of the entire hall. In front of the king. What a fool she'd been. She couldn't have found a better way to make an enemy if she'd planned to.

She twined her fingers in Fire-eyes's mane, trying to allow the horse's warmth to steady her. It didn't work.

As she watched Mord, he twitched his horse's reins and rode into the trees. She had no choice but to follow.

Once they were under the forest eaves, the woods became a mixture of fir and ash, water from the morning mist dripping down on them from the few brown leaves that still clung to the branches above. Notches cut into tree trunks here and there blazed the trail, but this close to the Wolf-holt's edge, the path was wide and trodden enough that they could have found their way without the marks.

On the forest floor, pine needles and leaf mold covered the ground and muted the sound of the horses' hooves. A lone squirrel skittered up a trunk and disappeared. The quiet seemed ominous. No birds called from the tree limbs that loomed overhead. Hild thought she might have preferred to hear wolves howling or the grunts of bears than to feel creatures were watching her silently, just out of sight.

Directly in front of her, the two younger Geatish warriors

rode side by side behind Thialfi, the Geat with the damaged arm. They carried themselves with the ease of young men accustomed to the saddle, their backs straight and tall, their blond hair tied back and emerging from under their helmets. One was taller and more broadly built than the other, his hair darker blond, but they wore their cloaks identically, thrown back over their shoulders. She regarded the cloth critically; it was well made, if unadorned. Whoever had woven it was skilled, which surprised her. It must not be Geatish work—she wondered if the seaweed-eaters stole cloaks and tunics during raiding parties, not just gold and weapons and slaves the way the Shylfings did. It seemed like the kind of foolishness they might resort to.

Behind her, Unwen moaned. Hild knew the slave must be hurting, but there was nothing she could do. Yet she, too, was relieved when they rode into a clearing and Mord called a halt.

As she began to dismount, one of the Geats, the smaller of the two who'd been riding in front of her, stepped to her side and offered his hand to help her. Angrily, she brushed it away. As if she needed help getting off a horse!

The Geat stepped away, bowing briefly to her as he did, a hank of his white-blond hair flopping into his eyes.

She gave him a curt nod, then slid from Fire-eyes's back. As her feet touched the ground, she stumbled and inwardly cursed herself, certain the Geat was still watching.

Not that it mattered. The Geats would all be dead—or

slaves—soon. And she would be . . . Well, she supposed she would be dead, too.

Another Geat was helping Unwen from her pony. Hild turned her head away and leaned against Fire-eyes's flank. After so many days of being cooped up inside, of having so little activity, the long ride had left her shaky.

As she rested her head against the horse, something odd caught her eye—a flap of leather that she didn't recognize, a part of the saddle that seemed out of place to her. She reached for it and then stopped.

From the angle where she stood, she could just make out the edge of a blade hidden under the leather flap.

She wasn't weaponless after all. Arinbjörn had armed her.

THIRTEEN

They didn't rest long. Before Hild's body felt ready, she was in Fire-eyes's saddle again. She could hardly keep her fingers from reaching for the sword hilt. Her father's lessons, the time she'd spent practicing with Arinbjörn— she was grateful for them now. Before, they had been nothing but pastimes, amusements. Now they might mean her survival.

Nearby, one of the Geats helped Unwen onto her pony. It wasn't just herself she was responsible for, Hild thought. She could protect Unwen, too, when her uncle's army came to do its deadly work.

She drew alongside the slave. "Sit back a little more," she said. "And don't hold the reins so tightly."

Unwen relaxed her grip on the reins for a moment but immediately clenched her hands around them again, scrunching her shoulders up to her ears and sitting forward as if the pony were about to break into a gallop.

Hild reached over and touched the other woman's shoulder. "Sit back," she said again. "The pony isn't going anywhere—it's just going to follow the horses."

Unwen lowered her shoulders but Hild could see how taut her body was. She leaned down, took the pony's reins from Unwen's hands, and held them loosely in her own. The pony didn't change its pace but ambled along beside Fire-eyes.

"Oh, my lady," Unwen said, looking up to catch Hild's eyes. She pursed her lips as if she was about to say something else.

Hild waited, but Unwen took hold of the reins again and looked away just as the jingling of a bridle announced that Brynjolf, who had been riding in the rear, was catching up to them.

"By Balder's pretty toes, looks like you'll be sore tonight!" he said, grinning so broadly at Unwen that Hild could see his chipped front tooth. She remembered when he'd gotten the chip, falling off his horse during the midsummer races a few years earlier. He'd grinned when he'd broken it, too, even though it must have hurt. And that silly saying about Balder's toes—it had been on all the boys' tongues recently. Hild and Beyla had teased Brynjolf mercilessly about it.

She wished he would look at her, but she knew how difficult his position was. Even if he wanted to be friendly with her, this was his first time to ride out with the men. The warriors would be judging him, and they would have plenty to judge. With his helmet tucked under his arm and his dagger in his hand, Brynjolf trotted past Unwen, then maneuvered his horse around the Geats and up to where Mord was leading the party.

Hild cringed, knowing exactly what would happen next. Mord's voice rose in anger, allowing all of them, maybe even the scouts, who were riding somewhere nearby, to hear him berating Brynjolf for leaving the women unprotected.

Unprotected? She smiled grimly. Mord didn't know about her blade. Could she pull it out without cutting the horse—or herself? And if she could, would she be able to defend herself on horseback? The Shylfings preferred to fight on foot, but if she stayed on Fire-eyes's back, she would gain both height and power. Could she do it?

As Brynjolf made his way back through the other riders, an abashed grin on his face, Hild imagined him coming at her with a sword and tried to determine how long it would take her to unsheathe her own weapon. Once she did, her height—and the length of her arm—could give her an advantage if someone as short as Brynjolf ever attacked her. So would the element of surprise: nobody expected her to be armed, nor would they expect her to fight from Fire-eyes's back.

She wished she could tell Brynjolf about the sword and have him practice with her. She wished . . .

She stopped herself. Wishing was pointless.

The day went on forever. The trail wound past an endless succession of trees, with nothing to distract her except the dread of what lurked unseen in the forest. Every tree appeared to be watching her, hiding behind it a slavering wolf—or worse. She tried not to think of the creatures she had heard about in Ari Frothi's lays. In the safe confines of her uncle's stronghold, she had enjoyed the frisson of fear those tales had caused. But now she recalled the warrior whose mangled body had been brought through the East Gate when she was a little girl. "Trolls," she remembered people saying before her sisters had rushed her away from the scene.

Still, she'd always been far more afraid of enemy warriors than the creatures of mountain, lake, and forest, and with good reason. It was only one winter past that Helmings had surprised the kingdom. The women and children had been rushed into Gyldenseld to wait out the violence, hoping no one would torch the hall, and Hild had held a weeping Faxi on her lap, trying to comfort him, wishing her nephew's warmth would comfort her. They had been lucky that time. Not a single Shylfing had died and the wounds had been minor, but Faxi still woke from nightmares.

Now, however, an enemy she could see, a *human* enemy, seemed preferable to the unseen creatures that might be watching her from behind the trees.

The day never brightened. The same solid gray that

had surrounded them when they left the stronghold followed the company, making it hard to tell whether time was passing. Finally, though, Hild grew certain that the light was fading and the Between Time was upon them. The evening song of a solitary bird confirmed it. Soon, she knew, Mord would call a halt.

She tensed at the sound of hooves, but it was only Hadding, back from scouting out the trail. He conferred with Mord, pointing, and Mord turned his horse in the direction Hadding indicated. The rest of them followed. As they rode, the trail narrowed and branches and underbrush began to grab at their cloaks. They splashed through a fast-running stream. Just beyond it, the woods opened out again. Mord stopped and dismounted, the signal for the others to, as well. Before she did, Hild gazed around her and saw a ring of fire-blackened stones surrounded by felled logs. It was a campsite stocked with fuel for hunting and raiding parties. Gizzur was already taking kindling from a pile near a tree to build a fire.

As Hild lowered her aching body to the ground, she realized Brynjolf was standing near her—but not too near. "Your horse, my lady?" he said, not looking at her as he reached for Fire-eyes's reins. She searched his face, the splash of freckles across his cheeks, his nose the same snub shape as his sister's. His jaw clenched, but he stood unmoving.

A wave of sorrow rushed over her and she dropped her

eyes. So this was how it would be: they would treat each other formally. She knew Brynjolf had no other choice, and for his sake, she would be distant, too, but it grieved her. Without looking at him again, she handed him the reins and stood with her head bowed as he led the horse away.

"My lady," Unwen said beside her, and the urgency in her voice made Hild turn. "Perhaps you should show me how to unsaddle a horse." The expression in the slave's eyes mirrored her tone.

Instantly, Hild remembered the hidden blade. Unwen must know about it, too. Without speaking, they hurried after Brynjolf.

The confusion was evident on his face when they approached him. "My slave will do this," Hild said, now glad for the formality between them, which would keep her from having to explain.

Brynjolf started to speak, then shut his mouth and bowed. He took a step back but hovered, ready to help them. She had to get rid of him.

"I'll need some water. Would you fetch it for me, please?" she said. He nodded and turned toward the stream, stumbling in his hurry to get away. Hild felt a twinge of sympathy. This couldn't be easy for him.

The moment he was away, she whispered, "Now, quick," and reached for the sword hilt.

"Here, my lady," Unwen said, holding out the blanket

that had been rolled up behind Hild's saddle. Hild laid the sword in it and stood shielding Unwen's body until she had wrapped the blanket around it. Then Unwen put it on the ground, and together, they unsaddled the horse.

By now, Gizzur had a fire blazing in the pit. A look of complicity passed between Hild and Unwen. Hild walked over to the fire and leaned down to warm her face and hands. She could sense Unwen's movements behind her as the slave made beds for the two of them, unpacking bags and placing them over the blanket with the sword in it. Both the Shylfings and the Geats were busy, none of them watching Unwen with suspicion, but Hild couldn't ease her tension.

Finally, the slave joined her beside the fire and Hild let out her breath.

"Here's water, my lady," Brynjolf said, coming toward them with a bowl in his hands.

"I'll take that," Unwen said, stepping forward. "Come, my lady, we'll go someplace private for you to wash." She looked at Hild with a pleading expression, urging her to do something, although Hild wasn't sure what.

"Yes, I'd like to wash," she said, keeping her eyes on Unwen's.

The slave nodded. "Come, then." She started for the woods and Hild followed.

"Where do you think you're going?" Mord strode forward, glaring at the two of them.

"Just a little way into the woods, sir. My lady needs privacy," Unwen said, her voice light. "We won't be long."

Hild stood silent, as pleasant an expression on her face as she could muster. She felt bone tired and wished she knew what Unwen intended. She wanted to glance back at the sword to make sure it was hidden under the blanket, but she didn't dare.

Mord stared at them for a long minute. "No farther than twenty paces," he said.

"Of course not, sir," Unwen said, and gave him a smile that couldn't have come easily to her. Hild couldn't remember ever seeing the slave smile before. Even when Unwen laughed, her habit was to give her lips a sardonic twist.

Mord turned back to the horses, and Hild followed Unwen toward the woods. Again, they were stopped, this time by Thialfi, the Geat with the damaged arm.

"My lady," he said in his drawling accent. He bowed, and when he raised his head, she saw the perplexed glance he threw at Mord. Then he focused on her again, and she had to struggle to understand his words. "My lady, you should have a guard." He drew out the *you* for the space of at least three words. "These woods, this time of night—" He shook his head. "It's not safe, my lady."

Hild looked toward the dark trees and tried not to think of what might be hiding in them. Reminding herself that there would be seven warriors close by, their weapons at the ready, she inclined her head toward the Geat. "I thank you, but I feel quite safe," she lied. "Now, Unwen?" She walked past the man, who stood watching her.

Unwen followed, water sloshing out of the bowl. "Oh, dear, my lady," she said. "Look at what I've done, spilling the water that way." She shook her head. "Shall we go back to the stream and you can wash there?"

Hild understood immediately. If they could only get a little distance away, the noise of the stream water might cover their voices. She followed Unwen to a place where trees crowded around the stream.

They looked back at the campsite. The Geat was watching them. So was Mord.

"This won't do," Unwen said. She pulled off her cloak and held it up to shield Hild from the men's view. "Now, my lady."

Hild knelt on the rocks beside the streambed. The water was icy on her hands.

"Here, my lady, look in my pouch," Unwen said, her arms spread to hold the cloak. She indicated the little leather bag that hung from her belt.

Hild shook the water from her hands and opened the flap, reaching into the pouch. Her fingers touched something cold and hard.

"Hurry, my lady," Unwen said, casting a glance behind her.

Hild pulled the object from the pouch and gasped. It was her mother's blue cloisonné brooch, the one Hild's father had given her. Hild ran her fingers over the runes that ran around the edges.

"She gave it to me for you," Unwen said, keeping her voice low. "Splash water, my lady. Like you're washing. And put the brooch back into my bag."

Hild cupped water in her hands and scrubbed her face with it, hardly noticing how cold it was this time.

"After you're there, the king will attack the Geats."

"I know. Arinbjörn told me." Hild splashed again.

"Your uncle has forgotten honor. Ari Frothi thinks he'll kill you, too, because he fears your power."

That part Hild had already started to work out, even if it was hard to bring herself to believe it. What to do about it, however, she didn't know.

"My people live south of here. There's a river we can follow, Ari Frothi says, if we stay with the men a few more days." Unwen looked over her shoulder again. "Wash, my lady."

Hild stared at her, then put her hands into the water again.

"Your mother wants me to take you there. Until then, my lady, we must act as if nothing is amiss."

Hild nodded. Her mind was on fire. She would escape after all! Hope such as she had never needed before flooded into her. She looked up at Unwen, her eyes shining. "You'll know when we get there?"

"I think so, my lady." She gestured toward the camp with her head. "We should go back."

Hild scrambled to her feet, brushing her skirt and pulling her cloak around her. The day's weariness melted away and she felt full of strength. "Come," she said, and led Unwen back through the dark woods toward the fire's light.

FOURTEEN

Nothing is amiss, Hild reminded herself, trying to curb her spirits. She and Unwen had a plan! The very idea of it made the corners of her mouth twitch. Best not to let Mord see, lest her smile raise his suspicion. She set her face in a neutral expression as she and Unwen returned to the clearing.

At the fire, Hadding bent his substantial frame over the flames, roasting a bird. A pile of feathers lay on the ground beside him and bits of fluff clung to his tunic. He must have wiped his hands on his tunic, too, judging by the dirt and grease that streaked it. He was still wearing his helmet. When he glanced up at her, his eyes hard behind the helmet's mask, Hild looked away. Yet the smell of sizzling meat made her realize how hungry she was. The day's riding—and Unwen's news—had whetted her appetite.

"Are you feeling refreshed, my lady?" the Geatish leader asked, approaching her.

Simple as the words were, it took a moment for Hild to untangle them. "Yes, I thank you, Thialfi," she said. She took a seat on the log near the fire and stretched out her hands, her fingers still tingling with her secret knowledge. Across the flames, the two younger Geats crouched in front of a meal they were making, and suddenly, Hild was ravenous. She stared at the bird Hadding was cooking, at the juices dripping into the flames. Her mouth watered. Hadding pulled the roasting stick out of the fire, poked at the bird with his meaty fingers, blew on it, then crunched into it.

On the other side of the fire, one of the Geats stood and Hild saw that he, too, was watching Hadding, an odd expression on his face. Anger? Surely he hadn't expected Hadding to share with him.

The second Geat stood and the two spoke in low voices as Thialfi joined them.

Hild tensed. Had the Geats already grasped the treachery her uncle was planning? She watched their faces but their expressions were foreign to her. What were they thinking?

Thialfi stepped around the fire toward Hadding.

Hild wished the sword Arinbjörn had given her was sheathed by her side, not hidden in the blankets several paces away. She moved forward on the log, ready to flee if a fight broke out. Was this the moment she and Unwen were waiting for? Would the distraction of a fight allow them time to saddle Fire-eyes and the pony? The river—she didn't know if they'd be able to find it on their own.

"Is it the custom . . ." Thialfi said to Hadding, who looked up from his meal, a feather hanging from his mustache. "Among the Shylfings," Thialfi continued, "is it the custom to not offer meat to the lady first?" *Cooa-stom*, he pronounced it, holding on to the first syllable for an improbably long time.

Hadding stared, his mouth too full to speak.

Across the fire the other Geats stood watching.

A movement behind Hadding made Hild look to see Mord coming forward. He kicked Hadding's foot, not hard, and said, "Didn't you serve Lady Hild before you ate?" Then he turned to Hild. "My lady, accept my apologies for this hungry warrior."

"Of course," Hild said, not meeting Mord's eye. He was playing along to pacify the Geats, she realized, and he expected her to do the same. There would be no fight. The tension that had gripped her body fled, leaving a deadly weariness in its place.

"Ah, I see your slave has a meal prepared for you," Mord said as Unwen stepped up to hand Hild a bowl of dried goat meat and a piece of bread, hard-baked to last on the journey. Hild took it, her tongue still hungry for fresh fowl, her body almost too tired to chew the cold, dry meal. Dutifully, knowing she needed to keep up her strength if she and Unwen were to escape, she ate, then let the empty bowl slip from her fingers onto the ground. Her head slumped forward to rest on her hands. The cold seeped around her, chilling every part of her body that was turned away from the fire. Her eyes closed and her mother's face swam before her, followed by a procession of people she loved: Siri and Sigyn, her nephews and nieces, Beyla, Arinbjörn, her father, dead these many years. She dozed.

A cry sounded in the trees, high-pitched and terrible. She jerked upright. Swords rang out as men unsheathed them and stood, their weapons raised.

Where was Unwen? Wildly, Hild twisted until she found the slave crouched motionless by the blankets, her eyes wide with fear.

"What *was* it?" Brynjolf asked, his dagger held high.

Mord held up his hand to quiet him and stood listening, firelight glinting off his eyes as he looked into the night.

The fire snapped. In the dark woods, stream water chuckled over stones.

"Just a bird," Mord said, and sheathed his sword with finality. He clapped Brynjolf on the shoulder. "You can't jump at every night noise you hear."

Brynjolf laughed, but he didn't sheathe his dagger.

"That was no bird," Thialfi said.

Mord gave him a dubious look. "Bird, animal, something in the woods, that's all."

"Something in the woods, yes," Thialfi said, his voice low and serious.

"What are you suggesting?"

Hild wondered if Thialfi could hear the anger in Mord's voice. He didn't like having his decisions questioned; that was obvious.

"Only that we ask the Hammerer for protection," Thialfi said.

The Hammerer? Hild wondered briefly before realizing it must be a Geatish name for Thor. She had heard they held the Thunder-God in high esteem, higher even than Odin, the All-Father, but she hadn't really believed it until now. She wondered what their temples looked like, and whether they even had one for Freyja.

Hild watched as one of the two younger Geats began looking through the logs stacked up as firewood, rejecting one piece after another until he found the one he wanted. He pulled out his belt knife and carved something into the wood—a rune, she supposed, maybe *thorn* for Thor. Another of the Geats held out an amulet. From where Hild stood, it looked dark enough to have been blackened by fire.

The three men each placed their hands on the wood and spoke in a low chant, too low for her to make out the words even if she could understand their accents, before they threw the log onto the fire, sending up a shower of sparks. *This* was how the seaweed-eaters supplicated a god? The practice seemed strange and primitive, something country folk might do, but hardly fitting behavior for a king's hall thanes. She shook her head and thought longingly of the temples at home.

· · ·

Never had Hild slept in the open before. She couldn't recall a time when she hadn't been able to crawl into the safety and comfort of her warm cabinet bed, except after Midsummer festivals when she'd slept amid a tumble of cousins in a hay barn. She told herself the trees made a protective roof, but she wouldn't have believed it even if she could have seen their branches in the darkness. The blanket shielding her body from the ground did nothing to keep out the cold or the stones that poked into her hip bones, her arms, her head. She turned and turned again, but no position was comfortable. Had Unwen chosen the rockiest place in the whole campsite on purpose? Hild pulled the blanket all the way over her head to block out the cold air, but doing so left her feet exposed. She sat up to rearrange the blanket. As she did, a movement made her turn. Brynjolf stood near the fire, staring at her.

She caught her breath. Now that everybody else was asleep, would he speak to her?

Then he turned away, but not before she caught the pained expression on his face. Deflated, she pulled the blanket over her feet and sank back down again, closing her eyes so Brynjolf didn't have to avoid them.

There would be guards every night, she knew, and they

wouldn't be watching just the woods; they'd be watching her, too. Her uncle must have expected that she would try to escape. How would she and Unwen ever get away? Once they made it to the river, she had no idea how far they would have to journey to get to Unwen's people. Would they be able to survive on foot, carrying their supplies? Or should they take Fire-eyes with them?

Whatever she did, if she was to have any hope of the men's relaxing their guard on her, she would have to convince them that she had accepted her fate.

She rolled onto her side. The cold and the thoughts that circled round and round inside her head kept sleep far away.

Near her, Unwen moaned from her own rude bed. The long day on the pony must have left the slave's body aching, and a night on the cold ground was hardly a remedy for a woman old enough to be Hild's mother.

Her mother. A wave of grief tightened Hild's chest and she shut her eyes tight. She would never be able to sleep.

Yet she did, for there is no waking without sleeping, and she woke to the sound of a bird that didn't realize it was too late in the year to greet the dawn with song. Hild blinked in the gray light and pulled the blanket up to her nose. She could feel every bruise where rocks and roots had bitten into her during the night. Nearby, the fire popped, and she could smell someone cooking meat. Footsteps sounded somewhere close, and she heard the clink of a mail shirt. Was she the only one who hadn't arisen yet?

She sat up and was grateful to see two blanket-covered bodies under the trees. One of them let out a loud snore.

On the other side of her, a figure crouched beside the fire. It was the smaller of the younger Geatish warriors. He was the one roasting the meat. The scent of it perfumed the cold morning air.

Unwen knelt beside her and Hild watched the slave as she placed her hand on the blanket between their two bed-rolls, then caught Hild's eyes with her own in a way unfitting for a slave.

Hild bridled, then relented as she understood Unwen's silent message. Arinbjörn's blade was still hidden under a blanket. They needed to be careful.

"My lady," a man said in that drawn-out Geatish accent. Hild looked up, her heart in her throat, to see the Geat standing beside her. He hadn't seen Unwen's hand, had he? Did he know about the sword?

"This is for you," he said, then set a bowl before her, bowed, and backed away. It was filled with the meat he had been roasting.

Calming her heartbeat, Hild picked up the bowl and called, "My thanks," to the retreating Geat. Then she took a bite. After the previous night's cold supper, the meal warmed her. She closed her eyes as she crunched the delicate bones, then licked every last bit of grease from her fingers.

As Hild ate, Unwen knelt behind her, combing her hair and tidying her clothes, before she began packing up their bedding. Hild kept the sword in view, hovering close to it even though she needed to relieve herself.

Unwen seemed to understand. "Help me carry this to the horses first, my lady," she said quietly before speaking to Mord, who had walked over to the men sleeping nearby. "My lady needs privacy. We're going into the woods."

"Twenty paces, no more," Mord growled, barely looking at them, before he yelled, "Hadding! Stop your snoring and get up. Brynjolf!" He kicked lightly at one of the figures, and Brynjolf shot to his feet, ready to fight.

Mord laughed and nudged Hadding with his foot. Brynjolf smiled sheepishly, wiping sleep from his eyes, while Hadding pulled his blanket away from his head and blinked suspiciously at the daylight. An indentation ringed his bare forehead where his helmet fit him. Hild had rarely seen him without it, and in the morning light, the skin around his eyes looked pale despite the dirt on his face.

She and Unwen picked up their gear and carried it carefully to the horses. Leaving it there, they walked into the woods, and Unwen held up her cloak to shield Hild from the men's view as she squatted. When she stood again, Hild looked at the slave. "Shall I?" she said, reaching for the cloak and feeling awkward. The king's sister-daughter doing such a task for a slave seemed wrong to both of them.

"No, my lady. Go back to the horses and I'll be right along."

Hild gave Unwen another look, but the slave shook her

head, so she made her way back to Fire-eyes, who stood patiently beside the pile in which the sword was hidden.

Between the two of them, they saddled the horse, and then, when the slave gave her the signal that nobody was looking, Hild slipped the blade back into place. Afterward, hands still shaking, Hild helped Unwen ready the pony. How long they would be able to keep up this ruse, she didn't know.

By the time they were finished, the men had doused the fire and cleared the campsite. None of them seemed to think it was odd for Hild to have saddled not only her own horse but her slave's pony. She doubted they had ever had a lady along on their travels before.

As they rode out of the camp and back onto the blazed trail, Hild tried to take particular note of directions. The sun remained hidden behind a gray sky, itself hidden by the trees, but she marked where the light was brighter. Once they got to the river, she told herself, they would be fine because all they had to do was follow it. But first they had to get away from the men. How?

She was lost in consideration of the problem when Thialfi fell back to ride beside her. "It's a fine horse, my lady," he said, giving Fire-eyes an appraising glance. *Fiine hooarse.*

Hild stiffened and kept herself from looking at the place where the blade was hidden. Was it showing? Could the Geat see it? She had to distract him.

"Fire-eyes was a gift from my cousin, the atheling," she

said, reaching forward to stroke the horse's neck, hoping Thialfi's eyes would follow her hand away from the blade.

He gave her a puzzled look and she realized with surprise that he hadn't understood her. She had thought the Geats were the ones with the strange accents, but her speech must sound just as odd to them. "My cousin, the crown prince," she said, enunciating carefully. "He gave me the horse."

"Ahh." Thialfi regarded Fire-eyes again, and she searched for another topic to divert his attention.

"Tell me about your king," she said. It was natural for her to want to know about the person she was supposed to be marrying, wasn't it? "What sort of man is he?"

"Our king?" Thialfi nodded and looked thoughtful, as if he was sorting through details, deciding what to tell her.

She tried to appear interested.

"Scarcely have we finished mourning at our old king's funeral pyre, yet already the bard celebrates our new king's deeds in song. I am honored to have served them both."

Hild's comprehension lagged a step behind the words themselves. *Bard* must be the word the seaweed-eaters used for skald, she decided. When she untangled *saarved them booath*, her eyes dropped to his sword arm, which rested uselessly in Thialfi's lap. The man really seemed to believe he served the king—two kings—despite his injury.

"Would that our bard were here to sing you the tale of the dragon fight," Thialfi said.

"Dragon fight?" She'd forgotten all about it in her sorrow at leaving her family, but now the memory came rushing back. In the hall, her uncle had said that old King Beowulf, who'd ruled the Geats for as long as Hild could remember, had been slain by a dragon. And hadn't he said that the new king had killed it?

A dragon! She wondered if the Geatish kingdom had been cursed. How else could such an evil fate have come to its people? She gazed at Thialfi, waiting.

"I have no skill in chanting," he said, "but I know the story well." When he looked at her, Hild saw the seriousness in his expression.

"After all," he added, "I was there."

She moved Fire-eyes a little closer to Thialfi's horse and settled into her saddle, ready to listen.

FIFTEEN

"A DRAGON, MY LADY . . ." THIALFI PAUSED AND LOOKED into the distance. Hild could see how rough and pitted his skin was, and his dark beard barely hid the gauntness of his cheeks. But his eyes, when he turned back to her, were clear and green.

"You hear about the creatures in stories," he said, "how big they are, how powerful, how they torch villages with their fiery breath."

She nodded, thinking of Ari Frothi's tales.

"What you hear in the stories is nothing. Compared with how it really is? Nothing." He looked away again, and his expression changed as if he was remembering some long-ago sadness.

Hild bent down to avoid a low-hanging branch. The

way was becoming rockier, making the clopping of the horses' hooves louder.

"I was asleep when the dragon attacked," Thialfi said. "We all were—it was the wolfing hour."

"Weren't there guards?" someone asked, and Hild turned to see Brynjolf edging his horse nearer. He'd always loved Ari Frothi's stories, begging him for just one more even after a long lay had left the old skald's voice ragged. She fought the urge to smile at him. Then she saw that he had left Unwen to ride last in the company. This was the second time Brynjolf had neglected his duties. His lack of attention might be exactly what she and Unwen needed to help them escape.

"Yes, there were guards," Thialfi said, "but it wouldn't have mattered if they'd all been asleep."

"I would have shot it." Brynjolf patted the bow he carried over his shoulder.

Thialfi regarded him for a long moment. Hild glanced back at Unwen, whose shoulders had risen to her ears. She held the pony's reins in a death grip. Hild tapped her own shoulder and rubbed her fingers together to remind the slave to relax, but she might as well have been talking to a tree for all the good it did. She turned back to Thialfi.

"It came out of the night with thunder and fire," Thialfi said, "the thunder of a thousand storms. Before I even knew what was happening, the hall was in flames and the cursed creature was gone."

"You didn't see it?" Hild tried to keep the disappointment from her voice.

"Not that time," Thialfi said. "I felt it, though."

"Did the ground rumble?"

"Did it?" Thialfi rubbed his beard, his eyelids lowered, in the manner of a man searching his memory. He looked up again and shook his head. "Maybe it did. I don't recall."

"But you said you felt it," Hild reminded him.

"Yes, my lady, and I pray to the Hammerer that you never have to endure such terror." He reached for something he wore on a leather thong around his neck—an amulet that had been tucked under his shirt. Immediately Hild thought of the fire-blackened ornament she'd seen the previous night. Had it been burned by dragon fire? The pendant Thialfi held was unburned metal, a small hammer symbol. The one she'd seen must have belonged to one of the other Geats.

"I'd heard the stories, just like everybody else," Thialfi said, "about how simply being near a dragon is so terrifying it can freeze your marrow."

Marrow took her a moment to interpret, but the longer she listened to him, the easier he was to understand.

He caught Hild's eye again. "I suppose I believed it, but it takes more than belief to understand what terror truly is."

Brynjolf snorted with derision and Thialfi started to

address him, then seemed to think better of it. "Like I said, my lady, I hope it never happens to you."

The smaller of the two Geats riding directly in front of them turned to Thialfi. "Did our father"—he gestured toward the other rider—"feel it? That terror?"

They were brothers, then, Hild thought. She should have guessed from the similarities in their features.

"I can't say what your father felt, Wulf. But he sought out the dragon and he looked his death straight in the eye."

Wulf inclined his head to Thialfi. "So the king told us," he said, and turned to the front again.

The dragon killed their father? The story suddenly took on a reality it hadn't possessed before. And if Wulf and his brother were still seeking details about their father's death . . . "How long ago?" Hild asked in a low voice.

Thialfi thought for a moment. "The moon was beginning to wane," he said. "A month, maybe."

A month? The ashy cloud of sulfurous smoke that had darkened the skies over the lake loomed in her memory. Ari Frothi had said it was dragon smoke. Could it have been from the very same creature?

Thialfi leaned toward Hild, so close that she had to keep herself from flinching backward. "They were out on patrol," he said softly. "They didn't know about their father until they returned."

Hild looked from Thialfi to the young warriors. She

closed her eyes briefly, remembering her own father's death and how she'd sensed it days before the news came.

"Killing the dragon robbed old King Beowulf of his life," Thialfi said, "but our fate would have been far worse if it hadn't been for our new king."

Ahead of them, the Geatish brothers had positioned themselves so they could hear, and Brynjolf brought his horse even closer. "King Beowulf claimed the dragon fight for himself. But when it proved too great a challenge, when he needed our help, we failed him. Even his most seasoned warriors fled. Even Dayraven."

"*Dayraven* ran from a fight?" Wulf asked, turning in his saddle, disbelief in his voice.

Thialfi nodded, his face sober. "Nor had he returned to the stronghold before we left."

"Who is this Dayraven?" Brynjolf asked, but the men ignored him, lost in the news of their own tribe.

"I can't believe he ran," Wulf said.

The other Geat, the larger brother with the honey-colored hair, turned to Thialfi. "I heard he accused our new king of trying to kill King Beowulf. Is it true?"

There was a moment of silence, punctuated by the sound of hooves clopping over rock, before Thialfi said, "Yes, Dayraven made the accusation." He turned to Hild. "It was the first time our new king saved our old king's life, but in the confusion, I think Dayraven misunderstood his intentions."

"The first time?" Hild asked.

Thialfi nodded. "When we were on our way to fight the dragon, he saved him from falling over a cliff."

There was obviously more to the story, and Hild waited while Thialfi hesitated, as if he was considering his words.

"Later, when the monster showed itself, whatever the terror was that kept the other warriors from coming to King Beowulf's aid, it didn't stop our new king." He paused. "It stopped me, my lady." His voice dropped. "When my king needed me, I ran." He looked away, his story guttering out.

Hild watched him, feeling a curious mixture of emotions. He might be a seaweed-eater, but the pain and honesty in his expression tugged at her.

"I ran," he repeated, this time meeting her eyes, "but our new king didn't. He saved our kingdom."

They rode on in silence for a moment, Hild trying to picture what their new king, who stood firm against such terror, might look like. He must be a powerful warrior, she thought, strong-limbed and confident.

"Whoa," Thialfi said, and Hild looked up just in time to rein in her horse before it overtook Wulf's. The men at the front of the party had stopped, but they hadn't dismounted.

Ahead of them, the trail continued through the trees, but a rocky outcropping rose on the right. They started up again after a few moments, but instead of following the marked path, the men in the lead turned, disappearing into what Hild saw, when she neared it, was a narrow cleft in the rocks.

"Wait, my lady," Thialfi said, and gestured at his companions. One of the brothers dropped back to ride behind her, with Thialfi, while the other stayed just ahead of her. She followed him as they made their cautious way forward, turning off the path and into a canyon of rock and brush, the way wide enough for only a single horse at a time. Above, branches reached out from fissures in the stone, making an arch above her. It was a tunnel of rock and wood, closing in around her. The horses' hooves echoed too loudly in the silence, and she flinched at the touch of a twig against her neck. Fire-eyes seemed to feel just as hemmed in as she did, judging from how he increased his speed when the way finally widened.

They emerged into a glade and paused to wait until everyone had come through. As Brynjolf, the last of the company, rode into view, Mord spurred his horse out of the open area and onto a narrow path. Again, they had to ride single file. Underbrush grabbed at Hild, and she had to duck one low-hanging branch after another. Where were the notches on the trees, the ones that marked the way? She saw none. When a bramble tore at her cloak, she bloodied her fingers freeing the wool.

"Halt!" Thialfi called from behind her.

Hild turned to look at him.

"Beg pardon, my lady," he said, and tried to push past her with his horse. But the path wasn't wide enough and he had to dismount and thread his way to the front on foot. Hild looked back to see Unwen and Brynjolf, their horses waiting patiently behind her.

Ahead, she could hear voices, Mord's and Thialfi's. She thought she heard Thialfi saying the word *dangerous*, but with his accent, it was hard to tell. She definitely heard him say, "Not the right way."

Then Mord's voice rose in anger. "I know my own kingdom's forest."

Hild looked at the thick stands of oak and ash that surrounded them. She might not be able to hear all the men's words, but their intent was clear. Mord had led them off the established track and Thialfi didn't like it. It wasn't long before he returned, the set of his jaw announcing who had lost the argument. The same bramble that had grabbed Hild's cloak snagged Thialfi's, and he yanked at it viciously with his good hand as he passed her.

The horse in front of her started forward again and Hild followed, paying close attention to the branches and rocks and fallen limbs that threatened to knock her from the saddle or lame her horse. While one part of her mind kept watch, another part ruminated on the situation. Could she use the tension between Mord and Thialfi to her advantage when they got to the river? Their anger seemed to have infected the other warriors, as well. Hild heard muttered oaths when branches lashed at men's skin or thorns caught on their clothing. They splashed through a stream, and the cheerful sound of water over rocks made the company's grim mood all the more oppressive.

Finally, when the light was beginning to fade, they came to a small clearing and Mord called a halt. Before he even dismounted, he began barking orders that didn't need to be given: where to hobble their horses, where to put their bedrolls. "Get a fire going," he said to Gizzur, who was already gathering kindling. Mord must still be rankling from Thialfi's challenge, Hild decided.

In such close quarters, she wasn't sure how she and Unwen would ever hide Arinbjörn's blade. She watched the men carefully as she and the slave unsaddled Fire-eyes and the pony, but they were all watching Mord, trying to keep out of his way. "Now," she whispered to Unwen, and together they got the sword off the horse and under the blanket.

As Unwen prepared the beds, hiding the blade between them, Hild sank onto a rock near the fire. She felt shaky with fatigue, even though she'd done nothing but sit on a horse all day. The warmth of the new flames lulled her into a doze and her head fell forward. She startled awake when Unwen put a bowl in her hands. Around her, the men were working or eating in the shadows, Brynjolf currying Mord's horse, Gizzur sitting before the fire, the straps from his leather cap dangling in front of him as he sewed a tear in his meticulously neat tunic. Had the same bramble that caught her cloak torn his tunic? Someone was cooking meat; she could smell it on the night air. In the dark at the camp's periphery, she could just make out the silhouettes of two men who leaned toward each other in conversation. The Geatish brothers, she thought.

The contents of the bowl in front of her—hard bread and dried goat meat again—made her think longingly of Unwen's famous cod and barley stew. She sighed and pulled her cloak more tightly around her shoulders.

When a figure approached, she looked up to see Thialfi. "My lady," he said, and held out a stick with a roasted bird on the end of it.

"My thanks," she said, and reached for it. It was as if he had heard her thoughts. She brought the bird to her lips and blew on it to cool it.

A noise made her jerk it away, almost dropping it. Something was crashing through the woods away from the campsite. The sound faded, but where the brothers were standing, she could see a hint of sword gleaming in the firelight. "What was it?" she whispered.

Thialfi crouched beside her. "Men do not belong in these woods," he said in a low voice, looking intently into the dark.

She followed his gaze but could make out nothing but warriors' shadows.

"Do your people not fear nightwalkers, my lady?" When

she didn't answer, he said, "There are fens not far from here. When the wind is right, you can smell them."

Hild sniffed, but if there was any whiff of rotting vegetation in the air, it was overpowered by the scent of wood smoke.

"Not even the wisest of men know the depths of the pools in those fens." Thialfi watched the darkness, his eyes seeming to track something.

Hild squinted in the same direction, but whatever he saw was invisible to her.

His voice a whisper, his gaze still on the woods, Thialfi added, "They say that night wonders have been seen there, fire on the waters, and creatures who do not welcome our presence." He looked back at her. "It's not a pleasant place."

Hild shuddered. In the safe enclave where she'd grown up, tales of nightwalkers had been mostly that—stories to frighten children. Now, with the dark pressing around them and two of the Geats mourning their father, killed by a dragon, such creatures took on a reality she had never felt when she'd sat in the firelit hall listening to Ari Frothi or Bragi chanting lays about them. "Do you think we'll see any of them?" she whispered.

Thialfi shook his head. "We should have stayed on the trail. Now we won't be safe until we've crossed the river."

"The river?" Hild's voice squeaked. She cleared her throat, trying to disguise her excitement. "How long until we reach it?"

"Soon. Two days, perhaps." He looked at her with concern. "I shouldn't have spoken—please don't worry yourself, my lady."

Hild nodded, reassuring him, her own fears melting into the night.

Two days until the river! Two days until freedom! She had to tell Unwen. They needed a plan.

SIXTEEN

Hɪʟᴅ ʜᴀᴅ ᴛʜᴏᴜɢʜᴛ sʟᴇᴇᴘ ᴡᴀs ᴇʟᴜsɪᴠᴇ ᴛʜᴇ ᴘʀᴇᴠɪᴏᴜs night, but tonight it was impossible. It was colder, the ground was rockier, if that were to be believed, and the woods were alive with strange noises. Far in the distance, a wolf howled and another answered, while closer to camp, branches creaked and nocturnal animals scurried through the underbrush. Hild's body ached so much from tension and fatigue that the cords in her neck felt like they might snap. Escape plans whirred through her head. She examined one, saw its faults, rejected it, and reached for the next, over and over again, until finally, she fell into a restless sleep.

A figure loomed over her, huge and menacing. It reached toward her and she flinched away. The movement woke her and she lay blinking in the dark, trying to calm her pounding heart.

When she turned her head, she could see a low fire still flickering and, beyond it, one of the Geats, the larger brother, whose name she didn't know, standing stiffly, staring into the night, his hand on his sword hilt. When she shifted to the other side, she could just barely make out someone—Hadding, she thought—slumped against a tree, a sword resting beside him. She could no longer hear wolves howling, but an unpleasant odor permeated the night air, making her nose twitch.

She closed her eyes again, pushing away the image from her nightmare and replacing it with thoughts of escape. How would she stop the men from following them? Could she scare the horses away and, in the confusion, run? Should she take Fire-eyes with her or leave him behind? No scenario she imagined seemed right.

At least she had been able to tell Unwen. While the two of them were preparing for bed, Hild had said, "You asked me how long the journey would take. I'm not sure, but Thialfi says we'll have to ford a river in two days. Surely it can't be far beyond that."

Unwen said, "Yes, my lady, thank you, my lady," the way a slave should speak to her mistress. But as she spoke, she met Hild's eye and gave her a nod so slight that anyone who wasn't watching for it would have missed it.

Hild pulled the blanket over her face to block out the dank smell and the cold. With two men on guard each night, how would they ever get away? Would daytime be better? She felt trapped in a whirlpool of plans that pulled her deeper and deeper down, as if she had fallen into a black and bottomless bog.

When she opened her eyes again, it was morning. She blinked at the triangles of sky visible through branches. It was the first bright day she'd seen since she'd left home. The air was so frosty that the end of her nose and the fingers of one hand, which had slipped out from under her blanket, were numb, and she could see her breath. She pulled her hand back under the blanket and rubbed it to warm it, feeling how rough her fingers had become. She could just hear Siri scolding her for not keeping her skin supple with the decoction of bear grease Aunt Var made for them. The lavender her aunt added to it never stopped it from smelling like rancid bear grease to Hild, but now even that odor would have been a welcome reminder of home. She shut her eyes tight, the better to keep her memories deep inside her. Then she opened them wide and threw off her blanket.

Despite the blue sky, she felt jittery from dreams that had disturbed her sleep, dreams she could only recall in wispy fragments. The smell of smoke—not the ordinary scent from a campfire, but choking fumes whose source she couldn't identify—had twined through her slumber, and she'd heard a woman speaking to her, the same harsh voice she'd heard before. Who she was and what she was saying, Hild didn't know, but the voice had offered no comfort. Packing her belongings, Hild dropped things more than once, causing Unwen to regard her with concern when she handed her the blanket-wrapped sword. Hild steadied herself, then gave Unwen a slight nod to signal that she was ready to transfer the blade to her horse.

Fire-eyes picked up on her mood. As they rode out of the camp, he pranced uneasily until she stroked his neck and spoke calming words into his ear. Even then, she could feel his tension. He was ready to bolt at a word. It wasn't just Fire-eyes. The other horses were equally skittish, and she couldn't blame them. Without a trail to follow, they had to pick their way over rocks and fallen logs that hid amid the bracken. One lichen-covered rock made Hild look twice to make sure it wasn't some malevolent dwarf crouching in the woods to watch them pass.

She scoffed at herself. She was letting the seaweed-eaters' superstitions infect her. Yet the Shylfings, too, were wary and their silence seemed ominous. Even Brynjolf had stopped his chatter. She glanced back to see him bringing up the rear, turning his head first to one side and then the other at noises in the trees. In the helmet and mail shirt he'd inherited from his father and not quite grown into, he looked like the boy he was, not a full-grown warrior. She wondered if he was afraid, riding alone at the back of the company. She wished that she could fall back to ride alongside him, that they could be friends again.

The Geatish brothers, ahead of her, must have been a few years older than Brynjolf, a more appropriate age for warriors. If they felt any fear, their erect posture and measured movements disguised it. They watched the woods so intently that Hild found herself glancing into the trees, too. Something flashed past her line of sight, making her jump, but it was just a bird.

Above her, bare branches met, caging her away from the sky. Below, the ground grew spongy, and once, Fire-eyes's hooves splashed through a place where Hild had thought the earth would be firm.

By the time Mord finally called a halt, Hild's body was taut with the strain of constant vigilance. Yet the rest period was no better. Mord and Gizzur walked a little way into the woods, talking quietly to each other, but the others stood silent and watchful, hardly eating. Hild saw Thialfi exchange glances with his companions. They nodded, and while Wulf pulled food from the bag on his horse, his brother took up a position near a boulder, his bow in his hands. The Geats were taking turns eating, two of them always on guard. Against what? A prickly sensation crawled up her back, as if something were watching her. She whirled, but only rocks met her gaze. She wished her sword were in her hand, not hidden on her horse.

"My lady," Unwen said, and presented Hild with bread and water. She ate mechanically, never looking away from the woods, whose shifting shadows held secrets she couldn't discern.

It wasn't long before they mounted again and began the

afternoon's weary ride. At least the woods thinned a little, making the going easier. There was nothing for Hild to do but think. She needed a plan and she needed it now, but her mind was blank. She imagined herself in the temple to Freyja, making an offering of mead at the altar, as she'd done so many times in the past. "Lady of the Vanir," she whispered. *Help me see a solution,* she prayed silently. *Let me find an escape.*

She quieted her thoughts, listening for an answer, but nothing happened. Tears of frustration pricked at the corners of her eyes.

Fire-eyes tossed his head and whinnied in protest.

"Sorry," Hild whispered, loosening her grip on the reins and leaning over the horse's neck. When she looked up again, she realized the two Geats in front of her were staring back at her. Feeling her face redden, she raised her chin and gazed into the woods, her bearing stately, her expression imperious, as if she were a goddess dismissing mortals, mere flies buzzing around her.

Amid the bare trees, a single oak caught her eye. Its leaves, red as a bloodstained blade, still clung stubbornly to its branches.

Fire-eyes's gait was steady, despite the rocks, and her two nights of slim sleep dragged at Hild's lids and sent cobwebs to wrap themselves around her brain. Slowly, her muscles began to relax as her head nodded in time to her horse's pace. Her eyes closed, fluttered open, then closed again. Her chin fell to her chest. She thought she could feel someone falling in beside her but she was too drowsy to look.

Behind her lids a scene took shape—a shadowy figure climbing toward her out of darkness, its body swathed in green ribbons. No, the ribbons weren't woven of cloth; they were seaweedy spirals hanging from a torso covered in dripping fur. The figure stood to its full, terrifying height and reached out its claws. Hild jerked away, her hand going up to protect her face.

"My lady."

Thialfi held her arm, keeping her from falling off her horse.

She looked at him, blinking. He held her gaze and she used the concern in his eyes to steady herself. They were still riding in the woods. She had just had a dream; that was all. She would need to get more sleep tonight.

She took a shaky breath, then gently disengaged her arm from his, nodding him her thanks.

He moved his horse a little away from her, but she could tell he was keeping a close eye on her.

As she rode, she watched the woods, the late sun barely visible through thickets of bare branches. A squirrel leapt from one tree to the next. In the distance, a cry pierced the sky. A hawk?

She glanced at Thialfi, whose eyes were on the woods, his head cocked. He, too, was listening.

The sound came again, nearer this time.

She looked up to where Mord rode alone. He didn't seem to be reacting, but she couldn't see his face.

The cry came directly above her and she looked up in time to see a hawk gliding fast overhead, its breast feathers dusky above, white below. Suddenly, it plunged into the trees. For a moment, she couldn't see it behind the branches. Then it emerged again, something struggling in its powerful talons.

The squirrel.

Bird and prey disappeared beyond the trees. As they did, a final long hunting cry hung in the air. The sound unnerved her.

They continued onward as dusk settled around them, but Mord didn't call a halt. Hild strained to see ahead of her but no camping area with a fire pit or piles of kindling greeted them. Soon she strained to see at all as Mord kept pushing them on into the dark. Trees crowded close and rocks and boulders made the footing difficult.

"We need to stop before we lame a horse," Thialfi said in a low voice to Hild.

"Is this a good place?" she asked, keeping her voice just as quiet as his.

"As good as any."

Well. Whatever the men thought of her, she was still the king's sister-daughter. She still outranked them all. Steadying herself, she sat up tall and called out, "We'll make camp here for the night. Gizzur, see to a fire. Unwen, where are you? I need you here."

She heard a grunt from up ahead, but Mord couldn't argue. Riding in a trackless wood in the dark was dangerous in more ways than one.

Wulf was at Hild's side instantly, ready to help her dismount. She started to send him away, then caught herself. If she and Unwen were going to escape, the Geats needed to think she was pleased to marry their king. She took Wulf's hand.

When her feet touched the ground, she gave the young warrior a slight curtsy of thanks and even graced him with a semblance of a smile. *Don't overdo it,* she told herself as he bowed and moved away.

In the half-light, boulders hunched like goblins amid ghostly tree trunks. This forest was no place for humans to be in the Between Time, she thought, then laughed at herself. She sounded just like a seaweed-eater.

Leading Fire-eyes, she stumbled over a rock. As she righted herself, a branch scratched at her, and when she skirted it, another rock made her lose her footing. Finally realizing it would be easier to stand still until there was a fire to see by, she stopped and waited until light sprang into the night. Not far away, Gizzur was feeding sticks to the new flames. They cheered her despite the eerie shadows the boulders cast. She looked around to find Unwen, and together they unsaddled Fire-eyes and the pony.

Slowly the camp took shape, Brynjolf picking up fire-wood, Unwen unrolling blankets, Hadding digging for something in a leather pouch. Hild knelt in front of the fire, warming her hands and face, and watched both Wulf and his brother standing guard, their hands on their weapons. Were they still near the fen?

And where was Mord? She glanced around but saw only boulders crouched in an irregular group like a circle of trolls who had lingered too long in the night, until daylight had surprised them, turning them to stone. It made her think of the grassy place where she and Arinbjörn used to play. The place where she had killed a man. She blinked the memory away. This place wasn't anything like that. It wasn't grassy, and it was surrounded by woods. A tree grew out of a cleft in the boulder nearest her, and in the flickering firelight, she could see roots grasping at the stone like ancient, knobby fingers.

She stood, turning to find Unwen and something to eat, but the slave was hidden somewhere in the rocks.

Hild scanned the area again, an idea taking shape in her mind. She couldn't see Unwen, she couldn't see Mord, and now that she was paying attention, she realized Brynjolf had disappeared, too.

Thialfi stooped over a leather bag near the fire and Hild approached him.

"Will the way continue as rocky as this when we near the river?" she asked.

He looked up at her. "Yes, my lady. Our journey tomorrow won't be any easier than today's."

She nodded and looked at the huge pile of stones not far from them. Putting a hint of dismay in her voice, she said, "There will be boulders this big?"

"I'm afraid so, my lady. We'll have to walk the horses at times. But after we ford the river, our path will be much easier."

"Thank you, Thialfi." She turned so he wouldn't see the gleam in her eyes, then mouthed a quick prayer of thanks to Freyja.

The goddess had heard her request. The rocks were the answer. They would help them escape.

Again she looked for Unwen and saw the slave emerging from the shadows, a bowl in her hands. Unwen had become hidden among the stones without even knowing it. How easy it would be when they actually tried to make themselves disappear.

Hild stepped forward to meet her accomplice.

SEVENTEEN

THEY PACKED CAREFULLY THE NEXT MORNING. THE ROCKS might have dug into Hild's body all night, chilling her and once again keeping sleep far away, but now they provided cover as Unwen stuffed food into a bag they could grab at a moment's notice.

Exactly what they took with them would depend on the circumstances of their escape. They would have blankets ready, but if they couldn't get to them when they needed them, cloaks would serve. As long as they had food, they would be all right, Hild told herself. Food, cloaks, the bag tied to Unwen's belt—and the sword riding next to Fire-eyes's saddle.

Her fingers fumbled over the saddle's straps. She felt as feverish with excitement and cold and lack of sleep as a child at a Midwinter festival. Strange dreams and a feeling that she was being watched had woken her again, but now the night's terrors faded into the morning light and the promise of freedom ahead.

The others were moving so slowly that Hild wanted to scream. At the same time, she knew she needed to be calm and methodical, pay close attention, and use the extra time to make sure everything was ready. She made her hands into fists to quiet them, pressing so hard that a fingernail broke. She picked at the jagged edge, trying to smooth it—and her nerves.

When they finally broke camp, the rocks made their path as difficult as Thialfi had predicted, and time and again they had to dismount to lead the horses past treacherous spots or down steep declines. The way was thick with stones, thorny brambles, and leaves, dry and brown. Gnarled trees grew out of fissures in the rocks, and branches curved in weird patterns, blocking their passage. All morning, the land descended gradually. By the time they stopped at midday, Hild had to tilt her head up to see the path they had come from, and look down to see where they were going. Were they nearing the river? She listened for the sound of water but heard only the clattering of bare branches.

As she sat to eat, Thialfi squatted beside her. "We're past the fens now, my lady, and no harm to us."

Hild looked a question at him.

"The horses are calmer. Haven't you noticed?"

She'd been so focused on guiding Fire-eyes through

the treacherous territory that she hadn't paid attention to the change in atmosphere. Looking at the horses now, she saw that they were standing placidly beside each other, and when she sniffed the air, the dank odor that had trailed them for so long was gone.

Thialfi sat as calmly as the horses, munching an oatcake.

"When will we reach the river?" As soon as the words were out, she regretted them. Would he think her interest odd? Would he begin to suspect? No, she told herself, it was a normal question.

He gave the downward slope a glance, then regarded the sky. "Not long now. Before sun-wane, surely. Maybe in time to ford it today."

Hild's heart quickened. She busied herself with the strips of dried goat meat she'd been given, to keep Thialfi from seeing her excitement.

She finished eating before the others were ready to ride again. Why was it taking them so long? Unable to contain her fidgeting, she went in search of Unwen. The slave was bent down, a cross expression on her face. Immediately, Hild saw why. A dried blackberry vine had caught in the bottom of her skirts.

"Ow!" Unwen pulled her finger away from a thorn and sucked on it.

"Here, let me," Hild said, stooping to help her. "Stand still." She gently pulled one thorn from the wool, then another, careful not to scratch her own fingers, which were still sore from the brambles she'd battled the previous day. She held the tangled vine aside and the slave stepped free.

"Thank you, my lady."

Hild glanced around to make sure they were alone. "Today," she whispered.

Unwen's narrowed eyes opened a little wider than usual. "Today," she mouthed.

At that moment, Mord mounted his horse, the signal to the rest of them that it was time to go. As she climbed into her saddle, Hild reached to touch the hidden sword, then pulled her hand back. Had Mord seen her? *Be more careful,* she admonished herself. No unnecessary risks when escape was this close. Subdued, she fell into line behind the Geatish brothers, Unwen behind her, Thialfi and Brynjolf bringing up the rear.

As they descended, loose rocks, prickly bushes, and a path that wound around and through boulders and trees made the going even more difficult than before. Bits of shale tumbled down from the horses behind her, and she knew Fire-eyes was sending it showering onto the men ahead of her. When Wulf dismounted, she did, too. The first time it happened, she almost resisted the hand Wulf offered to help her. But by the third time they had to lead the horses, she was glad of the assistance.

Finally, the path opened out enough that they could ride. Hild could see the sky, although the trees hid the sun. To either side, sere trunks rose like an army of spears, receding into darkness. Her spirits lifted a little when she heard Brynjolf begin to chant a walking song, one she and Beyla used to sing as little girls when Siri took them berry picking. Recalling the warmth of the sun on her head and the pleasant plink the berries made as they fell into the pail, Hild closed her eyes, the better to savor the memory.

Goat's breath! She pulled up short, almost running into Wulf's horse. She'd thought they were through with having to lead the horses, but the way had narrowed yet again. Brynjolf's song trailed off. In silence, they led the horses through stones that rose as tall as Hild herself. Would they ever get to the river? She looked at Fire-eyes, who was picking his way delicately over the rocks, and checked her impatience. It would slow them much more if one of the horses was lamed. Besides, Thialfi had said they'd make it to the river today.

It wouldn't be long now.

A horse whinnied. Brynjolf's, she thought as she guided Fire-eyes between two standing stones so high they almost met overhead. The horse pulled at his reins, tossing his head. "It's all right," Hild whispered to him. "You don't like these rocks, do you?" He pulled again and whinnied, causing the horses in front of them to respond.

"Control your horse," Mord called from somewhere ahead.

I'm trying! Hild thought, but there was no point in saying it aloud. Fire-eyes whinnied again, then reared, and

Hild had to jump out of the way to keep from being kicked. "Whoa, there, steady, boy!" she said, grabbing for the reins, which had pulled loose from her fingers. His eyes rolled back in fear. "It's just rocks," she told him soothingly.

"The way widens ahead," Thialfi said as he came running up to help her, but then the horses ahead of them began whinnying again and someone cried out, "Thialfi!"

As she turned, a movement caught Hild's eye. She glanced up, but there was nothing to see, just a tree shadow against the stones.

Fire-eyes reared again and Thialfi caught his reins with his good hand. "Get ahead of me," he said, and led the horse forward.

Hild looked back at Unwen. Her pony, as wide-eyed with fear as Fire-eyes was, struggled against the slave. Ignoring Thialfi, Hild ran back to take the pony's reins and pulled, crooning to it.

It balked, but with Hild pulling and Brynjolf pushing from behind, it came through the rocks as they widened into a glade. Thialfi handed Fire-eyes back to Hild. The horse had quieted some, but all of the horses were skittish now, prancing and rolling their eyes.

Hild glanced at the trees and standing rocks. The clearing wasn't natural. Somebody had made it. "What is this place?" she asked, and when nobody answered, she repeated her question.

"We should keep moving," Thialfi said.

"Just somebody's old campsite," Mord said, but he, too, seemed eager to depart.

Hild regarded the leaf-covered ground, the way the trees and stones leaned in, encircling them. She tilted her head back and saw the trees crowding toward each other, bare branches crisscrossed like thatch. She stretched out her senses but smelled only leaf mold, felt only the cold air against her cheeks. Branches clacked together above her, sounding like wooden swords in a practice match. When she glanced at the men, they seemed as nervous as the horses. Brynjolf passed her, Unwen and the pony directly in front of him, and she could tell they were eager to move on.

"Come, my lady," Thialfi said, and motioned her to mount again. She took another look around, then climbed into the saddle.

She had reached the edge of the clearing when she saw the wooden stave, half her height, planted in the ground. Atop it was a head carved of wood and darkened with age. A woman's head, hair knotted in back, nose worn away, eyes wide. Hild stared at it, curious. Who was the carved woman? The goddess of some heathen tribe? She moved her horse to have a closer look.

"Please come, my lady," Thialfi called again, his voice the sharpest she'd heard it.

Reluctantly, she followed, but she couldn't help taking one last look back at the carved head. As she did, a shadow on a rock caught her eye, making her think for a fleeting moment that she had seen someone. She squinted at it, but the shadow didn't move. It was just a tree trunk blocking out the light. She turned, tugged on Fire-eyes's reins, and caught up with the men.

Past the clearing, the path became easier, allowing them to ride slowly. They were still descending, but the ground wasn't as steep. The low sun had trouble piercing the thickets of twiggy branches.

When Mord called a halt and dismounted, irritation rippled through Hild. Why stop now when there was still enough light to make it to the river? It seemed as if Mord was deliberately trying to foil her plans.

She rode a few steps forward as the wind rushed in the branches overhead. Then she stopped and looked up. There was no wind; the branches were still. She listened again. It wasn't wind; it was water. Narrowing her eyes, she tried to see between the trees where something broad and brown blocked their way.

They had reached the river.

Hild's breath quickened and she slid from Fire-eyes's back, rushing to meet Unwen as soon as her feet hit the ground. It was exactly as she had hoped. The men would be too busy searching for a place to cross to pay attention to the two of them. Now was their time.

Brynjolf spurred his horse past them, joining the men who stood staring at the river. It was all the signal Hild needed. She handed a blanket and a bag to Unwen, who took another bag from the pony. Then, with quick, sure movements, Hild reached for the sword, pulled it from Fire-eyes's back, and slid it under her cloak.

Over the sound of the river, she could hear raised voices—Mord's, Hadding's, now Thialfi's pushing into the fray. *Good,* she thought, *let them argue.*

"Which way?" she whispered. Unwen inclined her head to the left. In the dying light, Hild could see a strange expression on the slave's face, but she didn't stop to question it. Instead, she stood for a silent moment, praying, *Goddess, be with us.*

They started walking.

EIGHTEEN

Unwen's feet snapped twigs and sticks as she rustled through dry leaves, her movements far too loud. With every second step, the slave's skirts brushed against Hild's. Hild didn't look back but kept her pace steady. *Give the men nothing to suspect,* she told herself. But every muscle in her body screamed at her to *run.*

She wove behind a boulder and started making her way closer to the river, trusting Unwen to follow. Had the men noticed yet? She strained her ears and heard the sounds of sharp words. They were still arguing. Underbrush caught at her skirt. A stick broke with a sharp crack behind her—too far behind her. She stopped and waited for Unwen to catch up, listening for a change in the men's voices.

"Here, let me have that," Hild said, reaching for one of the blankets. She rolled it tight, tucked it under her sword arm, and starting going again, hoping the slave would move more quickly without it.

A bird shrieked. Hild heard Unwen gasp, but she herself barely started, so focused did she feel. Dark was descending and she intended to get as far away from the men as she could while it was still possible to see. Trees came at her in the half-light and she moved around them, swift and sure-footed. A boulder rose before her and she easily skirted it. A sense of exhilaration flooded through her, filling her with strength and confidence. The goddess was with her; she felt sure of it.

Unwen must have felt it, too. Her footsteps were quieter now, but Hild could hear her breathing heavily. Hild turned and, without speaking, took the food bag from the slave. The sword and the blanket were under one arm, and carrying the bag left her with no free hand, but it didn't matter. She increased the pace. She felt as if she could go forever, as if she could take all the bags in the world and still move faster than Odin's eight-legged steed.

Birds called to each other from the trees. Behind her, Unwen panted. The steady rushing noise of the river came from her sword-hand side. She could no longer hear the men, nor was there any sign they had been missed.

A stone bit through her shoe, and a cobweb caught in her hair, but she ignored them. She felt like a nightwalker from the old stories, strong and certain in the dark woods. If only Unwen would hurry! She heard an "oomph" and turned to see the slave, no more than a shape in the darkness, coming around a tree. Hild waited, then started forward again.

Shouts sounded in the distance. She smiled and kept moving. The men would never find them now.

The darkness grew total, but Hild hardly slackened her pace. She leapt over a stone, yanked her cloak from a branch that grabbed at it, and kept moving.

A scream shattered the night.

Hild stopped so fast that Unwen bumped into her.

They stood without speaking, the noise of Unwen's breathing masking the sounds Hild listened for: footsteps, voices, bodies moving through the forest.

The scream came again. Then a sound Hild didn't know, an inhuman cry that sent a shiver down the back of her neck. Something flashed like fire in front of her eyes. She blinked, but nothing was there.

Suddenly, she knew she had to go back.

No! she argued. *I won't!*

But her desires didn't matter. A summons drew her like a royal command.

"No!" she whispered through clenched teeth. But even as she said the word, she turned to grip Unwen's shoulder. In a low, urgent voice, she said, "You have to keep going. Don't stop until you get to your people. Here." She pushed the food bag into Unwen's hands. "I'll catch up with you."

The slave didn't answer. Hild fought the irritation that surged through her. She didn't have time to explain, even if she could have; she needed Unwen to do what she said, and do it fast. "Do you understand me?"

Unwen stared at her, and in the starlight filtering through the tree branches, Hild recognized not the fear or the protest she expected in her eyes, but a strange, fierce joy.

Hild drew back as if she'd been slapped.

More than ten winters of loyalty and what Hild had taken for love—gone in an instant. Unwen had no care for Hild, not anymore. Instead, she was intent on finding her home, her people, her far-minded daughter.

Unwen was no longer a slave.

"Go, then. And the gods go with you," Hild said. As she spoke, the powerful compulsion took hold of her. She couldn't fight it. She had to leave *now*. Without another glance, she tore off through the forest, heading back toward the men she'd escaped.

.   .   .

Hild passed tree, stone, bush, and bramble, leaping, dodging, running full tilt, the sword in her hand. The blanket lay somewhere behind, snagged by branches. In the darkness, she could somehow feel her way without slowing, without stumbling, as if something was guiding her feet. What she was running toward, she didn't know.

But she recognized the same feeling she'd had before, back when she'd saved her cousin's life. She might not be able to control it, but this time, she was still aware of herself. A part of her was still Hild.

And despite the desperate urgency she felt, there was room in her heart for the hurt of Unwen's leaving. "*I* didn't make her a slave," she whispered angrily. "The gods did. She knows that." Yet another part of her knew that if the gods had made her a slave, she, too, would have done everything in her power to go home again.

"How could she leave me?" she asked herself, then remembered that she was the one who had commanded Unwen to go. "But she could have argued, just a little!"

A branch sliced at her face, grabbing at her hair and pulling strands of it free from its knot. Ahead she could hear confused noises, muffled shouting, a horse neighing in terror, and someone—or some*thing*—moving through the woods.

Hild ran faster, the sword gripped tight, all thoughts of Unwen banished from her mind. Her senses focused on what was before her. She couldn't stop if she wanted to, but now she didn't want to stop. Whatever it was, she needed to get to it.

Through the trees, she could see the glow of fire. A smell like rotting meat assaulted her nose, and ahead of her, something grunted angrily. She heard a terrified whinny and the sound of hooves—a horse was crashing through the woods toward her. She stepped out of the way just in time as it passed her.

Closer now, nearer the campfire, she could see another

horse, lying on the ground, entrails spilling onto the dirt. Near it lay a man, face turned away from her. She didn't stop to see who it was.

Gripping the sword hilt, she wove past a tree. Thorns yanked at her cloak, pulling her up short. She fumbled with the brooch that fastened the cloak, tugging at the pin until it came loose, and let the cloak fall to the ground as she ran. She stepped on something that made her foot recoil—someone's arm. She didn't look down.

As she burst into the space where the campfire blazed, a movement caught her eye. She turned.

A shadow lurked in the trees. A bear? It was too big to be a man.

Sword out, Hild ran.

"My lady! Stop!" someone yelled, and a hand reached for her. She pushed it aside and kept going. A rancid smell threatened to choke her, but she gulped air through her mouth. Ten sword lengths away now, she could see how enormous the creature was. Five sword lengths and the flickering firelight illumined the green fur, matted with gore. The creature raised a huge rock in its claws, bigger than any man could lift. Below, on the ground, lay Mord. Firelight reflected in the whites of his eyes.

He's nothing to me, Hild told herself. *Why should I help him?* But the words didn't stop her, even as someone grabbed her arm. Thialfi. She shoved him away with strength she knew wasn't hers and kept going.

The stench made her eyes water, but she blinked and focused on a spot just under the creature's raised arm.

Around the tree, and *now!* Her sword met resistance but she pushed and pushed again as Mord twisted out of the way of the falling rock.

She didn't have time to watch him—he'd have to take care of himself. The creature roared. It turned toward her, wrenching her sword arm. She gasped in pain.

She tried to pull the blade free, but it was too deeply embedded in the monster's body. The creature moved toward her, its fangs so close she could see the spittle dripping from them. The terrible red maw leered down at her, its fetid reek making her retch. Again she pulled, but now, when she needed it, her strength was ebbing away.

She dropped her hand from the hilt and took a step back, stumbling over a root and righting herself. Horror threatened to overtake her.

The creature stopped and Hild stared at its green fur hanging in clumps like seaweed.

She'd seen it before—in her dream.

It raised its head and screamed, the sound ripping through the dark woods. Her eyes cringed shut. She backed away but a tree blocked her escape. She was hemmed in.

She forced herself to open her eyes. Even if she'd had the sword, her strength was no match for the creature's.

She was going to die.

It peered at her through red, inhuman eyes set far back in its face, then swung its claw.

Hild didn't move. There was no place for her to go.

The creature screamed again, and Hild thought her skull might shatter from the sound. Maybe it had shattered. She couldn't get her breath. She watched the creature as if from a distance, as if she weren't standing a hand's breadth from it. As if she were already dead.

It brought its claw to its chest, then turned and loped away, melting silently into the darkness.

Hild swayed. Her knees buckled and she sank to the ground.

"My lady!" a man called out.

Blackness enveloped her.

NINETEEN

A CRACKING SOUND INTRUDED INTO HER DREAMS, WAKING her. It was still night. A black sky pressed down on her; fingers of cold pinched at her scalp, her face, her feet. Rocks dug into her hip bones and shoulders. Her wrist ached.

The cracking noise came again—somebody breaking sticks for kindling. Sparks from a campfire floated into the trees, and above the bare branches, she could see stars, hard and bright. A voice reached her ears, one man speaking softly to another.

Memories rushed back: a man lying on the ground, a horse with its belly slit, the arm she'd stepped on, the creature she'd fought.

The creature! What was it? Where was it now? Hild sat bolt upright, heart pounding, pain flaring in her ribs and her arm.

She blinked in the darkness, the scene around her coming into focus. A few footsteps away, Mord sat by the fire. Seeing her sitting up, he raised himself and limped toward her. On the other side of the fire, Thialfi sat with a stick in his hand, his face lit a lurid red by the flames.

Hild moved her hand to the ground beside her, under the blanket, hoping to find her sword. It wasn't there. Then she remembered where she had last seen it: buried in the monster's chest.

Mord lowered himself to one knee beside her, grimacing as he did.

"Is it still alive?" she whispered.

He gave her a curt nod.

"And the men. Did . . . did we lose anyone?"

"Your slave is missing."

Hild looked at him. Did he not realize what she and Unwen had done? Did he not know that she had almost escaped him? His face, contorted by pain, revealed nothing.

"And—" He stopped. It wasn't just physical pain he was feeling. Hild held her breath, waiting to hear.

Mord shook his head, his eyes cast down, his thumb going to the scar on his lip. "Brynjolf's dead."

Hild stared at him. Brynjolf? Not Hadding, not Gizzur, not the Geats, but Brynjolf? She closed her eyes for the space of a breath. Then, locking the information tightly away, refusing to think about it just yet, she looked back at Mord. "How badly are you hurt?"

He shook his head. "I'll be right by sunup."

She doubted that. "What about the horses?"

"Gizzur's horse was killed, my lady. The others—if they're alive, they'll come back."

"And the other men?"

"They'll mend." He looked into the dark, and when Hild followed his gaze, she could just make out the shapes of two men, shadows against the darker shades of the trees, the firelight barely revealing their presence. When he turned his head in the other direction, she understood that they were surrounded by guards, even if she couldn't see them. She would never be able to get away.

She lowered her voice to a whisper. "What was it that attacked us?"

Mord shook his head. "I've never seen anything like it. Thialfi says his people speak of a creature that lives in the fens. . . ." His voice trailed off.

"Will it come back?"

"I don't know. All I know is that I'm alive thanks to you, my lady."

The sincerity in his voice took her by surprise and she gazed at his dirt-streaked face. He had a cut on his cheek, but it didn't look deep. Firelight gleamed on the white scar above his lip. His eyes, usually so evasive, were trained on hers and she looked into them, trying to understand him.

"I don't know how you did what you did," he said. "But Bragi's wrong. The gods are with you."

There was an awkward silence. Mord rose to his feet, grunting as he did so, and limped back to the fire.

She watched him go and saw that Thialfi was looking at her, an expression on his face that she couldn't read. Suddenly, it hit her. Mord might not know that she'd tried to escape, but Thialfi did.

Someone had thrown a blanket over her and she rearranged it before she lay back down, shaky from the effort of sitting up. Firelight glowed on the branches above her and she watched it flickering.

Had the gods been with her? Saving her cousin, the atheling, the heir to the throne, *that* she could understand. But giving up her freedom to save Mord? Why would the gods want that?

The creature was out there somewhere, alive. And so was Unwen, armed with only a knife. It didn't matter what weapon the slave had with her—she was no match for the monster's strength if it found her. Hild closed her eyes to banish an image of Unwen being attacked, her body ripped open by the creature's claws. She hoped what she was seeing was a product of her own fear, not a vision.

She trembled and pulled the blanket up to her chin. Her cloak was gone; she remembered dropping it in the woods. She would have to wait until morning to find it.

Finally, carefully, she allowed herself to think about Brynjolf. Only it wasn't Brynjolf she was thinking of; it was Beyla. Who would tell her about her brother? Hild wanted to pull her friend into an embrace, to protect her from the pain. She pictured a crowd of women—aunts, neighbors, cousins—enveloping Beyla like a flock of crows, mourning with her, trying to ease her sorrow. It wouldn't help.

Had the arm she'd trodden on been Brynjolf's? She shuddered and tried to push the memory away, but it kept coming back.

How could he be dead? Although he'd been made a member of the men's troop, he was still a boy, full of fun and merriment. If it weren't for the endless fighting, and the unceasing need for new warriors, he'd be at home in the boys' troop, practicing the kinds of moves that might have saved him. He'd still be alive.

She could hear the way he'd snort with laughter when she and Beyla teased him, and see his broken-toothed smile. She'd always envied Beyla for having a brother. She still envied her, even with the pain she would carry with her for the rest of her life, the empty place Brynjolf had left behind. Brynjolf! How could he be gone?

Tears spilled onto her cheeks and wet her hair.

Birdsong woke her. She raised herself to her elbows, blinking her swollen eyes open. Shafts of sunlight broke through the trees, illuminating autumn mist. Hadding, standing beside the fire, saw her sitting up and limped over to put something on the ground beside her before retreating again. Her cloak. She reached for it gratefully, burrowing into it against the cold.

In the daylight, it was both harder and easier to believe that the previous night's events had been real. Harder because the creature seemed like something from a story told to frighten children, or from a nightmare, not something a person should ever truly encounter in this life. But when Hild looked around her, at the broken branches, the blood on the ground, it was all too easy to believe what had happened. Especially when she saw Brynjolf's body in a little clearing not far from her, his hands and sword arranged over his chest to hide his terrible wounds. She took a ragged breath and looked away.

Behind an oak, she could just make out Gizzur sitting on the ground, his palm resting on a mound of rock, his knees drawn up, his face pressed to them. She watched him curiously for a moment before she realized the mound was his horse, its belly split open. Quick, foolish tears pricked at her eyes. He must have felt the same way about his horse as she had about Fleetfoot.

She shook the tears away and rose, moving to the fire. Hadding stood beside it, an oatcake in each hand, chewing on one of them and eyeing the other. She glanced at him to see if he was wounded, but the limp she'd seen earlier appeared to be his normal clubfooted gait. Below his helmet's mask, his beard had more bits of twigs and leaves in it than usual.

"Here, my lady," he said, offering her the oatcake he'd been just about to bite into.

She took it, forcing herself not to cringe at the layers of

dirt on his fingers. With Unwen gone, had he been assigned to her? *Brynjolf would be a better choice,* she thought, then remembered that Brynjolf was dead.

Hadding pushed a log nearer the fire for her and she sat, looking around for the other men. Mord and Thialfi were over by the riverbank, but the other two Geats were hidden from her view. Wherever they were, she knew their weapons would be in their hands. They were the ones who had warned Mord not to take this route to the river; they were the ones who had heard stories of a creature that lived in the fens.

A bird warbled somewhere in the woods, unconcerned with the secrets hidden behind the trees.

As the fire warmed her, Hild's strength began to return. Her eyes finally detected the Geatish brothers standing watch, as motionless as trees. The horses had returned, too. Some of them, anyway. When she looked more closely, she saw that Fire-eyes wasn't with them. Nor was the pony.

Mord and Thialfi came back, Mord grimacing from his wounded leg. Not far from where Hild sat, Gizzur and Hadding started to dig a grave. *In this hard ground?* She knew the blaze from a funeral pyre would call too much attention to them, but she wasn't surprised when Gizzur finally set down the rock he was using to dig with.

"We'll cover him with stones," Mord said. Something in his voice made her wonder if this was the first time he had lost someone under his command.

She stood, beckoning to him. "Your leg," she said when he limped up to her.

He nodded and sat on the log she'd just vacated so she could examine the place above his knee where the creature's claws had raked him. Thialfi brought her water and handed her a little bag of herbs. When she washed the blood away to see how deep the wound was, Mord gritted his teeth but made no sound. She crumbled dried leaves of heal-all into her palm, mixing them with ashes and spit to make a paste. As she stirred them with her fingers, she chanted the words Aunt Var had taught her:

> *Take the poison, cast out evil.*
> *Be strong against venom.*
> *You are heal-all.*

Then she patted the concoction onto Mord's wound. He knew as well as she did that the wound would fester or it would heal, depending on what pleased the gods. If they looked kindly on him, the herbs might help.

As she leaned over to tie a cloth around the wound, a sound from the woods drew her upright.

Mord rose, unsheathing his sword, the bandage hanging from his leg. The other men stood alert, weapons in their hands.

Steps came toward them through the bracken. Mord pushed her behind him.

Something moved behind an oak tree.

She clenched her fingers. If only she had her sword!

Then the pony nosed out from behind a tree, followed by Fire-eyes.

Hild let out her breath, her knees wobbly with relief. Forgetting Mord's half-wrapped bandage, she ran to the horse, pressed her face against his warm neck, and wrapped her fingers in his mane. When she could breathe easily again, she looked him over. He had cuts and scratches, but nothing worse. Thialfi stepped forward to help her take off the saddle.

When she turned back to the fire, she saw that Mord was trying to finish tying the bandage himself, and making a bad job of it.

"Here," she said, pushing his hands away. She rewrapped it, tying it neatly.

"My thanks, Lady Hild." He dipped his head to her. "Will you see to Gizzur's arm?"

Her own wrist throbbed, and every time she moved, she could feel the bruises on her side, but she nodded. If Mord could ignore the pain a deep cut like his must cause, she wouldn't let herself be bothered, either.

Gizzur approached her reluctantly, pulling his cloak back to reveal the cut on his wiry arm, just below the band of twisted metal he wore. It looked like a claw had gotten him, too, but it wasn't as bad as Mord's wound. She made another paste of heal-all, spit, and ashes and chanted while she applied it to his arm. He endured her ministrations silently, never meeting her eyes, and stood the moment she finished tying his bandage.

"Gizzur," she said softly, touching his shoulder.

He looked at her through his narrow eyes.

"I'm sorry about your horse."

For an instant, his face changed, his eyes widening, the thin line of his lips softening. Then he nodded and moved away, returning to the cairn Hadding was building.

Hild rose. She couldn't bear to look at the body up close. But she had to, for Beyla's sake. She moved uncertainly toward the cairn. As she approached it, Gizzur stopped his work and elbowed Hadding. The two of them backed away, leaving Hild alone with Brynjolf. Keeping her eyes away from his bloody tunic, she knelt beside him. Dirt streaked his forehead just above his brows and Hild reached to wipe it off, trying not to recoil at the feel of his cold skin. She slipped off the silver band Beyla had given her and tried to work it over one of Brynjolf's lifeless hands. It wasn't easy and she almost gave up. But he'd earned an armband, even if he hadn't lived long enough to receive it from the king. She tried again, and this time she got it over his stiff fingers and onto his arm. Softly, she called on Odin, saying, "Receive this warrior into your hall." She hoped the silver band would help Brynjolf find a place among the warriors who had died in battle.

When she rose, Gizzur and Hadding stepped forward

again. "That was a good thing you did, my lady," Hadding said, nodding toward Brynjolf's arm. Then he placed another stone on the pile.

Hild turned away. As she did, Mord approached her. "We've found a place to ford the river, my lady," he said. "Now that the horses are back, we can go. As soon as we've done right by Brynjolf." He dropped his voice, his tone uncertain. "Would you sing him out, my lady?"

Hild looked at him, startled. Of course they would need a woman to sing for Brynjolf. She nodded.

While the men finished their grim work, she combed her fingers through her hair, struggling to bind it up, finally resorting to braiding it the way slaves wore their hair, in order to wind it around her head. Doing so made her think of Beyla's unruly curls falling out of their knot. How many times had she had to retie it for her friend? "Oh, Beyla," she whispered. She wished that none of this had happened, that the two of them were standing in the stables at home, making each other laugh, that Brynjolf would come around the corner at any moment, smiling his broken-toothed smile at them.

She closed her eyes for a space, then opened them and turned back to the men.

Thialfi was kneeling, arranging the cloak around the body. Brynjolf's sword was clutched in one of his hands and his bloody fingers had stiffened. Mord struggled to loosen the weapon, but in death, Brynjolf held fast. Finally, Mord worked it free and replaced it with the dagger Brynjolf had been so proud of, polished again to a high gleam. Holding the sword, Mord looked from face to face, Hadding standing at the dead warrior's head, Gizzur at his feet, the three Geats at his shoulders. "It was his father's before him. Now it will go to his cousin Borr," Mord said.

Hild felt tears threatening. If she didn't start now, she was afraid she wouldn't be able to at all. She stepped forward. Without waiting for acknowledgment, she squared her shoulders, drew in her breath, and began to sing.

She'd never sung the funeral rites before, but she knew them; she'd heard them often enough. She thought of her father's funeral and Aunt Var standing beside the pyre, singing him to the gods. Her own voice sounded high and thin, like a child's, not rich and resonant like Var's. Would the gods accept her song, so ill-sung? There was nothing to do but press on, her eyes closed against the wound on Brynjolf's chest.

As the last word lingered on the cold air, Mord leaned down to place the first rock over the young warrior's body. Hild stepped back and stood in silence as, stone by stone, the men covered him. Brynjolf had still had so much to learn about being a warrior. Hild smiled a little through her tears, remembering how often he had forgotten his task as a rear guard. He'd always been so good-natured when she and Beyla teased him, laughing along with them. She recalled the way he had played with his little sister Inga and his puppy outside Freyja's temple in what now seemed like another life. She wished she could have found a sprig of holly to lay on the cairn.

A bird trilled from a nearby branch, the sound incongruously joyous to Hild's ears. Then, as if it recognized her thoughts, it fell silent. Somewhere in the woods, she saw something move. She listened but heard nothing. It must have been the bird.

A horse whinnied. Brynjolf's horse? Did it know its master was dead?

She turned her attention back to the cairn. An edge of Brynjolf's cloak peeked out from the rocks, and Hild hoped they wouldn't leave it uncovered.

She pulled her own cloak more closely around her. As she did, she saw Mord rising from the head of the cairn, his mouth open in surprise. At the same time, a potent stench reached her nostrils, making her think of the leather tanners at home. She turned.

Something ran at her—something huge. It was on her so fast she couldn't react. A powerful arm wrapped around her torso, lifting her from her feet. Twisting, biting on thick hide, she tried to free herself, but her arms were pinned to her sides.

She kicked, then kicked again, wrenching her back. She was tight in the creature's grip, her face mashed against its wiry fur. She couldn't get away. And now it was running. Out of one eye, she could see trees passing in a blur. Where were Mord and the others? She could hear them but she couldn't see them.

She struggled, but it was no use.

Moving with incredible speed, the creature headed into the forest, Hild tight in its grip.

The shouts of the men faded into the distance.

TWENTY

Fur as coarse as horsehair scratched into her cheek and neck, scraping them raw. The creature leapt over stones and glided around trees, moving silently through the woods.

Hild stopped struggling. It did no good and it was tiring her out. She tried to watch where they were going, but fear crowded out thought. She heard a whimpering sound, then realized it was coming from her own lips. She willed herself to stop.

The terrible smell threatened to overwhelm her. She couldn't breathe. Or was it fear that kept her from getting her breath?

It could have killed me if it had wanted to, she told herself. She knew she needed to pay attention, to watch where she was being taken, but even if she could quell her terror, she could barely see.

She could hear, though. Her ear was pressed into the creature's chest, and its heart beat almost like a human's. Its breath came in sharp inhalations, but it didn't sound tired or even winded. Its feet made hardly any sound at all, which seemed improbable for a creature so huge. It must have been half again as tall as she was.

Where were they going? She tried not to think of animals that liked their meat fresh.

Inside her head, she imagined herself curling into a ball to protect herself. "Lady of the Vanir, Freyja, help me," she whispered.

Her legs dangled helplessly, hitting against the creature's knees as it ran. She tried pulling them up, but that took more strength than she wanted to expend.

How long had they been going? It could have been a moment or a lifetime. She forced herself to stay alert, to breathe despite the unbearable stench of the creature's hide. Trees rushed past. Light flickered through branches, but she couldn't look up to see where the sun was. If the creature set her down that very moment, she wouldn't know where she was or how to find her way back to the men. Not that she had to worry about that. The creature's grasp was so tight that she'd lost all feeling in her arms—it wasn't about to let her go.

Sharp pain shot through her side where something dug into her. She tried to shift her position, but the creature's grip was too strong. It couldn't keep running forever, could it?

A shudder ran through her. Better to keep running than to stop, because who knew what would happen then.

Twigs and branches scratched at her legs as they moved through dense woods. The pain in her side grew harder to bear. If only she could get away from whatever was digging into her side—but she couldn't. She closed her eyes and slipped into an endless stupor of fear and pain.

She was barely aware when the creature began to slow, but she woke fully when she heard splashing. The creature was holding her differently now, and whatever had been hurting her side was blessedly gone. She had almost grown accustomed to the foul odor and she could open both her eyes now, although her head was turned to the side, limiting her view.

She saw what she thought were giant legs until they resolved into tree trunks, alders, rising out of dark water in the pool the creature was splashing through. Either the sun had gone down or they were in a place that got no sun, but from her position, all she could tell was how little light there was.

Ahead of her she could make out the edge of the pool and, beyond it, the massive roots of a giant oak, coiled like a dragon's tail, earth packed around them. Below the roots, something dark. She stared until she understood the vision. It was the mouth of an earth cave under the oak roots.

. The creature's grip changed, loosening a little.

Hild tensed, readying herself to flee, but the claws tightened around her again. The creature stooped, then plunged them both into the darkness.

She stifled a scream. Her heart pounded so hard she thought it would burst through her chest. She couldn't think; she was too afraid. "Oh, Freyja," she whispered, the words coming out like a moan.

The creature dropped her. The ground hit her with a cold shock. She tried to scramble away, but her body betrayed her. She lay where she'd fallen. *Let me die now,* she begged the goddess, not knowing if she said the words aloud. *Let it be over.*

Snuffling noises reached her ears. She brought her knees to her chest, pulling herself into a ball, and waited to die.

Nothing happened.

She blinked. In the middle of the cave, coals glowed red. In the eerie light, roots dangled like snakes from the earthen roof and walls. She strained her eyes to see what was on the other side of the cave. Something crouched in the shadows, its eyes gleaming.

Hild scuttled backward. She hit a cold earth wall and hunched like a wild animal, watching. The feeling was returning to her arms, sending agonizing prickles to her fingertips. She squeezed her fingers into fists against the pain and kept her eyes on the shape in the shadows.

Something cried out.

She flinched and pushed herself farther into the cave wall.

The cry came again, not as loud this time, and diminished into a noise that made Hild think of one of her nephews whimpering.

The thing on the other side of the fire rose, towering, and moved toward her.

Hild brought her arms up to protect her chest and face.

The creature stopped. It bent down in front of the coals and blew, sending ash flying into the air. Flames leapt up, illuminating the creature and the cave.

Hild stared, incredulous. The creature had a woman's shape, like a troll-wife from one of Ari Frothi's stories. Behind it, against the other wall, lay a pile of something, a large heap, indistinct in the murky gloom.

The heap moved.

Hild shrank back, keeping herself from yelping. She tried to watch both the heap and the creature beside the fire, not knowing which threatened her the most.

The heap moved again. A noise came from it, a snarl, followed by a sound like a child's sniveling.

Hild's eyes widened. It was another monster. It held its legs and arms to its chest just as she had done moments ago. It was crying.

The female creature raised its head from the fire. It cast a glance at the monster on the ground. Then, with a movement so swift that Hild could barely follow it, it stood and crossed to Hild, swept her into its arms, carried her to the other side of the fire, and dumped her on the floor—directly in front of the crying monster.

She couldn't get away. There was no place for her to go. She tried not to weep. She didn't want to sound like the monster as she died. Her mother's face filled her mind. Instead of giving her courage, it sent tears streaming down her cheeks, stinging the raw places where the monster's hide had rubbed her.

The female creature pushed her from behind.

Hild raised her hands to her face and lowered her head to her chest. If she had to die here, why couldn't it be faster? Horrified, she answered her own question. The monsters would want to play with her first, like a cat with a bird, before they ate her.

"Freyja," she whispered, and gulped back a sob.

The monster pushed her again, not as hard this time.

Hild raised her head, sudden anger filling her. "Stop it!" she croaked, her voice rough from tears and tension.

This time, the push was more like a nudge.

Bracing herself, curiosity fighting with her fear, Hild turned to see what the female creature was doing, to see what form her death would take.

It moved forward.

Hild jerked away, but she needn't have bothered. The creature went past her to the monster on the floor and raised its claw. For a terrible moment, Hild thought she was about to witness one monster killing another. The claw stopped at the monster's chest.

Hild squinted in the firelight, blinking, fighting her fear and pain in order to concentrate. The monster's claws clutched at something, but she couldn't see what.

Then it shifted position and she saw fur, dark and matted. Dried blood? Yes, she was sure there was blood, and then she saw something else.

Something buried deep in the monster's chest.

It was her sword.

TWENTY·ONE

THE FEMALE CREATURE LOOKED AT HILD THROUGH RED eyes set deep in its matted, wiry fur. It turned back to the sword hilt, dabbing at it gently while the monster on the floor moaned.

Then the female raised its claw toward Hild.

She flinched. In an instant, she looked around, taking in her position. The fire was behind her, too high to jump. On one side, an earth wall. The wounded monster lay on the ground in front of her; the other crouched beside her. There was no escape.

The claw came closer. Hild held her breath.

It stopped so near her face it was almost touching her.

Hild stared, mesmerized, at the dirt-encrusted talon.

Then it moved back, away from her face. She remembered to breathe, gulping in air.

The claw dropped to the sword hilt. As it did, the monster on the ground roared, twisting its body in agony.

Hild hunched into the wall, screwing her eyes shut in horror.

The sound died away. Cautiously, she cracked open one eye, then the other.

The female creature was holding its claw near the sword hilt, looking at it—and now looking at Hild. Did it know what she had done? Whose sword it was? Hild watched as it stared down at the weapon, then looked back at her, reaching out with its talons. She flattened herself against the wall again, but the claw stopped an arm's length away.

It was pointing at her. Then it pointed at the sword.

Like a rush of clear water, comprehension flowed through her. It wanted her to remove the weapon from the wounded monster's chest.

Perhaps it had seen her tending to Mord and Gizzur. Perhaps it believed only the blade's wielder could draw it free. Perhaps it had motives Hild would never fathom. Whatever the reason, the creature wanted her to heal the wound she had caused.

She'd been brought here to nurse a monster.

She could have laughed, the notion was so far-fetched. She felt momentarily giddy. She wasn't going to die, not just yet.

Then she looked back at the monster on the ground

and the feeling fled. Didn't the female creature realize that pulling the sword out was the surest way to a quick death? No, of course it didn't. That was why she was here: because it believed Hild had the power to heal. And if she was going to stay alive, she had better start believing it, too—or at least start convincing the creatures that she knew what she was doing.

"All right," she said. "I'll try." Keeping her eye on the female creature, moving the way you would to calm a skittish horse, Hild eased herself onto her knees in front of the injured creature. As she did, pain flared in her side and she gasped. She waited until she could stand it, then moved again, this time more carefully.

The closer she got to the wounded creature, the harder it was to breathe. She had thought the female smelled bad, but its stench was nothing compared to this. The fur was matted with dirt and blood. Not just its own blood, she realized. Brynjolf's blood.

She couldn't think about that now.

She glanced at the female monster. It crouched beside her, firelight playing on its coarse fur, its face in shadow. It was watching her.

Steeling herself, she reached a trembling hand toward the wound, then darted a look at the female again. It didn't move.

Hild extended her hand farther. She could see how deeply the blade was buried in the creature's body, how complete her work had been. Her fingertips brushed the sword hilt.

The injured creature howled, swinging out at her. She pulled back to the wall again. It was a moment before she could get her breath, a moment before she realized that the female was holding the injured monster's claws, keeping them from hurting her.

The female monster made a noise, a grunting sound. It made it again, then again, until it was a continuous grunting. What did it mean? What was Hild supposed to do?

Then it leaned toward the injured monster with an intimate motion that made Hild gape. It looked like nothing if not a mother crooning to her injured child. It was singing to the wounded monster, comforting it.

She caught her breath. Were these two mother and son?

Hild's heart sank. If she couldn't help the monster, its mother would kill her. But she couldn't help it. Nothing could.

That didn't matter, she told herself fiercely. The mother believed she had the power to heal. If it had seen her tending to the men, she would need to do something that looked convincing. Her life depended on it.

She had no herb bag like the one Thialfi had lent her. She glanced around the cave, but no herbs—not even moss—grew here. Bones and piles of what looked like animal droppings littered the cave floor. There was nothing she could use.

The mother made a threatening sound, a low growl in the back of its throat, like a dog preparing to attack. Hild backed away. As she did, something dangling from the cave's roof caught in her hair. She looked up and saw a wide web of tiny roots woven to the cave's roof. She stared at them, then cautiously reached up, her heart beating loudly. Her side throbbing, she rose to her knees and worked the earth with her fingers, digging out the roots, keeping them together like a piece of loosely woven cloth. Bits of dirt showered into her eyes but she blinked them away and kept working at the roots, glancing at the mother monster. Its eyes were on her, but it didn't move.

Hope surged through her and she tore at the delicate edges, gently bringing the tapestry of matted roots to her lap. Making sure the creature was watching her, Hild looked at the sword hilt, then back to the roots, and then to the fire. She didn't know whether the monster had seen her mixing ashes with the heal-all, but she wasn't going to take any chances. She scooped warm ash into her hand and began sprinkling it over the roots.

As the sooty flakes fell onto the roots, she started to chant the heal-all charm but stopped before the second word. Mixing roots she couldn't identify with ashes was harmless enough, but charms had power. Yet if the creature had watched her earlier, it would expect her to chant something. Hild took a shaky breath and then started again, grabbing at the first lines that came to her panicked mind, from the lay she had asked Aunt Var to sing so often, the scene she'd been making into a banner for her uncle's hall.

"Her babe in her arms, the elf-bright lady ran," she sang, her voice ragged and quavering. Surely the monster wouldn't be able to tell the difference between a lay and an incantation of power. Would it? She swallowed and kept going.

> *Tossing waves welcomed them, woman and child;*
> *The sea-steed stood ready, its sail eager for wind.*
> *The boat's beams embraced her boy. The woman*
>   *turned back.*
> *Slaughter-greedy warriors searched for her child.*
> *The web of fate had been woven; only one would*
>   *survive.*

A quick peek showed her that the monster wasn't reacting to her song. *Good.* She spat into her hand and used the saliva to make the ashes adhere to the roots.

She looked up at the mother again. It watched her closely, but it shifted backward, making room for Hild to come close to the injured creature.

Holding her breath, she edged forward inch by inch, careful not to damage her pretend poultice, or to set off a ripple of agony in her own side. She moved as calmly as she could, trying to keep from startling the creature on the ground. The closer she got, the more danger she was in. If what she did caused the monster any pain, she wouldn't survive.

She glanced back at the mother. Its red eyes were trained on her. She had to keep going.

As slowly and gently as she could manage with her

trembling hands, she stretched out the lace of twining roots, floating it softly down to the wound, draping it around the place where the blade emerged from flesh.

The roots caught on the matted fur. Hild held her breath.

The injured creature didn't move.

Tentatively, she touched the roots, tucking them together to keep them on the wound. She peeked at the mother. It moved its eyes from the wound back to Hild, as if it was waiting for her to continue. With what? She'd already put the roots on the wound—what else could she do? There was only one thing she could think of that didn't mean touching the monster again. Kneeling in front of it, her voice gravelly with fear and fatigue, she sang the words from the lay a second time. Then, without looking at the mother, she scuttled back to her place against the wall, wrapped her arms around herself, and watched.

The mother monster stared at the roots before it reached out to touch them with a gentleness that surprised Hild. Then it sat back on its haunches as if it was waiting for the wound to heal.

It seemed to have believed her ruse. She didn't think it would kill her quite yet. Her muscles relaxed the tiniest bit and she let out her breath.

Sitting on either side of the wounded creature, like women in a king's hall tending a battle-weary warrior, Hild and the monster settled in to wait.

TWENTY·TWO

HILD STARTLED AWAKE. HOW COULD SHE HAVE LET HER-self fall asleep? She glanced furtively around her, blinking in the dark. The fire had burned to coals. She could just make out a heap on the ground—the injured monster. Its mother hunched between her and the cave mouth. Were they asleep?

Keeping her eyes wide for movement, she listened for regular breathing and thought she might have heard it.

She had to take a chance. As quietly as she could, she started to stand.

The monster turned so swiftly that Hild stumbled and fell to the ground in astonished fear, agony knifing through her ribs.

She *had* to get away. The injured creature could die any moment now, and when it did, its mother would kill her. She had to do something.

Looking to the mother for permission, Hild rose to her knees, gritted her teeth against the throbbing in her side, and moved carefully toward the creature on the ground.

The mother grunted and Hild stopped. She gestured toward herself, then at the injured monster, unsure of how well the mother could see her in the dimness. Keeping her eyes on the female creature, ready to stop at the slightest movement, she pushed forward again until she was so close to the injured monster she could see its wound and hear its labored, raspy breath.

She couldn't make herself touch the poultice she'd made, but she bent closer as if to examine it, wrinkling her nose. On top of the monster's foul smell, she detected the sweeter odor of decay from its wound, the smell that meant death was imminent. Time was running out—she had to get out of this cave.

Thinking as fast as her fear-muddled mind allowed, she turned to the female creature. The wounded monster was far beyond needing food, but Hild had to trust that its mother wouldn't know that. Careful not to startle it, she brought her hand to her mouth and pantomimed chewing, then pointed at the creature on the ground. She repeated the gesture, watching the mother for a reaction, but it didn't move.

Forcing her agitation away, Hild tried again. This time she gestured as if she were tearing meat from a bone and chewing it.

The mother grunted. As Hild watched, it shifted position. Over the red glow of the coals, it looked at her. She pointed at the creature on the floor again, trying to make sure the mother didn't think *she* was the one who wanted meat. Then, horribly, she realized she *was* meat.

Scrambling back to her place by the cave wall, she cowered, watching. The mother moved, and Hild pushed herself into the wall, hands ready to protect her face.

The mother crouched in front of its offspring. It grunted, reached out its claw, and gently poked at its son.

Then, as Hild watched, it turned. Moving with incredible speed, it rushed from the cave.

Had the ploy worked? Hild listened, not daring to breathe. Was the mother gone? No, she could still hear it. Scraping sounds came from just outside the cave mouth, and a loud rumbling she couldn't identify. Her spirits fell as she realized the creature could be gathering food from a stash. If it was, Hild's plan had failed. Only if the monster went away to hunt would Hild be able to escape.

She strained her ears, trying to interpret the noises the creature was making.

Had they stopped? She concentrated and heard nothing, no sound at all.

Quietly, cautiously, she rose and crept toward the cave mouth.

It must be night; no light spilled through it.

Taking a deep breath as if to arm herself, she gathered her skirts and started forward, ready to run.

Something barred her way. When she reached out, her fingers met cold stone.

Panic set in and she pushed, but the stones didn't give. The sounds she had heard were the piling up of stones. The monster had walled her in.

"No!" she cried, and pounded on the stones, bruising her fists, scratching them. A sob of frustration rose from her chest. There was nothing she could do. She was trapped.

She retreated to her corner in the cave, cupping her hands against her aching side. She brought her knees to her chest, her face to her knees. "Freyja, help me," she whispered, knowing that no help would come. She closed her eyes. Tentacles of despair wrapped themselves around her.

The sound of the injured monster's breathing intruded into the space her arms made around her head. She wished it would stop. It was labored and painful-sounding, and she didn't want to hear it.

She tried to think of her mother's face, the sound of Arinbjörn's laughter, the taste of Unwen's cod and barley stew, but blackness crowded out thoughts of home. She was going to die in this cave and even her bones would never be found.

She fell deeper into the darkness. Her head felt too heavy for her neck and she let her chin drop to her chest.

All light and sound retreated except for the monster's gasps, the sound grating and horrible. Why couldn't it be quiet?

She burrowed her forehead into her arms and wished she were already dead.

Now even the sound of breathing stopped. Maybe the gods had heard her desire and granted it. Maybe she was dead.

She raised her head, listening. There was only silence.

The truth came to her with a jolt. She wasn't the one who was dead. The monster was. And its mother would return at any moment.

She moved toward it and stretched out a foot, kicking it gingerly. It didn't move. She tried again, and again it was still. And now she knew that she couldn't stay here in this cave waiting to be killed. She had to at least try to escape.

She knelt before the coals and blew on them until little flames sprang up. She looked behind her and gasped. The monster's mouth hung open, yellow-stained fangs visible in the new light.

It took her a moment to calm her wild heart, to convince herself that it was truly dead.

She looked toward the cave mouth and tried to think what to do. Bones littered the ground and she reached for a large one, ignoring the bit of gristle still clinging to it. She told herself firmly that it had belonged to a bear, not a man, but a shudder ran through her nonetheless as she stepped to the stones that blocked her escape. She ran her fingers over them, feeling for their edges, looking for chinks.

One huge stone covered most of the cave mouth. It was far too heavy for her to move. But at the top, smaller rocks had been piled. Careful of her throbbing ribs, Hild started to work on them, using the bone to push them free.

When the first one fell, it made such a noise that Hild was afraid it must have resounded through the entire forest, alerting the monster's mother to what she was doing. She had to hurry. She fingered the rocks again, feeling the space she'd just made, then pushed with the bone.

Nothing happened.

She repositioned the bone and tried again. This time she thought the rock moved just a little bit. She pushed harder. Yes, it definitely moved.

Using her hands now, steeling herself against the pain, she worked at the rock, shoving against it with all her might. It was bigger than the first one, and it took every ounce of her strength, but finally, it fell crashing down.

Hild stopped to rest and peered through the hole where the rock had been. She blinked, then blinked again. If her eyes weren't deceiving her, she saw black branches and, beyond them, the deep purple sky of half-light, whether dusk or dawn she didn't know. And piercing her heart with its promise, a white star shone steadily through the branches.

"Oh, Lady of the Vanir," she whispered in thanks before she set to work again.

The next two stones came out more easily, and now there was only one more. She pushed, but it didn't budge. Hardly daunted, she attacked it a second time, again with no result. She peered at it and saw that a number of little rocks were helping wedge it into place. Painstakingly, she worked at them, but they were hard to reach. She needed a tool, but the bone was too big.

Near the fire, there were smaller bones, but none of them was as long as she needed.

Her eye fell on the heap against the wall—the dead monster with her sword stuck through its chest.

Hild swallowed, then moved swiftly to take the hilt in her hand. She pulled.

The monster's body held tight to the blade.

Hild pulled again, but again the sword stayed fast.

Wincing with revulsion, trying not to gag, Hild planted one foot on the monster's chest, took the hilt in both hands, and pulled.

The sword moved.

She repositioned her grasp, put her foot more firmly on the creature's body, and tugged as hard as she could.

The blade came free, sending her staggering backward into the fire, agony flaring in her ribs.

Pushing the pain aside, she danced free of the flames, slapping them from her skirt, and ran to the rocks. Arinbjörn's sword did the work she needed it to. One by one, the tightly wedged rocks came loose. Dropping the sword,

Hild reached up and pushed the final rock free, sending it tumbling to the ground.

She gazed at the cave mouth, measuring. Even in the best circumstances, it wouldn't be easy to climb over the single huge stone that blocked her way. The space at the top was still narrower than she would have liked, and she feared she might get stuck. But there was no other way.

She peered out again, looking up to find the star, but she didn't see it—it must have already dipped below the trees. *Never mind,* she thought. Preparing herself for the pain to come, she grabbed the sword and scrambled up the stone, her fingers trying to find places she could grip.

On the first attempt, she fell to the ground, hitting her backside, but she got up again. She'd found a handhold; she was sure of it. Yes, there it was, and below it, she found a ledge for her foot.

She climbed, her fingers feeling for spots to grab, her toes scrabbling on the rock. Every movement made her think hot daggers must be piercing her ribs, but she had to keep going. She was almost to the top, almost ready to launch herself into the breach she'd made, almost ready to wriggle through. One more push and she would make it.

A splash made her stop. Silent as a rabbit, her limbs straining to keep her from falling, she listened.

Was it a fish?

It stopped just outside the cave and made a snuffling noise. Definitely not a fish.

Though her muscles were on fire, Hild didn't move. Her fingers began to slip and she grasped the rock more tightly, desperate not to fall.

The snuffling came again.

Her calves started to cramp, and she was losing her grip on the sword. In another heartbeat, she would drop it.

The animal, whatever it was, could probably smell her.

She resisted the urge to blink—she didn't dare close her eyes. She strained them in the half-light, watching, waiting for it to move away.

It made another noise, this time fainter. Was it leaving?

She readied herself to push over the rock, every muscle stretched to its limit. She was going to make it.

A claw shot through the gap.

The creature was back.

TWENTY·THREE

HILD FELL, HITTING THE GROUND HARD. THE SWORD FLEW from her grasp.

She scrambled to her feet and grabbed the weapon as the huge stone began to move. She watched in horror. The taste of blood flooded her mouth—she'd bitten her lip clear through. The new pain helped her focus. She gripped the sword hilt in both hands and positioned herself, knees flexed, just inside the stone's edge. As it moved, she moved with it, keeping herself hidden.

The stone stopped. So did Hild's heart.

An eternity passed and she waited, eyes wide, muscles strained.

The creature started through the cave mouth, a stag hanging limp in its arms.

Hild rushed forward and thrust the blade upward with

every ounce of strength she could muster, aiming for the creature's eyes.

It roared, dropping the stag and reaching for its face.

Hild pulled out the sword and leapt over the stag's body. The antlers snagged on her skirt, yanking her back. She tugged but her skirt was caught.

She tugged again, hard, and heard a tearing sound as the cloth ripped.

She was free.

She raced from the cave, splashed through the pool of icy water, pulling her sodden skirt out of the way of her legs, and ran.

Behind her, the monster kept roaring. She didn't know how badly she'd hurt it, but she wasn't going to stay to find out.

Her legs carried her forward and she pelted through the woods, not thinking, just moving.

The monster's roar took on a different tone, a howl that rose to a shriek of rage and grief so loud and long the trees quaked to hear it. It had found its dead child.

As cold and bruised and exhausted as she was, Hild stretched out her stride, running faster than she'd ever gone before. Branches whipped at her arms, vines reached out to trip her, and twigs slashed at her face, but she kept going, leaping over stones and dodging trees. She knew how fast the creature could move, and now revenge would fuel it.

She prayed that fear would fuel her own speed—yet

she felt no fear. Instead, exhilaration flowed through her and she gulped in the cold, clean air. It tasted sweet on her tongue, her throat. The pale light of dawn lit her way. Birds chittered in the branches, a group of them lifting into startled flight as she neared. Through the trees she could make out a hint of the sun's glow, drawing her forward, telling her the way. As if she was guided by the goddess, her feet took flight.

The sun rose and still she ran, sword in one hand, skirt held up with the other to allow her legs the freedom of their stride. Deer trails appeared before her and she took them when she could, always heading into the sun.

She wasn't sure how long ago the creature's howls had faded. The only sounds now were her feet hitting the ground, the crackle of branches and bracken as she pushed through them, and her breath, strong and steady. The scream of a hawk hunting for its prey barely startled her.

As the sun climbed, the ground fell, becoming rockier as it descended.

Hild's breath came in gasps now, and the strength that had carried her forward began to diminish—while her side began to throb insistently. "Just a little farther," she told herself, but she stumbled over a rock and hit her hands as she fell, the sword tumbling from her grip.

She grabbed it, clambered to her feet, and kept going, sliding on loose rocks, grasping at tree trunks to hold herself upright.

A steady rushing sound like wind in branches pulled her onward a few more steps. One foot after another, she moved forward until the rushing sound resolved itself into water.

She stepped out of the trees. In front of her, the river sparkled in the morning sun.

She crumpled into a heap beside the brown water.

．　．　．

At the sound of a jay shrieking, Hild roused herself. She couldn't stop yet; it wasn't safe. Still, she'd made it this far, and that was something. She whispered a prayer of thanks to the goddess.

A terrible thirst gripped her, but getting to the water was no simple matter, the bank was so steep. The river was swift and broad, and in places, the bank crumbled, dirt and leaves swirling into the current. She found a likely spot, but even then, she had to leave the sword above and grasp at weeds and bushes to steady herself.

The water was icy. Hild scooped one handful after another into her mouth, feeling it dribble down her chin and onto her gown. She knew she would regret it later when her wet garments made her cold, but for now, the water tasted too good for her to be more careful.

Sated, she climbed the bank again and gazed down the river.

A movement caught her eye and she stepped behind a tree, clutching her side to hold in the pain. In the distance, a figure led a horse to the riverbank. Someone else joined him, a bow in his hands, his blond hair gleaming in the sunlight. Wulf. The first figure was Thialfi, she felt sure.

She stepped farther into the woods, her heart thumping. She didn't think they had seen her. Surely they would have reacted if they had. If she was going to evade the creature and find Unwen's people, she had to get away from here. *Now.*

Keeping the river on her sword-hand side, she started walking, going as fast as she could while weariness, hunger, and pain dragged at her. Her feet were cut and bruised from her wild run through the forest, her hands from her battle with the stones. The throbbing in her side grew sharper with every step. A cold wind whipped off the river, catching at her wet clothes and chilling her through.

All the exhilaration that had buoyed her as she'd fled the creature was gone. In its wake, fear crept in, and she watched and listened for the monster—and for the men.

How far would Unwen have gotten by now? Would she have already found her people? Or—Hild hesitated, not sure she wanted to admit the possibility—could she have met the same fate as Brynjolf?

A bramble caught her skirt. As she struggled to get loose from the thorns without tearing her already scratched and bruised fingers, she remembered the change that had come to Mord after she had saved him from the monster. She thought of the way his eyes had looked and the way he had spoken to her.

She thought of the two Geatish brothers, grieving for their father, and of Gizzur sitting beside his dead horse.

She thought of Hadding looking after her in Unwen's absence, and Thialfi riding alongside her to keep her from falling off Fire-eyes when she fell asleep in the saddle.

They would be looking for her, as they should be, waiting in the woods in case she returned. And every single moment they waited for her made them vulnerable to attack by the creature.

She shoved the thought aside and kept going. Unwen might have already reached her home, and if she had, her people would be watching for Hild. Maybe they would come along the river to find her. They could be waiting around the next bend.

The farther she went, the slower her pace became, until finally, she slowed to a walk, dizzy with fatigue and hunger. As she leaned against an oak trunk, light-headedness made her sway. The world darkened. She bent down, hands on her knees, fighting the sensation. Behind her closed lids, a dark shape rose: the monster, loping through the trees, its gait awkward and jerky, half its face covered by its claws.

Hild stood upright, heart pounding. Where was it? She blinked, staring into the woods, straining her ears. And then she knew, in the same way she'd known about her cousin. The monster was headed toward the river. Toward the men.

What did it matter? Let it have them.

Brynjolf's face came to her, and the sound of his laughter,

now forever silenced. Sudden anger filled her. Why were they still waiting for her? They should have left and not put themselves in danger.

She took a step toward Unwen, toward freedom, then stopped and looked behind her. They needed to be warned. But if she went back now, she'd give up her last chance of escape. She wouldn't do it. She couldn't. The bend in the river wasn't far now, and Unwen's people could be just beyond it. She started moving again.

A root snagged her foot and she stumbled, catching herself just before she fell. Had she heard something? She listened, but the only sounds were the rush of wind over water and the rattle of dry leaves in the branches. She tasted blood and licked her lip where she'd bitten it in the monster's cave.

Then, angry tears stinging at the corners of her eyes, she turned toward the men.

With half her mind, she could see the way ahead of her, the tree branches that reached out to grab at her. With the other half, she sensed the creature, crashing through the woods, heading for the camp. She had to hurry.

She picked up her pace, stumbling as she ran, the vision urging her on. She didn't know how far away the monster was, or how soon it would reach the men. She only knew that it was coming.

When the trees thinned, she moved back to the riverbank. Surely the men would see her, or hear her movement through the woods. But now that she wanted to be seen, none of them stood by the bank. If they were guarding their camp, she thought irritably, they weren't doing a very good job of it.

She tripped over a rock and went down, dropping the sword. She grabbed for the hilt and lay panting on the ground. She was spent. She couldn't go any farther.

The monster growled.

She was up before she realized it, running again, not knowing if the sound had been in her ears or her mind. It didn't matter. The creature was on its way.

"Just a little farther," she told herself, "a little farther," but her footsteps grew plodding and leaden. She couldn't do it.

She grabbed at a branch, then at another, and found she could pull herself along. It helped, propelling her forward a step, and then another, until the trees parted before her.

She had made it. She was in the camp.

The men were mounted, their backs to her, looking as if they were just about to ride away. One of them shouted and they wheeled their horses, turning toward her. Before she had a chance to speak, they raised their weapons—arrow, sword, and spear.

All of them were aimed directly at Hild.

TWENTY·FOUR

THE MEN STARED AT HER, THEIR EYES WILD BEHIND THEIR masks, their mouths open, as if they were afraid of her. What was wrong with them, that they had their weapons trained on her? "Hurry, it's coming," she said, but her voice was too weak for them to hear.

"It's a spirit, sent back to haunt us," one of them whispered with a Geatish accent.

"It's angry because we failed her," someone else said. Mord.

Mord? Didn't he recognize her?

"Don't say anything and maybe it will go away."

"Why should I go away?" Hild asked, her voice cracking with incredulity.

"My lady?" Thialfi asked. He dismounted and rushed to

her side, Mord directly behind him, both of them catching her as she swayed.

"My lady!" They spoke the words simultaneously, the two of them lowering her to the ground and crouching before her.

"We have to hurry," she said. "The monster, it's coming."

"You need rest, my lady," Mord said.

"We have to go. *Now*."

They stared at her and then she saw the two men looking at each other, a silent agreement being negotiated, but she was too tired to care what it was.

"Can you stay on a horse?" Thialfi asked, and she nodded, hissing in pain as he gently pulled her to her feet.

Gizzur had already dismounted from Fire-eyes and was readying the horse for her. As she came close, Fire-eyes whinnied, shying away. Hild didn't have the strength to wonder why. Instead, she concentrated on getting into the saddle as Thialfi and Gizzur lifted her.

She heard Mord giving orders, but she didn't listen; she just focused on not falling off the nervous horse as they moved out, guards before her, behind her, on either side of her.

She let her head drop to her chest and trusted Fire-eyes to know his own business. All she had to do was stay on his back.

The landscape passed in a haze of pain and exhaustion. She heard water splashing as they forded the river, and felt the slope of the land pushing her backward in the saddle as they began the climb into the rocks on the other bank. She wished she'd thought to ask for something to eat before they started, but changed her mind when the thought of food made her gorge rise.

Her eyes closed and she swayed back and forth with Fire-eyes's stride. Occasionally she felt hands gently nudging her back to the middle of the saddle, and she thought she might have heard someone saying her name, but none of it roused her from her stupor.

The sun was gone when they finally stopped. Hands she didn't bother to look at helped her down from the horse and led her to a blanket, where she fell into a sleep so deep she might have been dead.

"My lady," an urgent voice whispered, and Hild opened her eyes a slit to see the gray light of dawn in a rocky landscape devoid of trees.

"The horses are ready. We must go." She closed her eyes again and allowed the two men on either side of her to lead her to her horse and get her into the saddle. When one of them handed her the reins, she let them slip from her fingers. Fire-eyes was on his own again. She slumped back into her trance, waking up enough to refuse the dried fish Thialfi offered her. At first she felt hungry, but then she felt as if she would retch. She put her hand over her mouth and closed her eyes.

When they stopped, the sun had just begun its downward climb. Hild looked around her as Mord helped her from the horse. Why were they stopping during the daylight? The monster could still be out there, following them.

Mord must have understood what she was thinking. "We've ridden the horses hard, and this is a good place to rest," he said. "A hideout of the Geats' that's easy to defend."

It took all her strength to nod. They were in Geatish territory now—but she was too tired to care. Mord led her to a rock outcropping that made a natural roof, and she saw a stack of firewood that had been left by the previous visitors.

"You must eat something, my lady," Mord said, but Hild shook her head. Her stomach felt tight and peculiar, as if she'd been ill for a long time, but at least the pain in her side had dulled.

"Just sleep," she whispered.

When the scent of roasting meat woke her, she realized she was ravenous. She sat up, blinking in the firelight, and saw Thialfi kneeling beside a fire, looking at her. When he saw her sitting up, he smiled, then turned to reach for something—a bowl.

"Broth," he said as he handed it to her. "Drink it slowly, my lady."

She tried to do as he said, but she couldn't get it down fast enough. "Is there more?"

He smiled again and shook his head. "Not broth, but I think we could find you some meat, if you wanted it."

She nodded enthusiastically, then looked around as she heard a chuckle. Wulf was sitting near her, grinning broadly, and across from him, Hadding stood up, a skewer in his hands. "Here, my lady, take mine." He beamed as he gave her the roasted bird.

She didn't have time to thank him, because she was too busy chewing, unconcerned by the fluff and feathers that still clung to the bird, sucking on her fingers when she burned them in her haste.

Eating exhausted her and she had barely swallowed the last bite before her lids closed again. She felt someone settling a blanket over her, but she was too comfortable and too sleepy to see who it was.

It was morning when she woke again, and cold. She sat up and looked around at the campsite. The larger of the Geatish brothers, the one whose name she still didn't know, saw her and gave a small bow, which the others must have noticed, because one by one they inclined their heads or offered her smiles.

She stood unsteadily and made her way closer to the fire. The Geat backed away, giving her the best spot—a stone that made a comfortable seat just close enough to the flames that she could warm her fingers and toes without singeing them.

"Here you are, my lady," he said, and Hild looked up to see him presenting her with another bowl of broth.

She took it gratefully, thanking him as he backed away,

and tried her best not to slurp it down. As she drained the bowl, he took it and handed her a sloshing skin of water, then moved away again.

"You needn't be afraid of me," she said. "I don't bite."

He colored and looked down, then busied himself with something on the other side of the fire that she couldn't see.

She already knew he was quiet; he must be shy, too.

She turned at the sound of footsteps—Mord was coming up a steep path into the camp. He stopped to talk to Gizzur, who left the way Mord had come. They must be keeping a heavy post of guards.

Mord lowered himself to the fire a little way from Hild and stretched out his hands to warm them. He looked at something on the ground, then looked up at Hild.

"What is it?" she asked, unable to read his expression. If she didn't know better, she would have said he was embarrassed.

"My lady," he said, and then looked down again and cleared his throat.

The Geat rose from his position across the fire and hurried away.

Hild heard movement behind her—Hadding had joined the Geat, the two of them almost racing each other down the path away from the campsite.

She looked back at Mord.

"My lady," he started again, looking into the flames. "We, uh, we can stay here for another day."

She waited.

"There's a tarn not far from here, a little pool with good, fresh water," he said brightly, pointing and looking off as if he could see the tarn from where he sat.

"We'll have plenty to drink, then," Hild said, thinking that they sounded for all the world as if they were sitting in comfort in her uncle's hall, making pleasant conversation. Why was Mord avoiding her eyes?

His expression grew troubled and he looked back at the fire. The red-brown hair of his beard, she saw, wasn't entirely hiding the red of his face. He was blushing.

"What is it?" she asked again.

"Well, we thought . . . ," he said, and then stopped, his cheeks now flaming.

"Thought what, Mord?" She didn't have the strength for games. What was he getting at?

"It's just that you, uh, might want to, well, wash, my lady," he said, rising to his feet. "We could bring water here and heat it for you," he called over his shoulder as he fled from the fire.

Hild felt her own face growing warm. She looked down at her skirt and raised her hand to her face, her hair. Her clothes were stiff with blood and dirt, and her face must be streaked with them, as well. Her hair was falling out of the slave's braid she'd made when she'd put it up for Brynjolf's funeral so long ago, and she could feel twigs and cobwebs and bits of things she'd rather not imagine in it, too.

Hadding's beard must look positively tidy compared to her hair. No wonder they'd thought her a spirit.

Her appearance was bad enough, but now that she took a whiff of herself, she understood instantly why the men had tried to keep their distance. Even Fire-eyes had objected, and now she knew why. She must still bear the foul odor of the creature from when it carried her to its lair. She smelled terrible.

She turned to see Mord standing at the edge of the campsite, Thialfi beside him. She stood, pulling herself to her full height, and spoke in her most dignified voice. "I wish to bathe."

The two warriors glanced at her, and the fear in their eyes made her smile. The smile turned into a grin, and the grin into a laugh.

Mord laughed, too, and as he did, Hild heard the laughter of the other men, who had been hiding behind the rocks, awaiting her reaction.

Monsters they were ready for, but telling a lady she smelled bad? That was beyond their experience.

TWENTY-FIVE

THE BATH FELT BETTER THAN ANY HILD HAD EVER HAD in her life. In the pony's saddlebag she found a clean linen shift and her best gown, the one made of wool dyed a deep red, its neckline embroidered with gold thread. It was no easy task pinning the brooches that held it together on either side of her chest, something she'd never done by herself, but she could hardly ask one of the men for help. When she finally got the brooches fastened, she sat in front of the fire, combing her wet hair with her fingers to dry it and luxuriating in the feel of clean wool socks.

Once she was dressed, the men who weren't on guard duty returned to the campsite. She pretended not to notice the way their eyes widened when they saw her, but their expressions told her she must have looked even worse than she had realized.

Gizzur approached her and bowed more formally than seemed necessary before he held out a small leather bag.

Hild looked at him, puzzled.

"We found it, my lady, when we were searching for you. Back on the other side of the river." He laid it in her outstretched hand.

"Thank you, Gizzur," she said, and was surprised by the way her words made his thin face brighten.

She looked at the bag, a pouch of plain leather. When she opened it, her breath caught in her throat. Her mother's brooch. The whalebone comb Unwen had used to comb Hild's hair since she'd been a child. It was Unwen's bag, the one she'd carried at her belt.

It didn't mean anything, Hild told herself. Unwen could have dropped it. The leather cord that had tied it closed was still intact; the bag could have come loose and fallen without Unwen ever knowing. She still could have gotten away.

"Gizzur?" she said, and the warrior looked up. "Was there any other sign of her?"

"Not that I saw, my lady."

Hild turned her attention back to the bag, running her fingers over the leather. That was good, wasn't it? If the monster had killed Unwen, they would have seen something, wouldn't they? She picked up the comb, staring at its smooth surface as if it could tell her the slave's fate, but it revealed no secrets.

"Pardon me, my lady," someone said, and she raised her

head to see the taller Geatish brother, the shy one, standing in front of her with a dripping ball of cloth in his hands. It took her a moment to realize it was her linen shift, the filthy one she'd been wearing.

"You washed it?" she asked, not meaning to sound quite so surprised. It wasn't a task a warrior should concern himself with—didn't these Geats know anything? She rose and tried to take the sodden garment from him, but he held it back.

"Don't, my lady, you'll get yourself all wet. Just tell me where to put it to dry it."

She looked at him, his lean, tanned face, the dark circles under his blue eyes. Like the rest of the men, he must not have slept much since the first monster attack. "I don't even know your name," she said.

"It's Wake, my lady."

"Wake. Thank you."

He shrugged. "It's what I'd want someone to do for my sister."

"You have a lucky sister, then," Hild said, smiling despite her disapproval. "You could spread it on those rocks over there, in the sun." She followed him and supervised while he stretched the shift out in a sunny spot where it would get air. Before she could thank him a second time, he slipped away in the direction of the tarn.

Hild went back to her place by the fire. On the ground beside the stone she'd been sitting on, a blade gleamed in the sunlight. Her sword! How could she have forgotten it?

She looked around to see who had put it there, but Gizzur was sitting alone by the fire, a needle in his hand, his nose wrinkled as if in distaste. She looked more closely. He was mending the tear in her gown where she'd snagged it on the stag's antlers. Unlike her shift, the gown hadn't been washed.

"Gizzur," she said, and he looked up. "That must smell awful."

He regarded the cloth in his hands, then nodded. "But don't worry, my lady. Wake said he'd wash it as soon as I'm finished." He returned to his work, but not before he blushed at her smile of gratitude.

The sound of footsteps came from the path, and Hild turned as first Mord and then Thialfi climbed into view. Seeing her, they approached. She stiffened. The sword lay naked on the ground beside her—she couldn't deny its existence.

"My lady," Mord said, and she looked at him, trying to decide what to say about it. But before she could speak, he said, "Will you tell us about the creature?"

She opened her mouth, then shut it. "The creature?" She swallowed her surprise. "Of course."

The three of them sat down in front of the fire, Hild's eyes straying to the sword and then back to Mord, but it might as well have been invisible—he neither looked at it nor mentioned it.

"What do you want to know?"

Thialfi leaned forward. "Everything, from the moment we failed you."

"Failed me?" It was the first time Hild had considered the events from the warriors' perspective. Of course they would blame themselves. She shook her head. "You didn't fail me—none of you did." She looked from Thialfi to Mord and beyond them to Gizzur and then Wake, who had just walked back into the campsite, her cloak dripping in his hands. "However it might seem to you, you did everything you could have."

Thialfi grumbled something she couldn't hear and Mord looked away.

"I mean it. You waited for me, and you got me safely away—to here." She gestured around the campsite. "I thank you for it, all of you."

Not one of them met her eye, and she knew she wouldn't be able to convince them. Not yet, anyway. "Listen, then, and I'll tell you what happened."

As she began the story of being taken to the monster's lair, Gizzur moved to a closer rock, followed by Wake, who had been spreading her cloak beside her shift to dry. She raised her voice to include them in her audience. At first, only Mord and Thialfi asked her questions, but then Gizzur began to, as well.

She couldn't tell them where the cave was, but she described it as well as she could—the alder trunks growing out of dark water and, on the other side of the pool, the oak tree's sinuous roots hiding the cave mouth. She told them about the fire in the cave and the dying monster, the sword buried in its chest. She paused, looking from Mord to Thialfi, expecting one of them to ask where the sword had come from, but neither of them did. Had it been less of a secret than she'd supposed?

Thialfi leaned forward to stir the fire, but his face gave nothing away.

Hild settled more comfortably on the stone and continued her story. When she explained the way she had made the poultice of roots and substituted Aunt Var's lay for a healing charm, Mord said, "Just as well that you didn't heal the monster, my lady," drawing a chuckle from the others. They nodded appreciatively when she told them how she got the monster's mother to leave the cave by convincing it its son needed food, and again when she explained how she pulled the sword from the monster's chest to help free herself from the rocks. She thought she heard one of them—Wake?—draw in his breath when she told about the creature returning just as she was about to escape.

"How badly did you wound it?" Thialfi asked.

Before Hild could answer, Mord said, "Would you have stayed around to find out?"

They pressed her for details about her flight from the cave to the river, and she told them as much as she could remember, but she knew it wasn't enough to help the

Shylfings know where the cave was, or how to avoid it on the return trip.

At the end of her recital, the men fell silent. Then Thialfi spoke. "In years gone by, King Beowulf defeated a monster like the one you fought."

"I've heard that tale," Mord said. "It was the Danes, wasn't it, that the creature attacked?"

Thialfi nodded. "Grendel, they called it. Our king killed the monster and its mother, too." He looked at Hild. "Do you know the story, my lady?"

She didn't. Her uncle's skalds usually sang about the exploits of her own people and those of their allies, not the deeds of hostile tribes.

"It's said that the king had the strength of thirty in his hand's grip. But you, my lady . . ." Thialfi paused, shaking his head. "You have strength of a different kind."

The other men nodded. They rose, talking among themselves, and returned to their duties, Gizzur heading down the hill to relieve Hadding, Wake taking the path for the tarn, her newly mended gown in his hands.

Hild felt drained from reliving the memories. She stared into the flames, seeing the fire in the monster's lair, the wounded creature lying on one side of it while she'd huddled on the other. She didn't realize Thialfi was still standing near her until he spoke.

"You'll need a sheath for that."

She looked up, her face frozen.

"We have Brynjolf's sword belt. She could use that," Mord said, walking back.

Hild sat in front of them, feeling like a child caught stealing apples.

"It wouldn't be the right shape, but we could make it fit," Thialfi said, stooping to pick up the blade. "Wulf's good at that sort of thing."

The two of them looked at the sword, Thialfi testing its heft in his single working hand. He held it to his eye and sighted down the blade. "It's a fine weapon," he said before he laid it on the ground beside her again. The two warriors walked away, their conversation back on the monster and whether it would cross the river.

Hild watched them, wondering whether they'd been charmed into forgetting she'd had the blade before she'd gotten to the monster's lair.

Then Thialfi glanced back and their eyes met. He remembered. He knew she'd tried to escape, too. And from his expression, she thought he might understand the options she'd been given—and the choice she had made.

He turned to face her and bowed—not a polite nod to a noblewoman, but the full bow of a warrior to his queen.

TWENTY-SIX

THEY PREPARED TO RIDE OUT THE NEXT MORNING, HILD dressed in damp but clean clothes, her red dress packed away again. Her sword slapped against her leg—it would take some time before she was accustomed to wearing it. Thialfi had been right about Wulf. The young warrior was good at leatherworking, and she had watched, impressed, as he'd adapted the belt and sheath to her and her sword. It comforted her to have a memento of Brynjolf with her.

As she readied herself for the day's ride, she tied Unwen's leather bag to the belt, her fingers stiff with the cold morning air. Then she struggled with her hair. When Unwen arranged her hair, the knot in the back was always perfect. How had she done it? And how many other things had the slave done for her that she'd never noticed? The men helped, bringing her food and water, but nobody rolled up her blankets for her or helped her pin on her gown. And who was there to hold up a cloak for privacy when she needed to relieve herself?

When she was finally ready, frustrated at how long it had taken her and aware that Hadding was patiently waiting to escort her, she made her way down the path to the grassy place where the horses had been hobbled. This time Fire-eyes didn't shy away from her, but Wulf had to help her into the saddle now that the sword was in her way. As she labored to arrange herself on her horse's back, she wondered how the men wore their weapons with such ease.

The sun was climbing above the distant hills when they rode into the cold, clear morning. Glancing back, Hild could see how defensible their camp had been, with its boulders for guards to hide behind, and the campsite at the very top of the hill, hidden from view. Her eye fell on the pony, its saddle empty. She swallowed a lump in her throat.

It wasn't just that she had to do everything herself. It was Unwen, too—her wry expression, the way she muttered to herself as she went about her work and bossed the other slaves around. The way she took care of Hild. "Lady of the Vanir," Hild whispered. "Watch over her."

With sudden clarity, her own future spread before her like a landscape viewed from a height. She hardly needed a vision to tell her that whatever had happened to Unwen, whether she still lived or not, their paths had been inviolably sundered. Escaping to the slave's people was no longer a possibility.

Yet if she had followed Unwen, what would her fate have been? What place might she have had among Unwen's tribe? Surely Unwen would have vouched for her—assuming that she had a voice among her people. Then she remembered the look on Unwen's face when they parted. She might have ended up an outcast among Unwen's tribe. She might even have been enslaved herself.

She shook the thoughts away. None of that mattered anymore. The company had crossed into the land of the Geats, and whether she wanted to or not, Hild would marry their king.

As if a cloud had covered the sun, she felt the day darken. She bowed her head, letting Fire-eyes follow the men.

They rode down the hillside toward the valley, the warriors' helmets giving them a menacing look, their weapons poised against sudden attack. Every stone could hide an unknown threat. No one joked or even spoke. They kept close together, the men in formation around Hild.

She was the one who broke the silence, her words surprising her. "The creature. It's not here." As she spoke, she realized how certain she was. Just as she'd known it was racing through the woods to attack the men back on the other side of the river, she could tell that the monster was no danger to them now.

Thialfi, riding next to her, looked at her and she nodded

to reassure him. The other men exchanged glances and the mood shifted. They still rode without speaking, keeping a close guard around her, but Hild felt as if their mail shirts had been given permission to jingle.

She eased into the ride through the stone-filled valley, her fingers barely touching Fire-eyes's reins. He needed no direction. What a handsome gift he had been. Her young cousin's generosity humbled her. Could she have given Fleetfoot away, even to Beyla, who loved the horse so dearly? She didn't think so. Perhaps Arinbjörn had been more cognizant of what she'd done for him than she'd thought when she'd been sunk in her misery.

She recalled the day it happened, and the way she'd known the Bronding had been about to kill her cousin. The compulsion that had overtaken her had been so strong that she had half believed it when Bragi said she was possessed. But now she knew her uncle's skald had been wrong. She hadn't been possessed; instead, she'd been so overwhelmed that she'd lost all sense of herself.

Brynjolf's sheath slipped, digging into her leg, and she reached to adjust it. Fire-eyes tossed his head to ask what she was doing and she put a palm against his neck, warming her fingers. They were keeping a quick pace, and cold air buffeted her cheeks.

Again the sword worked itself into an awkward position and she moved it back, the touch of the weapon making her think about the first time she'd used it, when the monster attacked the men. A compulsion had filled her then, too, just like when she'd saved her cousin. Yet it had been different. How? She gripped the hilt, letting the sensation in her fingers remind her of that night. When she'd left Unwen, she hadn't lost herself in the compulsion. She'd known who she was and what she was doing, even if she hadn't understood why. Of that, she still wasn't sure.

She glanced at the men who surrounded her, their helmets hiding their faces. Then Hadding looked her way and beamed, his eyes bright behind his helmet's mask, his teeth bared in a grin below it. She smiled back.

She might not know why she'd run to help the men, but she recognized that the vision she'd had by the river, of the creature coming for them, had been different yet again. She'd been given knowledge, but whether to act on it had been left up to her. Was that what it meant to be far-minded? Was that the load her grandmother had borne when she'd envisioned her youngest son crowned king?

The company turned south, and Hild could see a forest thick with firs in the distance. Thialfi pulled ahead of Mord, taking the lead—after all, this was Geatish territory, and it was his prerogative to guide them along paths familiar to him. But as Hild watched, Mord maneuvered around him, signaling Gizzur to accompany him. Thialfi reined back, but she saw the anger in his eyes when he looked at Wulf and Wake, who brought up the rear.

Yesterday's easy camaraderie between Shylfing and

Geat was gone. Hild remembered Arinbjörn's warning. Her uncle's men weren't just watching for monsters and other threats. They were judging the best route to bring an army to conquer the Geats once they had been pacified by marriage—to her.

She would have to live with the Geats to the end of her days. Her only consolation was that her end would come quickly. When the Shylfing army attacked, she would be killed. Her uncle would see to that. He didn't like what he couldn't control, and over her far-mindedness, he had much less power than she did. He would wait for early spring, she thought, when the snows had lifted enough to allow an army through and the Geats were weak from hunger. And then he would attack.

She doubted she would live to see another harvest.

They passed the first trees on the edge of the forest, quickly leaving behind light and warmth. Hild pulled her cloak closer around her, wishing she'd worn her red dress instead of her damp clothes. They hadn't seemed bad when she'd put them on, and she'd felt sure they would quickly finish drying, but now she couldn't get warm.

The path widened and she looked up as they emerged into a bright glade. "We will stop here," Thialfi said, veering to the side and dismounting. Wulf and Wake did the same, but Mord signaled to his men that they should stay on their horses.

"We can stop later," he said.

"No," Thialfi said, and there was iron in his voice. He gave Mord a look that caused Hild to think he was made of much stronger stuff than she'd realized. "This is a sacred place. You should dismount." Without waiting for a response, he whipped off his helmet and strode to a massive oak at the edge of the glade, Wulf and Wake right behind him.

"All right, we'll let them have their little prayer," Mord said, his contempt loud enough for the Geats to hear. But he dismounted.

Hild watched the Geats as she clambered from her saddle, trying not to poke herself with her sword, but they didn't respond to Mord's provocation. They were standing in front of the tree, doing something she couldn't make out because their bodies blocked her view. All she could tell was that their arms were moving, and she thought they might be saying something.

She looked around her. A shaft of sunlight reached toward her but she couldn't feel its heat. The woods that surrounded them seemed dark and impenetrable, not a place that welcomed people. A small animal scuttled through the leaves, disappearing too quickly for her to identify it.

When the Geats finished, Thialfi and Wake returned to their horses and remounted quickly, while the Shylfings still rested on the ground. Mord leapt into his saddle, but he was too late. Thialfi had taken the lead down the narrow trail through the dark woods. He stopped to wait for the rest of them, turning his horse to block anyone from passing him.

Hild couldn't stop herself from smiling at his tactics.

"My lady?" Wulf said at her side.

She nodded, accepting his help back into her saddle. "Forgive me," she mumbled, coloring, as her sheathed sword hit his head.

"It's why I'm wearing my helmet, my lady," he said, and grinned at her before returning to his own horse.

. . .

Thialfi kept the lead for the rest of the day, both on the narrow paths through the woods and in the wide-open places they rode through. They splashed through streams and climbed rocky hills. The farther they went, the colder it got. The wind increased and low clouds blocked the sun. By afternoon, Hild's clothes were dry, but her teeth were chattering. She would have liked to stop to get out her hood and her mittens and to pull on her woolen leggings, but Thialfi pushed them hard. She knew he must have a campsite in mind, but knowing so didn't make her ears or her fingers any warmer.

By the time they finally stopped, she was so stiff with cold that she stumbled her way down from the horse, then fumbled trying to open the pony's saddlebags to find her winter gear. It was too dark to see what she was doing, anyway, Thialfi had kept them going so long. Unwen would have been able to find the hood immediately, but Hild couldn't even get the leather cords untied. She shouldn't have to do this to begin with—she was King Ragnar's sister-daughter.

"Goat's breath!" she whispered, tears of frustration stinging her eyes.

She laid her cheek against the pony's warm flank and ran her frozen fingers over its coarse hair. In her mind, she could hear Unwen *tsk*ing at her for her tantrum. She could see the slave shaking her head and giving her that twist of her lips that counted for a smile. She shook her own head at her foolishness. Then, more calmly, she tried again. This time, the cords came loose, and in the light of a newly built fire, she sifted through the saddlebag's contents until she found what she was looking for.

TWENTY·SEVEN

HILD WOKE TO THE SOUNDS OF MORNING IN THE CAMP, but she snuggled back under her blanket without opening her eyes. She was deliciously warm.

"My lady," she heard Mord say as she was slipping into a dream of summer and laughter.

"My lady," he said again, more loudly this time. She opened her eyes and blinked. No wonder she was warm. A thick layer of snow covered her blanket. Above her, the bare branches were lined with snow. As she watched, a little shower of it sifted off the end of a twig and fell in a clump to the ground.

"We need to leave soon," Mord said.

Hild sat up and saw that the men had already broken camp. She and the fire were the only things left. "Why didn't you wake me sooner?" she said, but Mord had already walked away.

Irritably, she shook the snow off her blanket and rolled it, then gathered her belongings, not bothering to comb her hair. She'd do without food until later, too. She wouldn't have them waiting for her.

Despite her hurry, all of them, even Hadding, sat astride their horses by the time she was ready. All of them except for Wulf, that is, who stood beside her horse, waiting to help her into the saddle. She wanted to refuse his help, but she knew that would make things even worse.

By midday they had left the deep woods behind them, and a snowy, rock-strewn plain lay before them. A single mountain rose far in the distance, its summit lost in clouds. A fierce wind knifed around them and Hild pulled her furred hood close to her face.

As they crossed the plain, she began to see what looked like farmland, and perhaps a farmstead, but it was still too far away for her to see clearly. The light was fading as they drew nearer, making Hild distrust her eyes. Yet the closer they got, the clearer things became—and the more bewildering. It was a farmstead, but not the large, prosperous sort of place she was accustomed to. Only three small buildings, one of them a mere hut, sat amid meager fields. The farmhouse itself was blackened, its walls crumbling, its thatch burned off. Even the fields seemed to have been scorched.

The dragon must have done this. She shivered.

She saw no people as they passed, nor any animals. Had they all died in the flames?

Thialfi clucked to his horse, hurrying them along, and Hild was glad to follow.

The next farmstead they came to had been spared the flames—but it was just as poor and ramshackle as the last, a few small structures in the center of tiny fields.

This was the kingdom of the Geats? Hild glanced at Mord and saw that he looked just as shocked as she was. They would hardly need an army to conquer these people. In fact, she thought, maybe Mord and Gizzur and Hadding should just take care of it now and be done with it.

They rode a distance before they passed another farm. This one, at least, seemed more prosperous, and she wondered if it was only the outlying farms that were in such bad shape. Yet as they drew closer, she could see that the snow was hiding the truth; this farm, too, had been scorched by the dragon. Its blackened timbers lay open to the winter sky. There could be no inhabitants.

A movement against the snow made her turn to see a dead goat on the ground, a dark object on top of it. A raven pulling at the goat's entrails.

She swallowed and looked away.

"We can stay in the barn if it hasn't been too badly damaged," Thialfi said, his voice scarcely audible over the wind.

Hild looked toward the building Thialfi pointed at, and turned her horse. Even Fire-eyes seemed dispirited, his gait weary and plodding.

At least the barn still had a roof to stop the snow and

even enough hay for the horses. The dragon must have struck at harvest time, when the people who had lived here had just finished their haying. What had become of them? She wrapped herself in her blanket and burrowed into the straw for warmth. As she drifted toward sleep, she tried to keep the dragon out of her dreams, but it flew through them, spewing fire, destroying fields and people with indiscriminate malice, always accompanied by the smell of smoke, bitter in her throat.

In the morning, as she brushed the straw from her cloak and combed it out of her hair, the dragon still hovered in the back of her mind. Even though she knew it was dead, seeing the evidence of its violence put her on edge.

More snow had fallen in the night, which slowed their progress. Thialfi led them down tree-lined valleys, where they splashed through fast-running streams, and up through farmland, the dwellings no more impressive than the ones they had seen the previous day. Some of them were built into hills or had sod walls, while others were rickety wooden structures. Her uncle would have had them torn down.

Mord caught her eye and gave her a look she couldn't decipher. Sympathy?

At least the wind had died down. It was a bright, crisp day, the sun shining on the snow and on the mountain that loomed in the distance. People watched them as they passed farmhouses now, sometimes raising their arms in greeting. Thialfi waved back with his good arm, but Hild just watched. She felt as if the scene were unreal, as if she weren't a part of it. She knew she wasn't dreaming it, but she wished she were.

They came to a wooded place where the path narrowed and they had to ride single file. When they emerged from the trees, Hild could see another group of buildings in the distance. It didn't look like a farmstead. She squinted at it and then saw Thialfi turning in his saddle. "The king's stronghold," he called out.

She kept her mouth from dropping open. That tumble-down collection of buildings was the king's stronghold? It didn't even have a defensive wall surrounding it. And where was the hall?

She stared, trying to make out the details. She could see a structure in the shape of a hall, but it was far too small to be the king's hall. Yet when she scanned the stronghold, she saw no other.

This was to be her home. This was her uncle's vengeance on her—for daring to act without his permission. For saving his son's life. She blinked back angry tears.

Thialfi led them forward, and as they approached the first structure, a tall thin guard stepped out from it, a spear in his hand. Thialfi dismounted and the two men greeted each other with an embrace.

Hild sat watching, not bothering to listen, while they talked, Thialfi occasionally gesturing back at the rest of them. When he mounted his horse again, she followed dutifully, doing her best to keep her emotions in check.

But it wasn't easy. The ugliness of the place overwhelmed her, and the smell. Didn't they ever clean the ashes from their fires? An acrid odor made her nose wrinkle, and the narrow dirt lanes through falling-down houses made her want to look away.

As they rode, a young warrior who was still pinning on his cloak came running toward them, grinning. "Thialfi! You're back!" he said, and Hild saw how misshapen his nose was, as if it had been broken. When he added, "Come this way," Hild didn't miss the look he gave Thialfi, who nodded. She wondered what had passed between them.

Though the stronghold was small, it seemed to take them a long time to get to the hall. When they finally approached it, she saw that she had been right. It was as puny as it had seemed from a distance.

Wulf was immediately at her side, helping her dismount. "The dragon burned the old hall," he said, and she knew he must have seen her expression of disdain.

She made her face blank and followed the men.

In the antechamber, they stamped the snow from their shoes and laid aside their weapons. Hild could smell how new the wood was; the walls were as blond as the Geats themselves, not yet darkened by smoke and age like her uncle's hall.

They arranged themselves to march in, Mord and

Hadding leading the way, Thialfi and the young Geatish warrior with the misshapen nose on either side of them. Hild walked behind them, alone, followed by the others. Not until they had begun to move through the hall did she realize she still had her hood up, but she was glad of it if it hid her dismay at the hall's plainness. Where were the bright banners, the beams carved and painted by skillful hands, the embroidered tapestries hanging from the walls? Bare wood met her gaze, along with a single fire so small it hardly cast any light into the shadowy corners. Worst of all, the floor was packed dirt, not just in the antechamber but in the hall itself. Even if the old hall had burned down, it was hard to believe the Geats lived this way.

And where were they all? Only a handful of people were gathered in the hall—a few warriors near the fire, some slave girls by a door. Hild's group stopped in front of the dais. Three people faced them. One was a man with a close-cropped beard, wearing the finest clothing she'd seen so far in the kingdom. He had only one eye. A woman wearing a plain gown stood near him, her eyes flicking from warrior to warrior. Between them stood a dark-haired youth. His cloak swished around his legs as if he had just run in from outside. Where was the king?

Mord didn't wait. "Hail, Wiglaf, son of Weohstan," he called out in his strong voice.

Hild scowled in irritation. Why wasn't Mord waiting for the king? Was this part of some plan she wasn't privy to?

The young man with the dark hair stepped forward. "You are welcome to the land of the Geats," he said, as if he were some kind of spokesman, perhaps a skald in training. She wondered briefly why he wasn't fair-haired, like the other Geats, but she didn't have time to think about it before Mord spoke again.

"Our king sends you greeting."

Hild watched warily, trying to interpret Mord's actions. Hadding had made no movement that she could discern. What was Mord up to?

The young man spoke again. "You have journeyed far and returned our valued thanes, free from harm. We thank you."

We thank you? The words caught Hild by surprise and she shifted her attention from Mord to the youth. "*Our* valued thanes," he'd said. She stared at him—at his plain mail shirt hanging a little too low on his legs, his ordinary sword belt and scabbard, his bare head—and felt a prickling sensation, like a warning, as comprehension began to dawn.

"Past hostilities have divided our people," Mord was saying. "My king asks that they be forgotten."

"Your lord speaks wisely," the young man answered.

Thialfi had told her that the new Geatish king was a powerful warrior, that he had killed a dragon. She had thought of Thialfi as an honorable man, as someone she could trust. What else had she been wrong about?

There was a pause, and then she heard Mord say, "We thought we would find a king."

The young man nodded. "The coronation takes place tomorrow," he said, and added, "You will be our honored guests."

Hild had accepted the fate that had been woven for her, knowing the sorrow it would bring. But she'd made her decision believing the king of the Geats was a proven warrior, someone who faced danger when others fled. She'd pictured a dragon-killer—she'd thought he was a man.

Yet this clean-faced youth no older than she was, wearing a mail shirt too big for him—this *boy*—was the king of the Geats.

She had been tricked.

And she had no choice but to marry him.

TWENTY-EIGHT

NOTHING FELT REAL. MORD AND THE YOUTH CONTINUED speaking, but Hild barely heard them. ". . . peace pledge between nations," Mord was saying, but the words swam away like minnows Hild was trying to catch with her fingers.

Then he signaled her to step forward.

Woodenly, she moved, remembering belatedly to push her hood back from her face. As Mord said, "Hild, our king's sister-daughter," she sank into a low, stiff-backed curtsy. She would have stayed there forever if the young man hadn't taken a step toward her and reached for her hand.

As he raised her, he said, "Be welcome, Hild," in that drawling Geatish accent she'd grown accustomed to.

She should speak; she knew she should. But she couldn't. Instead, she looked at him, trying to read the expression in his dark eyes and failing. The two of them were matched for height, she realized, and he was still gripping her fingers in his shield hand.

He spoke again. "Be welcome, all of you. Sit and rest after your journey."

Then he guided her to the woman who had been standing beside him.

Hild dropped into another curtsy, glad of the custom, which took away the need for words. The woman, who must have been Hild's mother's age, her head crowned with a coil of braids, curtsied as well. As she did, the young man left the two of them together.

Hild glanced back to see him approaching the warrior who had led them to the hall, speaking to him, and shaking his head as the warrior grinned broadly.

She stiffened. Was he talking about her?

"Come and have a seat by the fire," the woman said. "I'm Thora, Wulf and Wake's mother."

Hild looked at her. She could see the resemblance in her eyes and the lines of her brows. She swallowed, searching for her voice. "Your sons have been kind to me."

Thora nodded without smiling and Hild remembered that her husband had been killed by the dragon. What relief she must feel to have her boys back again. Hild wondered if the sister Wake had mentioned was in the hall, but the only other women she saw were slaves.

She sat on a bench and watched as Thialfi led Mord and the others to a table on the other side of the fire. A slave hurried in with a load of logs, followed by another with a board full of meat and bread.

Thora had disappeared from view, but moments later, she emerged from behind the dais, a drinking horn in her hands, firelight reflecting off its silver rim. Was Thora the highest-status woman among the Geats? Her clothes were ordinary working-day wool, but the set of her shoulders, her measured step, the lift of her head—they all signaled her pride.

As Hild watched, Thora approached the dark-haired youth and held out the horn to him. He seemed surprised. Thora's lips moved as if she was whispering to him. Finally, he took the horn, drank, and returned it to her.

She moved on to the other high-ranking men, then to Thialfi—and then to Mord, who flicked his eyes over to Hild before taking the horn and drinking.

Hild knew she should be paying close attention, remembering the faces of the men Thora had taken the horn to so she would know their ranks—information that could be vital to her well-being—but she couldn't concentrate. Instead, she kept picturing the riverbank, where she had left behind any hope of freedom. What a fool she'd been. If she'd followed Unwen, she would be free by now. Instead, she'd squandered her chance, leaving her with nothing but bitter regret.

She looked up as someone approached her, but it was only slave girls, the two she had seen standing near the door, the older one with a bright blond plait down her back, the other with curls fighting to escape her braid. They curtsied to her, but she didn't acknowledge them. Didn't they know enough to wait until she summoned them?

"Welcome," the older girl said, and this time Hild did look at her, unable to hide her anger. Did the seaweed-eaters not even bother to train their slaves?

"Perhaps you would like to bathe after your journey. If you come with us . . ." The girl held out her hand to Hild, as if she were inviting her to join the two of them. It took Hild a moment to realize she *was* inviting her. Both slaves had started for the door, assuming Hild would follow them. She shook her head in exasperation. Although she hadn't expected much from Geatland, she had expected a great deal more than this. Even the slaves didn't know their places. Well, she could hardly teach them now.

Wearily, she rose and followed them.

In the antechamber, she retrieved her sword, strapping the belt around herself. She saw the slaves raising their eyebrows at the idea of a girl wearing a sword, but she pretended not to notice.

When they stepped through the door, the wind whistled around the corner of the hall, sending snow into Hild's face. She pulled her hood up, happy to be able to hide behind it again. The older slave directed somebody to bring Hild's saddlebags, and they hurried along a narrow lane, their heads bent into the sharp wind, until they came to a small house and ducked inside.

Hild stood beside the door as one of the slaves built up the fire and the other went out again for water. The anger that had gripped her was gone, replaced by numbness.

The fire flared and the slave girl looked up at her. "Sit, if you'd like," she said, gesturing toward the bed.

Hild was too tired to be affronted by the familiarity the slave showed her. She crossed to the bed and lowered herself onto the mattress. Straw, not feathers—no surprise in that.

"Did my brothers treat you well?"

Hild looked at the girl. With sudden clarity she saw the line of her brows and the shape of her eyes that linked her to Wulf and Wake. "You're not a slave," she said.

"A slave?" Now it was the girl's turn to be affronted. She stared at Hild, her lips parted.

"You're Thora's daughter."

The girl nodded, her gaze wary.

"Forgive me," Hild said. "In my uncle's kingdom, slaves wear their hair as you do." As she spoke, she realized why she'd misunderstood. It wasn't just the braid; it was the blond hair and something about the girl's features that made her think of the slaves at home, so many of whom had been captured from the land of the Geats. Yet her bearing and her behavior should have told Hild the girl's status. She lowered her face into her hand. How else could this day go wrong?

She raised her head again and stood, then moved to

stand directly in front of the girl and spoke to her in the formal language appropriate to someone of the highest rank. "I give you greeting. I am Hild, sister-daughter to Ragnar, King of the Shylfings." She curtsied low, her back straight; it was the kind of curtsy she would use for her uncle.

The girl watched her for a moment, as if she was trying to make up her mind. Then she said, "I am Wyn, daughter to Finn and Thora, sister to Wulf and Wake. Be welcome, Hild." She, too, curtsied. And then she smiled.

Hild tried to smile back, but to her horror, she felt tears spring to her eyes. She turned away, but not before Wyn saw.

"Here, sit while we wait for the water," Wyn said, touching Hild's arm lightly. "You must be hungry—we'll eat just as soon as you've bathed." She busied herself, turning to the fire.

Hild knew she was being given time to recover. She swallowed back her tears and took a shaky breath, followed by another, this time not as shaky. Finally, she felt her chest relax.

Hild rose again as the door opened and the other girl entered, escorting two men—real slaves this time—who carried buckets of water, which they set by the fire before they departed silently.

Wyn pushed the second girl forward. "This is my cousin, Gerd."

There was something about Gerd—her unruly hair,

perhaps, or the way her emotions played freely across her face—that made Hild think of Beyla. The thought warmed her. Again, she curtsied formally. When Gerd scowled in confusion, Wyn pushed her cousin into a curtsy of her own. This time when Hild met Wyn's eyes, her smile was genuine, and it extended beyond her lips. There was no denying that Geatland was more backward than she had ever dreamed possible, but at least she'd found an ally. And she knew that if she was to survive here long, she would need all the allies she could get.

.   .   .

A meal—a real meal, eaten indoors before a fire—followed the bath. Wyn and Gerd chatted companionably while the three of them ate, allowing Hild to sink into silence. She watched with amused detachment the way Wyn shepherded Gerd, not allowing her to ask the questions she really wanted to, especially about the terrible bruise she'd seen on Hild's side from when the creature had carried her. It didn't hurt very much anymore, and Hild had almost forgotten about it until she removed her shift and heard Gerd gasp. As she'd bathed, she'd seen Wyn give her cousin a stern look that forbade her from asking about it—just as Wyn was doing again now, while they ate.

The older girl was doing her best to make her feel welcome, Hild could tell, and she knew she should try harder to be sociable, but doing so was difficult. She kept slipping into her own thoughts, as if she were watching shadows on a wall. *Pay attention,* she scolded herself, and then was glad she had.

"Did you see how scared Rune looked in the hall?" Gerd said.

Hild saw the consternation on Wyn's face, and how much she wanted her cousin not to have spoken such words, but it was too late.

"She means King Wiglaf," Wyn explained. "That's his nickname—Rune."

"Rune," Hild repeated, in what she hoped was a non-judgmental tone. Not only was he younger than she'd thought he'd be, but his people called him by a *nickname?* She tried to imagine anyone using a nickname for her uncle, and failed. Didn't these people value honor?

"He wasn't scared," Wyn said to Gerd. "He just doesn't know all the protocol yet."

"And why doesn't he?" Hild asked.

"He wasn't brought up in the hall," Wyn said.

Hild waited.

"He was raised on a farm."

The cheese she had just swallowed hardened in her throat. It was even worse than they joked about back home. The king of the Geats really *was* a country bumpkin.

"He was raised by a far-minded woman," Gerd added.

Hild looked at her sharply. "What do you mean?"

"Nothing," Wyn said, giving her cousin an angry glance. "She means nothing. Pay her no mind."

"No, I'd like to know," Hild said. When neither of them spoke, she added, "I . . . I, too, am far-minded."

"You are?" Gerd said. "So was Amma, the old woman who raised Rune. And she could interpret dreams, too." She got the words out in a rush before Wyn could stop her.

But rather than quiet the younger girl, Wyn took up the story. Being far-minded seemed to carry no stigma here. "Amma wasn't from the farm," Wyn said. "She wasn't even a Geat. She came here a long time ago seeking refuge from a feud. They say she was a peaceweaver, but—"

Wyn stopped. She didn't need to say more for Hild to know what had happened—that the peaceweaving had failed. Just like it would now. She ran her thumbnail along a crease in the wooden tabletop, stopping when she reached a dark knothole. Had the tribe who married Amma to their enemy truly intended peace? Or had they been full of treachery, like Bragi and her uncle?

"She died, though," Gerd added, her voice a whisper. "The dragon killed her."

Hild nodded and turned to Wyn. "Like your father."

Wyn looked down as if she was steadying herself. Then she met Hild's eyes. "Yes. Like my father."

"Thialfi told me," Hild said. She reached out to touch the other girl's hand. The fire snapped, but there was no other sound. "My father was killed when I was young," she said. "I remember when they brought him home."

They fell silent, and Hild knew Wyn was working to

control her grief, still recent and raw. When the other girl raised her head again, her eyes were bright.

"Come. You must be tired. Let us take you to the guest quarters."

Hild nodded, even though her exhaustion had fled. The king had been raised by a far-minded woman? A peace-weaver? As Wyn and Gerd escorted her down the narrow lanes, she couldn't stop her mind from working.

At the cottage where they left her, a fire had been laid, and her baggage brought inside. She blinked in the flickering firelight, then walked across the small room to test the bed. It might not have been a cabinet bed, whose doors she could close for warmth, but this mattress was stuffed with feathers, not straw. She was almost ready to sink into it when she heard men's voices outside the door. Mord's voice.

She rushed to let him in. "Gizzur and Hadding will stand guard tonight," he said as he crossed the threshold.

"Do you think it's necessary?" Hild asked.

Mord looked behind him, waiting until the door was shut. "Have you taken a look around you? Do you trust these people?" He closed his mouth, but Hild could tell he had more to say. She watched him, waiting.

"My lady," he said, giving her a slight bow.

"Go on," she said.

"Hild." He looked up beseechingly. "My lady, you can't stay here."

She kept her eyes on him, but she didn't speak.

"If we—the other men and I—if we tell your uncle what happened with the monster, he'll accept you back, I'm sure he will."

She stared at him, her heart racing.

"I didn't know, not about you, not about this place. But I know now—you don't belong here, my lady." He crossed to the fire and then back to her again. "Gizzur and Hadding, they agree. After your uncle hears what you did with the monster, how you saved our lives, *my* life—" He stopped and looked at her.

She needed no convincing. "When do we leave?"

"The coronation's tomorrow. After the ceremony would be the best time—we can slip away when they're all drunk."

"I'll be ready."

"My lady." He bowed lower than he normally did. When he rose again, he caught her eye and held it. Then he turned and strode from the room, barking an order at Hadding as he shut the door.

She stood beside the dancing flames, hardly able to breathe, she was so excited.

She was going home!

She picked up a pillow, hugged it to her chest, and twirled. Home! She would see her mother again, and Beyla, and her sisters, and Arinbjörn. Just wait till he heard what she'd done with his sword. She'd see her nieces and nephews and Aunt Var and Ari Frothi. Even her cousin Skadi seemed dear to her now. She'd be with everyone in the hall, a real hall, in a real kingdom once again, far away from this place where people didn't know what a hall was, or a king.

She could practically feel her fingers on her loom, and for the first time in weeks, she remembered the pattern she'd been weaving, the one she'd been so excited about.

Home! She hugged the pillow tighter.

She'd seen Mord's eyes and she grasped the implications of his plan. He wanted to marry her himself—it would put him closer to the throne than he'd ever been before. She swept the details aside. She'd have the whole journey home to dwell on them. But at that very moment, all she cared about was that Mord might be able to get her back into her uncle's good graces. If he could, it was a compromise she might be willing to accept.

As long as it meant she was leaving Geatland far behind. As long as it meant she was going home.

TWENTY·NINE

HILD'S MIND SPUN WITH POSSIBILITIES. SHE CRAWLED under the covers, luxuriating in the warmth and the softness of the mattress—the first she'd slept on since the day she'd left home—and imagined the look on Siri's face when she rode through the gates.

Would Mord ride ahead to negotiate with her uncle? Or would they all walk into the hall together? It would be better if she didn't speak, she decided, but allowed the men to do all the talking. She would stand a little to the side, wearing her red gown, holding herself regally. She wouldn't look her uncle in the eye; he might take that as a challenge. Instead, she'd keep her gaze slightly averted from his face. It would be important to show him that their return had been the men's idea, not hers, but he also needed to see that she wouldn't be cowed.

What about Arinbjörn? she wondered, picturing her cousin standing with the men in the hall. Would he be uneasy with her? Ari Frothi wouldn't be. She was surprised by how much she missed the old skald. It would even be good to see Unwen— She shook her head at her foolishness and offered a prayer to the goddess that Unwen was safe with her own people.

Despite the thoughts that swarmed through her head, she found herself growing drowsy as the sheets warmed. She scrunched more comfortably into the pillow and pulled the blankets up to her ears. A log on the fire shifted and the flames hissed companionably. Hild blinked, then blinked again as sleep overtook her.

When she woke, comfort and hope still held her tight, and now woven into the pleasant sensation was the memory of the old woman she'd dreamed about. Had it been her grandmother? No, the woman hadn't looked like her grandmother, she didn't think, although it might have been her in the way dreams have of showing you one person hiding behind another's face. Whoever it had been, the old woman had gazed at her intently with strange eyes, one that looked directly at her while the other seemed to see beyond her. It was as if she could see right through Hild, challenging her, taking her measure. "You are home," the woman had said, her voice so harsh and commanding that the dream had been almost frightening.

But now, as Hild turned over in the bed and pulled

the covers over her head to block out the cold air, any fear she might have felt was banished by delicious warmth. If it hadn't been her grandmother, it must have been one of her ancestors, welcoming her back to her uncle's kingdom and proclaiming her right to be there. Starting today, starting now, she was no longer an exile from her people. Today everything would change, and she would be ready for it.

She recalled how things had been the day they left the kingdom, how the men had avoided her, fearing her, wanting to be rid of her. It wouldn't be like that on the return journey. She had their respect. And not just their respect; they believed they would come to power through their attachment to her. At least, Mord did.

But they'd be traveling without Brynjolf this time. The image of his smile made her heart hurt. At least now she'd be able to be with Beyla when she found out about her brother's death. Not that it would bring her friend much comfort, Hild knew.

The door creaked. Gray light crept in and, with it, a slave with logs in her arms. She built up the fire and slipped out again silently. Hild waited until the flames had established themselves enough to light the room before she got out of bed and dressed. Surely they would send a slave to help her later, but she'd become accustomed enough to doing it on her own that it hardly bothered her. She knotted her hair, the task easier with warm fingers and no men waiting impatiently for her. Fastening the sword belt around her waist, she grabbed her cloak and opened the door.

"My lady!"

Hild stepped back, startled, as Thialfi rose from beside the door, a spear in his good hand.

"What are you doing there?" she asked.

"Guarding you," he said, and from the way he shook his head, as if to wake himself, Hild could tell he'd been dozing.

"From what?"

"I'm not sure, my lady. Hadding was falling asleep out here, and he said you needed a guard."

She looked at the dark circles under his eyes and the way his tunic and cloak were crumpled. When Mord had left her the previous night, Hadding had been the first on guard. "You've been here all night," she said.

His lack of response was answer enough. "Thialfi," she said, touching his arm as he stifled a yawn. "You should get some sleep."

"I will, my lady," he said, but he didn't move from his post.

"Now, Thialfi."

He shook his head. "Not until someone relieves me."

"Let's go find them, then."

"They need their sleep, too, my lady."

It was her turn to shake her head. The man was exasperating. "Then come with me."

He nodded, not asking where they were going, and walked beside her down the lane.

Fresh snow lay on the ground and the thatched roofs, brightening the place and making it look less tawdry than it had the previous day. The sun was just rising, turning the snow rosy where it wasn't hidden in shadow. The hall stood high above the other buildings, and in the crisp light of morning, Hild could see how well it was built, how solid the joints, how secure the roof. The wood was so clean and unscarred that the hall looked impossibly new.

Beside her, Thialfi gazed at it, too. "Not a log had been cut when I left for your land," he said softly.

It was newer than Hild had realized. "Where was the old hall?" she asked, and looked in the direction Thialfi pointed.

"It was a grand place," he said, "a proud place. Bigger than your uncle's Gyldenseld, even."

She raised her brows.

"My grandmother wove a long banner that hung behind the throne," he went on, looking into the distance. "My aunt loved to tell about it—she helped when she was just a girl, or so she said." He looked back at Hild and the barest trace of a smile crossed his face. "She probably just got in the way instead of helping, but that banner was dear to her. To me, too."

Hild watched him as he returned his gaze to the empty space where the hall had stood. How much had the Geats lost when the dragon attacked? She looked skyward, wondering what it must have been like to have the winged monster swoop down on them unawares.

"It came at night," Thialfi said, as if he'd heard her thoughts. "If we'd seen it—well, it's almost impossible to look at a dragon in the daylight and not be overcome by fear." He shook his head, and Hild had the impression he had forgotten she was there. "I don't know where Rune found the courage," he said, in a voice so low she knew it wasn't meant for her ears.

Rune. He was talking about the king.

She looked away just as the sound of hooves drew Thialfi to attention.

They watched as two figures on horseback clopped toward the hall. Neither of them saw her or Thialfi. As they neared, she could see that the closest of them was the one-eyed man who'd been in the hall the day before. The other she couldn't see well enough to recognize. Then he reached down to stroke his horse's neck and she realized it was Rune. He looked older than he had yesterday. His dark hair was pulled back from his face, revealing an expression so somber it made her catch her breath. Today was his coronation day. Shouldn't he be happy on such a morning?

She watched until he disappeared behind the hall, the look on his face never changing.

Again, Thialfi answered her thoughts. "He didn't want to be king," he said.

Hild looked at Thialfi through narrowed eyes. What man wouldn't want to be king? "Why is he, then?"

"Doesn't have much of a choice, does he? He's King Beowulf's only living kinsman." Thialfi nudged his toe at a stone sticking out of the snow. "Not that he knew it until they'd killed the dragon." He looked up at her. "As I heard it, he didn't know who he was or even that he was well born until then. Must have been a shock when the king named him his heir."

They stood in silence, both of them watching the space where Rune—*King Wiglaf,* Hild corrected herself—had disappeared. He was well born? The old king's kinsman? What else had Thialfi not thought to tell her earlier?

"My lady!" a voice called, and they turned to see Hadding running toward them with his clubfooted gait, his helmet askew. "I didn't know where you were—are you all right?"

"I'm fine, Hadding. But Thialfi needs some sleep."

"Right. I'll take over now," Hadding said. "You're relieved."

Hild glanced at Thialfi, who gave her a quick bow before hurrying away.

"He didn't give you any trouble, did he, my lady?"

"Hadding," Hild said. "He stood guard for you and Gizzur all night long—which I won't tell Mord." She held his gaze until he looked down, abashed. "Shall we go back?"

A slave had brought water while she was gone, and

as Hild washed her hands and face, another slave entered with food. Hild took the hot bowl of porridge, thick with butter and honey, and sat on the bed to eat it. She shut her eyes and luxuriated in the soft mattress beneath her, the rich taste of the porridge, and the steam rising from the bowl to touch her cheeks and eyelids. She wouldn't be able to savor a meal in warmth and comfort again until they got home.

Just as she finished, someone knocked and the door opened. With a rush of cold air that set the fire dancing, a woman came into the room. Thora, mother of Wulf, Wake, and Wyn.

Hild stood and the two curtsied to each other.

"You slept comfortably, I trust?" Thora said, and Hild nodded, stifling a smile at the way the question didn't allow a negative answer. Thora, she could tell, wasn't accustomed to having her opinions questioned.

"And you've had enough to eat?"

"Thank you. It was good to have a meal inside, in the warmth." Hild sat on the bed again, gesturing to invite the older woman to join her.

"My sons told me about the journey—and about your deeds. You will make a good match for our young king." Thora nodded at Hild and looked her up and down as if appraising her worth.

A sense of discomfort flooded through Hild, and she lowered her eyes.

"This is for you," Thora said. She opened her fingers to reveal a golden bracelet that winked in the firelight. Delicate tracery ornamented the metal band, making it a rich gift. "It's an heirloom of my family. You are most welcome here, Hild." She held out the bracelet.

Hild reached for it hesitantly. "I thank you," she said, dipping her head. She was suddenly deeply aware that Mord had presented the Geats with no gifts in the hall when they'd arrived, a breach of honor and an insult—surely one planned by her uncle. She hadn't even noticed at the time, she'd been so overwhelmed, and she wasn't sure Rune had realized it, either. But Thora would have seen it. She would have known, too, about the gold necklace set with rubies that her sons had carried to Gyldenseld—where it had been added to the treasury, not sent back to Geatland to adorn Hild's neck as it had on the day her uncle pledged her to his enemies.

And now, just as her uncle had done, Hild was accepting a gift from someone she was planning to deceive. She turned the bracelet over in her hand as if she were admiring its finely wrought edges. She couldn't take it—but to give it back wouldn't just be an insult; it would announce her intentions. No, she would simply have to leave it behind when they departed.

"It's beautiful," she said, forcing herself to meet Thora's eyes. "I am honored." She winced, wishing she had chosen a different word.

"My grandfather's father gave it to his wife in the days of King Hygelac," Thora said. "You will wear it well."

Hild swallowed and slipped it over her wrist.

"Now, let me help you dress for the ceremony." Thora rose and turned to her.

There was nothing for Hild to do but follow. She took the red gown from the saddlebag, along with the embroidered linen shift that went under it.

Thora reached out to finger the embroidery. "This is skillfully made."

"As is the cloth of your dress," Hild said, glad that she could compliment Thora without stretching the truth. Unlike the day before, when the woman had been dressed in plain brown wool, today she was wearing what must have been her best gown, of finely woven wool dyed a deep blue. An expensive blue. The intricately decorated brooches just below each shoulder, which held up the gown, were wrought of silver, making Hild think of Siri's best gown. It was blue and she, too, wore it with silver brooches.

Thora folded the dress Hild had just taken off. "I don't know how much my sons or Thialfi told you about our king."

"Thialfi told me about the dragon—and that it killed your husband."

Thora nodded briskly and laid the dress on the bed. "He was the best of men. King Beowulf's shoulder companion."

Hild could hear the pride in her voice.

"And the best of husbands, too. As our new king will be to you, I know."

Hild clenched her teeth. How much could this woman test her? She forced her jaw to relax. Thora would expect her to want to talk about the man she was supposed to be marrying, she reminded herself. She should be asking questions, but she couldn't think of any that wouldn't lay bare her deception. All she could do was repeat what she already knew. "I heard that he was raised on a farm."

Thora nodded. "It's been hard for him, coming from the farm to the stronghold. But it's served us all well. When King Beowulf died, the bard urged him to have a new hall built straightaway, but our new king wouldn't allow it. Instead, he insisted that we bring in the harvest first so there would be food enough to see the kingdom through the winter." She glanced at the fire as a log shifted, sending up a flare of light. "And now," she said, turning back to Hild, "because he insisted on it, there will be."

Rune had ignored their bard's advice? Hild recalled how easily her uncle was swayed by Bragi's arguments. She brushed the thought away and tried to concentrate on the conversation. It was her turn to speak, but again she had to fall back on the things she'd heard. "Wyn said the king was raised by an old woman."

"Old? Well, I suppose Amma was old by the time Wyn knew her," Thora said with a wry smile. "She was an exile from another tribe. King Beowulf offered her a place in the hall, but she chose to live out on Hwala's farm."

Hild reached for her red dress and pulled it over her head. "Who was she to your new king—his grandmother?"

"No, no blood relation at all. Here, let me help with that." She took one of the dress straps and attached it to the brooch. Then she looked up. "Thialfi didn't tell you about our king's origins?"

"He told me he was King Beowulf's kinsman."

"Yes, that's true. But it's not what I meant." Thora turned Hild so she could attach the other strap. "Our new young king came to us when he was just a baby. Amma took him in."

"Came to you?"

"He washed up on our shores in a boat. All alone, just a baby surrounded by a warrior's weapons."

Hild stared at her, but Thora merely reached to adjust the embroidered neckline of her shift, running her fingers over the intricate pattern. "King Beowulf said the gods sent him to us. I say if they sent us Rune, they also sent us Amma."

"What do you mean?" Hild's voice dropped to a whisper.

"Well, she raised him, didn't she?" Thora turned Hild again, this time to arrange her shift in the back. "And all those years," she added, "Amma lived with her secrets, telling no one."

"What secrets?"

Thora gazed at the fire. "So many secrets, Amma had." She pursed her lips, then looked back at Hild. "That she was raising him to be king. And that she knew who his father was."

Something in Thora's expression told her there was more.

"She recognized the sword he had with him in the boat." Thora reached for Hild's shift again, her fingers working at something Hild couldn't see.

She waited.

Thora frowned and shook her head, whether at the shift or what she was thinking about, Hild wasn't sure. Finally, she spoke. "It was her son's sword."

Hild felt her mouth dropping open. She snapped it shut.

"Amma knew what the rest of us didn't find out until she was dead." Now Thora looked Hild in the eye again. "The baby she raised was the child of her own son's killer."

They stood silent, staring at each other.

Then Thora knelt, busying herself with Hild's hem. Hild stood unmoving. She tried to sort out the story, to assemble all the bits she'd heard from different people. Amma had been a peaceweaver but the peace had failed, leaving her an exile. So she had found a place here. And then a baby had appeared in a boat—the child of the man who had killed her son. And instead of demanding vengeance, as was her right, Amma had raised him to be the next king.

A knock sounded at the door and Thora crossed the room to open it.

"Thora? Can you come now? We need you in the hall," a man said in an urgent tone.

Thora turned back to her. "You look lovely, my dear. We'll send someone to fetch you soon." She closed the door behind her, leaving Hild standing beside the fire, her head thrumming, the blood beating against her temples.

The design she'd been weaving, the story Aunt Var sang about the baby in the boat—it was just a tale for a long winter evening, a legend of a brave woman saving her child from an enemy's attack. It wasn't true. It hadn't really happened.

Had it?

THIRTY

Hild picked up her comb and crossed to the fire, the image she'd been weaving clear in her mind. She'd been working on it when her cousin— She banished the memory, then allowed it to come seeping back as she recalled her uncle's reaction to what had happened that day. In his view, the only purpose of being far-minded was to help the king. As far as she could tell, the Geats didn't seem to see it that way.

She unknotted her hair and began to work the comb through the tangles.

Yet if the woman who had raised Rune had been far-minded, she, too, had been working for the king, hadn't she? Even if she had been the only one who knew Rune would be Beowulf's heir.

"Ow." She pulled too hard at a difficult tangle.

Hild, too, had been helping the king, by saving his son. Why couldn't her uncle see that?

Her thoughts skittered from her uncle to Rune. His real name was Wiglaf, she recalled. She thought about what the word meant: something—or someone—left after a war. Her own name meant "battle," even if no one ever thought of it that way; it was just a name. *Survivor of war.* Was that what Rune really was? Was that why he'd been in the boat, like the baby in the story? She'd always been so focused on the mother's courage that she'd never considered what had happened to the child.

She shook her head. Maybe it was more than a coincidence, but in the end, it didn't matter. Not to her, anyway. She wouldn't be here long enough to find out. She was going home.

Her hair untangled, she tucked the comb back into the saddlebag and tied it closed. Her sword she would have to leave here in the cottage when she went to the coronation ceremony. Her cloak, too, even though she would be cold on the walk to the hall. The knowledge of the cold journey to come was warmth enough.

She was putting her baggage in order when someone knocked sharply. Before she could speak, Mord entered.

Hild started to say something, then stopped herself, knowing he must be just as impatient to leave as she was.

"Good," he said, looking at her saddlebags, with the cloak and sword beside them.

No greeting? No *my lady* for her? Overfamiliarity had already replaced the respect he'd shown her after she killed the monster.

"Leave these here, just as they are," Mord said, glancing at her for the first time since he'd come in. He stopped, firelight glinting off his eyes. "My lady. You look like a queen."

Hild knew her dark hair was striking against the red of her gown, but it felt nice to have a man recognize it. Especially a man she might marry. She swallowed her irritation and smiled at him. There would be plenty of time on the journey home to remind him of his place.

"Now, here's what we'll do," Mord said, and the moment was over. He looked at the door as if he was listening for anyone outside it. "We'll go to the ceremony, just like we planned. It will be full of people—have you seen the crowds?"

She shook her head.

"The streets are busy out there now, and the hall will be, too. That's good for us."

Hild watched him, waiting. He was older than she would have liked, and too proud of himself, but he was a capable warrior from a high-born family. It would take work to make him into the kind of husband she could be happy with, but it was work she might be willing to do. She regarded his wind-reddened cheeks and his brown hair, curling above his strong shoulders. Her uncle thought well of Mord, and that would help her back into his good graces, if the gods allowed it.

Yes, she would marry him, if that was what it took to get her home again.

"Then, while we're at the ceremony," Mord said, "Gizzur will bring the horses to a place behind the hall."

Hild realized she'd missed part of the plan. "So when the crowd is cheering, we'll simply walk out of the hall and make our way around to the back?"

Mord nodded. "We'll find a good spot where no one will notice us leaving."

Hild ran through the plan in her mind, looking for problems. "When we ride out, the guards will challenge us."

"They'll be more interested in who's coming than who's going. And besides, they have no authority over us."

"Not over you," Hild said. "But you already announced me as a peace pledge. I'm bound to their king."

Mord made an impatient gesture. "Just keep your hood up and they probably won't notice. They'll think you're still in the hall."

Hild frowned. It was the part of the plan she disliked the most. Why couldn't Mord have waited before pledging her to the Geats?

"Don't worry about it," he said. "The seaweed-eaters? They have no honor."

No, Hild thought. It wasn't the Geats who lacked honor;

it was her own people. Her uncle. Sending her as a peace pledge when his real intention was to attack the Geats? There was no more honor in that than there was in sneaking away from the stronghold, hiding behind her hood.

She shook the idea away irritably and looked back at Mord. "How long till the ceremony starts?" If they were going to leave, she wanted it all to be over, now, and them to be gone from this place.

"You stay here—I'll find out." He slipped through the door, not bothering to bow to her.

As Mord left, troublesome thoughts crowded back into her head. She should have said something yesterday when Mord offered her to the Geats. She could have refused. But she hadn't. She'd just stood there, silent, allowing herself to become part of the ruse her uncle was planning. And now she was part of another scheme. *Where are your lofty ideas about honor now?* she asked herself. What did it matter? The important thing was that she was going home. The sooner, the better.

She eased the door open and peered out. Sun reflected on the snow, making her blink. A movement caught her eye as two people came around the corner, hurrying toward a house several doors down. Hild drew back so she could see without being seen. The two paused for a moment at the door, and she saw with a start that they were Thora's daughter Wyn—and Rune. As they disappeared through the doorway, Hild could see Wyn smiling up at Rune.

She felt the tiniest twinge—jealousy?—then scoffed at herself as she watched a raven, a shadow against a snow-covered roof, rise into the air and wheel out of sight.

When she looked in the other direction, she could see that Mord had been right about the crowds. Groups of brown-cloaked people, farmers from the look of them, were pushing their way toward the hall. The time must be getting close.

She stepped back inside and looked over her bags again. They were still ready, just as they'd been the last time she'd checked. Oh, why couldn't this ceremony be over and the journey already begun? She walked around the room, peering into corners. On one wall, a wooden shelf held a small stone figure. She looked more closely. It was a statue of Freyja. The shelf must be an altar to the goddess, right here inside the house. It was a good sign. "Lady of the Vanir, be with me," she said, dipping her head.

Just then, Mord looked in. He didn't have to say a word before Hild was across the room, through the door, and striding toward the hall, Mord beside her, Hadding falling into step behind them. The farther they went toward the hall, the more people she saw heading in that direction: mail-clad warriors, women of the stronghold wearing well-made gowns, farmers and their wives in brown wool, and everywhere, children running, shrieking, laughing, the sun reflecting off their blond heads. The smell of food cooking and the noise of the excited crowd—mothers calling to their children, a baby wailing, horses' bridles jingling—made the place seem like a real stronghold in a real kingdom, nothing like the ramshackle place it had been the day before.

Mord was right. With all this commotion, it would be easy for them to slip away unnoticed.

At the hall doors, guards stepped forward to clear space for Hild and her men. A white-haired woman moved back, smiling at Hild as she did and dipping her head in the only kind of obeisance the crush of people allowed.

Mord and Hadding pressed to her sides, guiding her through the antechamber, where the closeness made her wrinkle her nose at the odor of dirty wool and unwashed bodies. Once they were in the hall, where there was more room, Mord kept his hand on Hild's arm. She shook it off and quickened her pace, moving past farmers, town dwellers, and warriors alike.

She found a spot where they could see, close enough to the door that they would be able to get out easily, and stood silently while the men caught up with her. Mord came alongside her, but she didn't look at him. Instead, she watched the crowd as she let her eyes adjust from the bright outdoors to the shadowy interior.

Fires blazed. In front of the dais, Hild could see a figure in a magnificently embroidered green cloak that fell to his feet, his head down as he adjusted the golden torque he wore around his neck. Rune. He raised his head, and as

Hild watched, he looked into the crowd as if he was searching for someone.

He tugged at the torque again, the movement making his cloak ripple, reminding her of a woman's skirt. Not just any woman, but a woman with a baby in her arms running toward a boat.

Hild caught her breath. She studied Rune's face, his dark eyes framed by dark hair in this land of fair-haired people. The solemnity she had seen in his expression this morning was still there, and now she saw something else, too: steadfastness, she thought. Resolve. When he closed his eyes briefly, she recalled that he was the one who had wanted to bring an end to the long-simmering feud between Geat and Shylfing. He might have killed a dragon, but what he desired for his people was peace.

He turned, his eyes coming to rest on hers. She looked back at him for a long moment, until his eyes dropped.

She swallowed. She had to stay focused.

The sound of drumming began, startling her. Along one side of the hall, men were beating on hollow logs. The ceremony must be about to start. Hild glanced at Mord, who gave her a single nod.

She took a deep breath, steadying herself. Just a little while longer now and the journey would begin. Just a little while longer and she would be on her way home.

THIRTY·ONE

HILD WANTED TO LOOK BEHIND HER AT THE DOOR, TO SEE how difficult it would be to get through the crowd, but it was too late. Everyone was turned toward the dais, and if she looked back now, she would only draw attention to herself.

The smell of smoke made her nose twitch. It wasn't the clean smoke of hearth fires, but an unpleasant odor that she recognized from her dreams. Where was it coming from?

The drumming faded. A richly dressed man, the one with a single eye, walked toward Rune, a crown in his hands. The chief skald, she assumed, as he invoked Thor's name in a voice that carried throughout the hall.

A log on one of the fires shifted and the leaping flames reflected on the cheek guards of the warrior standing nearest it.

Hild tried to keep her attention on the skald's words and on Rune's answers, but she couldn't help thinking about the guards. Would they really be as easy to bypass as Mord seemed to think?

The skald stepped toward Rune, holding out the golden circlet.

Rune lowered his head.

"Stop!" a man called out, and the hall fell silent. Hild turned with the rest of the crowd, but there were too many people blocking her view. What was happening? She looked at Mord, but from the way he was craning his neck, she could tell he couldn't see, either.

"Dayraven!" someone else called out in a glad voice. "We thought you were dead!"

Dayraven? She'd heard the name before, in a story Thialfi had told that she couldn't quite remember.

People began talking all at once; there were too many voices for Hild to distinguish their words. What was going on? She stood on her tiptoes, but she still couldn't see over the crowd. When she glanced at Hadding, he shook his head to indicate that he didn't know, either.

She thought she heard somebody saying something about the ceremony. Then a voice snarled loudly enough to be heard throughout the hall, "There will be no ceremony."

No one answered.

Hild sucked in her breath. She didn't recognize the voice, but she thought it must be Dayraven's. It chilled her.

The snarl came again: "That boy, that cursed whelp, he tried to kill King Beowulf."

The words unlocked Hild's memory. Dayraven was the warrior who had run away when Rune had stayed to fight the dragon. Rune hadn't tried to kill the king! He'd tried to save his life! Why wasn't anyone saying anything?

She looked back at Rune. He was staring into the crowd, at Dayraven, she assumed.

"I will be your next king," Dayraven said, and as he did, Hild heard the unmistakable sound of swords being pulled from sheaths.

Mord gripped her arm. "We're leaving. Now."

"No, wait," she said, struggling to free herself, but Mord had already turned.

Dayraven barked, "Tie his hands. Take the cursed wretch away."

Over her shoulder, Hild took one last look at Rune. His face was pale, but he didn't look afraid.

"Hurry," Mord said, pulling her through the crowd. People paid them no attention; their eyes were caught by the scene unfolding before them. A man and a woman parted, moving out of the way without looking at Hild when she neared them.

Behind her, she could hear another man speaking in a loud, clear voice. "I heard King Beowulf name Rune his heir. I saw Rune save the king's life. And I saw Dayraven running—"

Good, she thought with relief. Finally, somebody was defending Rune. She wanted to hear the rest, to know what they'd do with the traitorous Dayraven, but she and Mord were through the wide doors and into the antechamber.

"This way," Mord said into her ear, and they walked unchallenged into the daylight, away from the commotion in the hall.

Mord was beside her, Hadding just behind her, and both of them were grinning. "They couldn't have made this easier for us," Mord said. "The gods are with us."

"Where's Gizzur?" Hadding said.

"Getting the horses." He looked at Hild, shaking his head and showing his teeth. "I told you the Geats had no honor."

"You're wrong," she said, her words exploding into the winter air in white puffs, their vehemence surprising her. "They do have honor." Maybe Dayraven lacked honor, but Rune didn't. Nor did Thialfi or any of the other Geats she'd met. Her own people, on the other hand, and Hild herself—

She lowered her head. All she wanted was to go home. But what she wanted and what was right warred against each other inside her. Now was her chance for escape, and she should take it—of course she should. Shouldn't she?

She thought about Amma—the woman who had raised Rune—a failed peaceweaver who had refused to take vengeance for her son's death. Who had found a new way to weave peace. *Am I really willing to let two kingdoms keep fighting?* she asked herself. *To allow people to be killed and enslaved, just so I can go home?* With her uncle being guided by Bragi, there was no hope of peace. But if she stayed here, she would be killed along with the Geats.

"I thought Gizzur would be here by now," Hadding said, his voice startling her from her thoughts.

"He'll be here," Mord said. "He doesn't know about the excitement in the hall—he won't expect us yet."

She looked at Mord, her eyes settling on the scar above his lip. She wondered how he'd gotten it—she'd never heard the story. She remembered how she'd thought he was a man with little honor, and how she'd bypassed him with the drinking horn in her uncle's hall. Yet now she was willing to set all that aside to get what she wanted?

She shook her head. She needed to think. She needed to be alone.

A shower of snow caught her eye as it sifted off a rooftop, falling to the ground. For a brief moment, a ray of sunlight glinted off it before the snow melted into the mud. She shivered, wishing she had her cloak. Gizzur was nowhere in sight. She turned to Mord. "I'll be back."

"Wait! Where are you going?"

She didn't bother to answer as she started for the lane that led to the cottage.

"My lady!" Mord said.

"I'll be back," she said over her shoulder. She hurried, hoping he wouldn't follow.

There was no one to block her way; everyone was in the hall. She heard someone call out, but instead of Mord, it was just a raven cawing at its mate. The snow had been trampled by the crowds, and mud spattered onto the hem of her gown as she ran toward the cottage. As she turned into the narrow lane and out of the mud, her way grew clear.

She had been pledged to Rune. Her uncle meant to break his word, but she wasn't her uncle. Rune wanted to stop the feud. He wanted to keep women from having to send their babies to unknown shores to save their lives. So did she.

And now that she had earned the men's allegiance, their trust, couldn't they help her convince her uncle not to attack? On their journey, the Geats and the Shylfings had put aside their habit of hating each other to escape the monster. Surely they could work together again. Both sides would be stronger if they were allies, not enemies. If she stayed here, she could send messages with the men for Ari Frothi and Arinbjörn. And if her mother tried hard enough, acting on the knowledge that Hild's life lay in the balance, maybe she could help sway the king, too. Wasn't it worth a try?

At the cottage, Hild paused in the doorway, blinded by the gloom inside. A slave must have banked the fire after she'd left for the hall. Coals glowed red, but there was no other light. Leaving the door wide open, she felt her way forward, reaching out to find her cloak. It had been hanging on a peg on the far wall beside the altar to Freyja.

Careful not to stub her toes, she inched across the room, her fingers reaching into the shadows and touching wood. She paused. It was the altar. Standing before it, Hild knew the goddess would approve of her decision. She would stay in the land of the Geats. She would marry Rune. And together, they would find a way to end the long feud between their tribes.

"Lady of the Vanir," she whispered, reaching for the statue. As her fingertips brushed the stone head, Hild gasped. Fury filled her, anger such as she'd never felt.

She whirled, ready to run, not knowing where or why— and stopped herself.

She breathed in, then out, then in again, taking control of her senses. What was happening? She hadn't felt like this since the Brondings had been about to attack her cousin. That time, she'd reacted without thinking. This time, she wouldn't.

Tentatively, she stretched out her hand again, touching the statue. Again fury filled her. She tamed it, lifting her hand from the stone, calming her mind. "Freyja," she whispered. "Tell me what to do."

Closing her eyes, steeling herself, she reached out her fingers a third time. Deadly anger surged into her mind and she fought to keep it from overwhelming her. As she did, an image took shape: a warrior's face, his features hidden behind his helmet's mask, his eyes glinting with malice through the holes.

She gripped the stone. Fire flared; swords clashed.

Her sword! She needed her sword!

No. She forced herself to focus. She had to act with knowledge, not blind anger.

The image came again and comprehension followed. The masked figure stepped forward and someone else backed up, almost tripping as a heavy cloak tangled around his legs. Rune.

The masked figure was Dayraven, she realized as she watched him raise his sword and bring it down heavily.

Rune parried, and as he did, pain surged through Hild's hand. She clutched it to her chest, gasping in surprise and stepping back. In her mind, Rune took a step back as well.

Dayraven's blade rose again. As it came down, Rune stopped it with his sword. Hild was ready for the pain this time, but not for whatever it was that tripped her, sending her down on one knee.

No, she was still standing. It was Rune who had tripped, and she was watching as Dayraven advanced on him, sword held high. Her view shifted and she saw the warrior's back—and the hole in his mail shirt.

She had crossed the room, pulled her sword from its sheath, and started running before she knew she had moved. At the threshold she stopped, daylight opening her eyes to her foolishness. It was too late. The goddess had been trying to warn her—Dayraven would have killed Rune by now. She lowered her head, shutting her eyes to the image of the warrior's sword rising into the air, of Rune's taut jaw, the resolution in his eyes. Then she pictured him lying dead in the hall, blood pooling from his wound. *"No,"* she whispered, her hand going to her mouth as if to hold in a sob. She didn't want him to be dead, but what she wanted didn't matter. Dayraven, not Rune, would be king of the Geats.

Something hit her hip. She jumped, suppressing a scream, and looked down. It was just a goat, butting its head against her. When she extended her hand, it danced out of reach. As it did, she saw how big it was, and how white. Someone's pet, perhaps.

She tried to clear her head, to think. She couldn't let her feelings about Rune overwhelm her. If he was dead and Dayraven was king, she was under no obligation to the Geats. She needed to get back to Mord to let him know what was happening. If Dayraven was taking charge, there would be no peace. They needed to leave now.

The hope of home rose in her again, and for an instant she saw herself raising her children alongside her sister's children, just like she'd always wanted, all of them secure in the web of kindred, uncles and aunts and cousins to protect them.

That web hadn't protected her father, or her sister's husband.

Nor would it be enough to protect her children when Dayraven continued the feud, for surely he would do so.

If he was king. If Rune was truly dead. But how could he still be alive?

A wave of dizziness made her grasp at the doorframe. She didn't have to close her eyes this time to see Dayraven's sword towering above Rune—and the hole in his mail shirt. It was the same image she had seen before, replaying itself in her mind. Her heart skipped a beat. Had it already happened? Or was it yet to come?

A splinter bit into her hand, making her realize how tightly she was gripping the doorframe. She let go, then grasped it again to steady herself.

She saw Rune's face, his dark eyes wide, his lips parted. She could see the masked helmet reflected in his eyes.

Freyja, tell me, she begged, but the goddess was silent.

She let out a shuddering breath.

She thought of her sisters, her mother, her cousin. If she didn't leave now, she would never see them again. But if Rune was still alive . . .

Again she saw Dayraven's mask reflected in Rune's pupils.

Slowly, her hand left the doorframe and fell to her skirt. She lifted it out of the way of her feet, grasped her sword, and ran.

THIRTY·TWO

HER WAY WAS BLOCKED. PEOPLE WERE SPILLING FROM THE hall, children crying, one woman shrieking and dashing after a little boy.

Where was Mord? She needed to tell him what was going on—but there was no time. There were people everywhere, standing with dazed looks on their faces, lumbering in confusion like a flock of goats missing their goatherd.

Hild fought her way through them, elbowing between men, women, and children, all of them going the opposite direction of the one she wanted.

Please, gods, don't let me be too late, she prayed, knowing that if she was, it was her own fault for taking so long.

Where was the back of the hall? That was where Gizzur was taking the horses. She spotted the side door and glanced wildly around her for Mord or Hadding. She couldn't see them.

A man ran into her and she stumbled, then righted herself and kept going, pushing through the people in her way.

Finally, she made it to the door.

A steady stream of people rushed through it, many of them looking behind them as they ran, none of them letting her through. She would never get in. Finally, she shoved against a woman, who stepped back in surprise, allowing Hild just enough space to duck between two farmers without skewering them with her blade.

Inside the hall, she stopped. Helmeted warriors were fighting near the fire, the terrible clash of metal on metal loud and jarring. In the back, more fighting. Where was Rune?

There, by the dais. He was still alive!

"You need to leave. Now!" a woman said, grabbing her sleeve, and she looked up to see Thora's angry face. "Hurry!"

Hild shook her hand away and stared across the hall, trying to take in the situation. Was this what she'd seen when she'd touched the statue? Had she misunderstood?

"You must leave," Thora said, pushing her toward the door.

Hild turned to her. "Thora," she said, meeting the older woman's eyes. "Your people need help. I don't." She glanced meaningfully at the sword in her hand.

Thora looked at it, as well. Then she took a step back, nodding. "May the goddess be with you," she whispered.

Hild watched as Thora turned and hurried to the door, urging people outside as she went.

A whistling sound followed by a thud made Hild jump. An arrow embedded itself in the wall directly behind her. She whirled back toward the hall. Was it a stray shot? Or had someone been aiming at her?

She ran toward a stack of firewood and crouched behind it. It wasn't high enough to protect her head, but it gave her a little cover.

Another arrow whizzed past and she ducked, her heart pounding.

Cautiously, she raised her head to peer over the wood. Where was Rune? She'd lost him. Then she saw him again, still near the dais. He was on his knees, struggling to loosen the folds of the cloak that tangled around his legs.

Directly in front of him stood Dayraven.

Hild gasped. Didn't Rune see the danger he was in? Of course he did; she knew that. She watched in horror as the fully armored warrior advanced on Rune, who wasn't even wearing a mail shirt. Dayraven's blade rose until it towered over Rune. He let go of the cloak to hold his own blade in both hands.

She watched, heart in her throat, as the sword thundered down. Rune parried, but Dayraven's sword slid off his, directly onto Rune's shoulder. Hild's hand rose to her mouth. Dayraven moved, blocking her view, but she knew Rune couldn't have survived the blow.

But there he was! And not even bleeding—what had happened? He was still on his knees, scrambling backward away from Dayraven. The brooch on his shoulder—it must have caught the sword blade. He was going to get away; she knew he was.

Then the dais stopped him.

Dayraven took two steps forward and planted his feet. He lifted his sword in both hands. Hild could see Rune's face as it tilted upward, looking at the sword. Something about it reminded her of her cousin's face—and of why she was here.

She gripped her sword hilt and raced for the dais.

Dayraven stood with his sword raised high—and now Hild could see the hole in his mail shirt, exactly as she'd seen it when she'd touched the statue. She narrowed her gaze, blocking out the sounds of battle, the yells, her fear of arrows, and focused on the hole. Her blade came up as she ran. She pointed it directly at the weak spot in Dayraven's mail shirt.

Dayraven's sword began its descent.

Using both hands and every bit of strength she could muster, Hild rammed her blade home.

The warrior in front of her lurched to one side, then crumpled, pulling Hild forward with him. Angrily, she yanked on her sword until it came free. This wasn't supposed to happen again. What had she been thinking? Killing people was no way to bring about peace. What kind of a monster was she?

She fought back a wave of dizziness and felt a hand catch her by the elbow, steadying her.

There was a hole in his mail, she thought—or maybe she said it aloud. A tremor ran through her body.

"My lady," someone said, and she looked to see Rune standing in front of her. He was holding her arm, keeping her from falling.

"I was supposed to weave peace," she said, as despair threatened to overtake her.

Rune looked down and she followed his gaze. Dayraven lay in a heap, blood spreading onto the dirt floor.

"Is he dead?" she asked dully, although she already knew the answer.

Rune nodded and led her a few steps away from the body.

Hild closed her eyes. This was what it had been like her entire life: men fighting other men; her uncle sending raiding parties or armies to the land of the Geats; the Geats retaliating, calling on their allies to avenge them. How long would it be before her cousin fell to an enemy sword, and then Siri's sons? How long would the feuds continue? If even she, who wanted an end to war, couldn't stop trying to solve problems with a sword, what hope was there for the men raised to be warriors?

She felt Rune looking at her and she raised her head. "I'm sick of all the killing," she whispered, whether to herself or to him she didn't know.

"Hild," he said. "You saved my life."

She swallowed. He hadn't understood. But before she could say anything else, he asked, "Where are your guards?"

Mord. She'd forgotten all about him. "Outside, looking for me," she said, and as she thought of Mord and Gizzur and Hadding searching for her, furious that she'd disappeared, a smile tugged at the corners of her lips. She'd have to find them and explain what had happened. But not just yet. She looked up, and as her eyes met Rune's, she found she couldn't get her breath. His hand felt impossibly warm on her arm.

He was the baby in the boat. She'd been waiting for him her entire life; she just hadn't known it.

A glint caught her eye. The crown, lying on the ground. She bent down to pick it up, then reached up to settle it on Rune's head. A lock of dark hair fell into his eyes and she pushed it back, tucking it behind his ear, the feel of his skin on her fingertips sending a shiver down her spine.

"Rune!" someone yelled, and they both turned.

Rune lunged for his sword, which lay on the ground beside Dayraven's body. Hild scanned the hall for danger. What a fool she'd been to forget the arrows and the warriors who wanted Rune dead. What fools they'd both been.

A young man was waving his sword—Rune's man?

Two bodies lay beside the fire, and near them, two men were bound and guarded. Another was trussed to a beam in the back of the hall. Noise from the side door made her turn to see people streaming back in, men, women, and children. The man waving his sword was grinning hugely, and now she recognized him as the warrior who'd led them to the hall, the one with the misshapen nose. She glanced over in time to see Rune smiling back at him.

When she looked at the door, she saw Thialfi entering. Behind him, Mord ran in, his eyes sweeping the hall. Looking for her.

She tried to catch his eye, to let him know she was all right, but he didn't see her.

As people rushed in from both doors, the noise mounted. A man held up his hand—it was the skald—and the crowd quieted enough for Hild to hear him call out, "Wiglaf, son of Weohstan, King of the Geats!" It took her an instant to remember that was Rune's name.

Then the roaring began, a joyous sound of people cheering. The drumming she'd heard earlier resumed and the noise of glad voices grew deafening.

Rune turned, his eyes meeting hers, and again she found it hard to breathe. She swallowed, unable to look away from his dark eyes, the line of his nose, the curve of his jaw. Much as she wanted to memorize his face, to look at him forever, she knew she couldn't. A king had responsibilities. She swallowed a second time, then inclined her head toward the crowd without taking her eyes from his. "Your people," she said. "They're waiting for you."

"They'll be your people, too," he whispered, and as he spoke, the crown slipped forward.

She reached up to straighten it and her fingers touched Rune's hair, sending a shiver of anticipation through her. For the first time since she'd saved her cousin's life, she felt hope for the future—and a hint of happiness.

Yes, they would be her people, too. She and Rune could work to stop the feuding. Her uncle might have forgone his honor, but that didn't mean she had to. With Rune's help, she would find a way to weave peace.

She reached for his hand and he took hers. Together, they turned to face the cheering crowd.

ACKNOWLEDGMENTS

My heartfelt gratitude to:

—the stalwart Ena Jones, whose words and ideas have enriched this book immeasurably;

—my gracious, thoughtful editor, Diane Landolf;

—the generous readers whose comments helped me see my way more clearly: Megan Lynn Isaac, Allison B. Wallace, Matthew J. Kirby, and Elizabeth C. Bunce;

—the wonder-working copy editors, designers, and behind-the-scenes team at Random House Children's Books;

—the ever-helpful Anna Webman;

—Dean Shearle Furnish of Youngstown State University, who allowed me a course release for writing;

—and, of course, the cheering section, especially Sid Brown, my parents, my brother, and the Gauses—my aunts, uncles, and cousins.

ABOUT THE AUTHOR

REBECCA BARNHOUSE is the author of *The Book of the Maidservant* and *The Coming of the Dragon*. She first read *Beowulf* in Old English at the University of North Carolina at Chapel Hill, where she earned her doctorate, studying Anglo-Saxon manuscripts and medieval literature written in Old and Middle English, Old Norse, and other fascinating languages. Originally from Vero Beach, Florida, she lives in Ohio, where she is a professor of English at Youngstown State University. To find out more, visit her website at rebeccabarnhouse.com.